Dear Reader,

Did you ever make up a secret code when you were a child? My girlfriend and I did. We liked to pass notes back and forth and didn't want anyone else to read the contents. We had great fun creating our secret messages. Our little codes and ciphers were simple and for the most part effective. I didn't realize how complicated the process of passing covert information could be until I starting researching the military use of codes for this book. The methods of conveying vital secret information during the world wars and Cold War were quite ingenious and helped save and protect lives.

I enjoyed spending time spent with Anne, Liddie, Ben and their friends while working on this book, but most of all I loved discovering new things about Aunt Edie and her colorful past. I hope you enjoy Anne's new adventure in *Cracking the Code* as much as I did.

Blessings to you,
Kelly Ann Riley
writing as Emily Thomas

Secrets of the Blue Hill Library

Nowhere to Be Found
Shadows of the Past
Unlocking the Truth
Theft and Thanksgiving
The Christmas Key
Off the Shelf
Gone in a Flash
All Sewn Up
If Walls Could Talk
The Rightful Owner

Cracking the Code

Secrets of the
BLUE HILL LIBRARY

EMILY THOMAS

Guideposts

New York

Cracking the Code

CHAPTER ONE

A nne Gibson tapped her pencil on the checkout desk as she studied the computer screen, which was opened to the budget spreadsheet for the Blue Hill Library. No matter how she tried to crunch the numbers, there was no room in this year's finances to pay for a major repair.

Wendy Pyle, a library volunteer and Anne's dear friend, leaned on the counter. "How's it going?"

"I just don't see how to squeeze in getting the elevator fixed without breaking the budget—let alone purchase a new one as Alex suggested. I'm going to have to appeal to the Library Guild or take out a loan. This is really bad timing with the county inspection coming up."

"They wouldn't shut us down for not having an elevator, would they?" Wendy asked, her blue eyes widening.

Anne pushed her glasses back up her nose and leaned back in her chair. "No, no, but they would write up a recommendation or sanction, depending on how you want to look at it. We would be listed in the directory as not being handicapped accessible. I really would like to avoid that."

"We'll just have to get it fixed by then," Wendy said with a determined nod that set her chin-length, dark hair bobbing. "God will provide. He always has."

"So true." Anne admired Wendy's steadfast faith and determined drive to get things done. Like the literacy program. In less than a month, Wendy had organized a whole new program, recruited a teacher to supervise, and enlisted volunteer tutors. This was in addition to her usual volunteer work at the library and duties involved in being a supportive wife to the local high school football coach and wonderful mother to seven children.

Anne glanced over at the back table, where her five-year-old daughter was busy coloring a picture for her kindergarten show-and-tell. "How's it going, Liddie?"

"I can't get Hershey's nose right." She held up her drawing. They were supposed to be drawing one of their pets or a friend's pet to share with the class in the morning. Since their only pet was a chocolate Labrador retriever they'd adopted from the shelter, Liddie concentrated on capturing his likeness in crayon.

"Maybe try drawing it a little bit longer, but I think you've done a great job already," Anne said sincerely. Liddie, with chocolate brown eyes and curly brown hair and blonde highlights, resembled her father so much at times that Anne's breath caught in her chest. Liddie had also inherited her father's talent for drawing.

Liddie's mouth pursed to a pout. "I want to start over."

"That's fine. We still have an hour until dinner." Anne appreciated Liddie's focus, although she hoped her daughter wouldn't get too stressed over getting the image perfect. Her original drawing was already well done for her age.

Wendy still lingered by the counter, straightening up some brochures for the local garden club.

"Did you need me for something?" Anne asked her.

"Not really. You already answered my question. I was going to ask if we had any more funds for advertising the literacy class, but I'm guessing that's out of the question right now."

"Unfortunately —"

" — the timing is terrible," Wendy finished for her. "I'm just concerned since we only have three people signed up. Surely there are more in need out there. Illiteracy is a national epidemic. I read someplace that thirty-two million adults in the United States can't read."

"Maybe word of mouth just didn't spread fast enough this time," Anne said. She was as excited as Wendy about the new literacy classes and had been praying that they would reach people who needed help the most. Teaching others to read had been a passion of her great-aunt Edie, who'd left her historic Victorian mansion to the town for a library. Anne wanted to make sure she made the most of her aunt's legacy to Blue Hill.

"But, again, there's no way around the need to get the elevator working again." Anne sighed. "That has to be our priority. Not only for the inspection, but we have patrons who can't climb the stairs. We're going to have to run up and down to get any books they want from the upstairs rooms. And it would be terrible if one of them got stuck in the elevator like I did."

"Yes, it would be." Wendy's lips twitched.

Anne raised her eyebrows. "Are you laughing at me?"

A giggle escaped Wendy. "I don't mean to. It's just you looked like a trapped bird, waving your arms under all those sheets."

Liddie looked up and giggled too. "Mommy must've looked funny."

"I was just surprised, that's all," Anne said with a laugh. That morning, Anne had been returning from the basement with a load of laundry to their private quarters on the third floor when there was a deafening boom of thunder. The elevator jerked to a stop, causing the sheets and pillowcases to fly out of the basket she was holding and land on top of her. She was stuck between the second and third floors without her cell phone and had to holler for Wendy who was downstairs shelving books.

"I'm just thankful you came in early and were there to get me out," Anne said with a shake of her head. Wendy had run out to the garage and brought in a ladder to rescue Anne.

Anne clicked the computer window shut on the budget and stood. "And I'm glad Alex came and took a look before he went to work."

When Anne had returned to her hometown of Blue Hill after the death of her husband and loss of her job in New York, she'd been glad to hire a familiar face, her high school buddy, Alex Ochs. He had done a marvelous job transforming the stately old house into a lovely library.

Alex was a contractor now, and Anne would forever be grateful for his skills and friendship. The library area now sprawled through the first two floors of the house with a portion of the second floor and entire third floor turned into living space for Anne and her two young children, Liddie and Ben. The house also contained an enormous attic and basement, as well as a detached garage.

Alex had originally inspected the house's antique cage elevator and determined it was up to code. But when Anne got stuck, she called Alex over immediately after Wendy freed her and he'd taken a quick look. The lightning had fried the elevator motor and damaged the cab control mechanism. It was fortunate that Anne's hands had been full with the laundry basket and that she hadn't been touching the metal sides or she might have been shocked. The magnitude of that lightning strike could have also set the house on fire along with taking out a circuit and the elevator. Anne kept thanking God for watching over the old Victorian and the people inside.

Alex was looking for replacement parts now but cautioned he may have to replace the entire motor. He also suggested that she compare the costs of a new elevator versus the repair and maintenance of the old one.

Anne loved the old elevator that she had used many times as a child. It was the jail when friends came over to play in the mansion on rainy days and a cage for her stuffed animals when she played zoo. She hated the idea of putting in a more modern one.

"I should know more when Alex gets back some estimates on the parts," Anne said. "Meanwhile, we could put up more flyers around town."

"I put one up in Coffee Joe's, Stella's Pizza, the diner, and the Senior Center. But I didn't put one up at the market."

"I'll do it." Anne made a mental note to get a flyer over to the grocery store. "Word of mouth should eventually help too."

Liddie set her pencil down. "I wish Beth's daddy would go to the class."

"You do, sweetheart?" Anne asked. "Why?"

Liddie nodded. "I told my friend Beth at church about the storybook you are reading to me at bedtime, and she says her daddy doesn't read to her."

"How sad," Wendy said. "Maybe he just doesn't have time or maybe he doesn't like to read."

"Beth said he can't read very well," Liddie said. "Her mommy used to read to her every night before she went away. Her daddy tried, but then he stopped. It makes Beth sad she can't hear stories."

Wendy raised her eyebrows at Anne. "Maybe all he needs is a personal invitation. What's his name?"

"Her father is Luke Norris. He's a carpenter and works for Alex occasionally," Anne said.

"I'll see what I can do." Wendy's eyes gleamed with determination. "Right now, I think I'll go upstairs and check on the Children's Room. I saw little Charlie Barnes going up there with his mother, and you know how he loves to take books off the shelves."

As Wendy started up the stairs, the front door opened and an elderly woman with a cane stood in the entry. It was Betty Warring, which meant her sister Nellie couldn't be far behind.

"Hurry up, Betty," Nellie Brown said over her sister's shoulder. "I don't want to get wet."

"Stop fretting. We beat the storm." Betty shuffled forward, leaning heavily on her cane. "Besides, a little rain won't melt you.

"Easy for you to say." Nellie stepped inside, patting her short white hairdo. "You didn't just get your hair permed. I don't want to lose the curl."

"Be careful, your vanity is showing," Betty teased with a wink at Anne.

"Vanity, my foot. I don't want to lose the money it took to get looking this good." Nellie set her book bag on the counter.

Anne reached inside and pulled out two library books and proceeded to check them back in. The octogenarians lived together and visited the library at least once a week. They loved biographies and took turns reading the books out loud to each other. Despite their excessive bickering, everyone knew the sisters adored each other.

Betty looked out the window. "It looks like our April showers are now May showers. We've gotten enough rain to last the rest of the year. We're lucky we're not all getting washed away."

Anne agreed. They were making up for their lack of rain earlier in the spring. The forecasters were predicting a stormy week.

"Hurry along, Betty." Nellie headed for the biography section. "That storm will be here soon."

Nellie's prediction was correct. By the time the sisters had chosen a book on Winston Churchill and checked out, thunder grumbled in the distance. The remaining patrons hurried with their selections, and soon a line formed in front of the checkout desk. Anne hurried as fast as she could. In addition to the looming bad weather, it was almost five anyway, which was closing time.

A rumble sounded as the last patron left. Anne hoped Ben was on his way in from playing outside. She was headed for the door when it burst open and Ben ran in.

"Mom! Come quick! Hershey took a package off the porch, and he won't give it to me."

Anne ran outside with Liddie at her heels. Dark clouds rolled close overhead and the wind stung her face. Hershey stood in the middle of the lawn, a large brown package hanging from his jaws.

"Hershey, here boy!" Anne called, slapping her thighs to get his attention. "Come."

The dog stood stock-still, his dark eyes shining mischievously as he watched her.

Anne knew that look and changed tactics. She advanced slowly down the stairs. "Be a good boy. Stay there!"

Hershey wagged his tail. Anne was about a foot away from him, when he suddenly bounced up on his hind legs, danced backward, and bounded away.

"That's what he was doing when I tried to get the package," Ben said with his hands on his hips. "He thinks we're playing."

Thunder rumbled louder. The storm rolled closer. Anne could smell the rain in the air. They had to hurry.

"Hershey. Bad dog! Come here," Anne scolded, but it had no effect on the playful mutt as he raced around them. She turned to her children. "We're going to have to corner him by the fence. Liddie you go that way." She pointed to her right. "And Ben try going around the other way."

Ben and Anne circled the dog that had now crouched down and watched them warily. They all edged in closer. Still Hershey didn't move a muscle, except for his wagging tail. Ben glanced at Anne and she nodded. He made a flying grab for the dog but only caught his tail. Hershey jerked away, evaded Anne's hands, bumped up against Liddie, and raced across the yard.

Anne shook her head watching their pet. At least he was having a great time. Normally she'd just wait until the dog realized they weren't playing a game, but she was worried about the package and impending storm. Could it be a delivery of new books? If they didn't get it soon, the rain would finish off any damage Hershey's teeth were doing.

"I'll go get a dog treat." Liddie sprinted back into the house.

"Hershey come. Now!" Anne was growing crankier with each passing moment. She looked at Ben. "Let's see if we can get him cornered again."

A flash of lightning illuminated the sky, and thunder boomed and shook the ground. Startled, Hershey twisted in midair and the package ripped. A cloud of green swirled into the wind.

Anne gasped.

The paper package was full of money!

CHAPTER TWO

"You go in, Ben. I'll get the rest of them," Anne said as rain pelted them and wind scattered money farther across the lawn. After her initial shock that the bag was full of cash, Anne and Ben leapt into action, trying to grab as many bills as possible before the storm blew them away.

Ben grabbed another ten-dollar bill on the grass. "I want to help."

Liddie ran out on the porch, a dog biscuit in her hand, and gaped at the sight of her mother and brother running around the yard in the pouring rain. Hershey spied the treat and raced up to her.

"Stay there, honey!" Anne called as she splashed through the pooling water on the already saturated lawn.

"What's happening?" Wendy called from the doorway. "Oh my! You're going to get soaked!"

"Too late. We already are." Anne sloshed up to the porch, clutching wet bills in both hands.

Wendy's eyes widened. "I–is that money?"

"Yeah." Ben trudged up the steps. "Lots and lots of it."

"I think we got most of it," Anne said, still in shock about the contents of the package.

"Stay there. I'll get some towels," Wendy said, clucking like a mother hen. She ducked back in the open door and hurried to the checkout desk, where Anne kept her key for the door into their living quarters. Wendy headed for the elevator and then veered toward the stairs. "I forgot it's not working," she said, then climbed the stairs two at a time.

Liddie examined Anne's appearance and giggled. "Mommy, you look funny."

"I'm glad someone finds this amusing." Anne dropped the money on the welcome mat. Hershey chose that moment to shake, splattering them all with mud. Liddie squealed and jumped back, bumping into Ben and they both fell backward.

"Liddie, watch it!" Ben pushed Liddie off of his legs and got to his feet. He grabbed Hershey's collar. "I'm sorry, Mom. Maybe Hershey should go to obedience school."

"Th-this isn't your fault." Anne's teeth were starting to chatter. "I think he just needs more attention." They'd been so busy lately with the end-of-school-year activities that they hadn't been taking Hershey for walks or playing with him as much as they usually did. No wonder he was rambunctious. She looked down at the sodden brown paper clutched in her hand. It appeared to be a large grocery bag closed with packing tape, which now had a huge tear in it, thanks to Hershey. "Did you see who dropped this package off?"

Ben shook his head. "No. Hershey was on the front steps with it."

"So he got it off the porch?"

"I think so. I don't know," Ben said with a shrug. "I didn't see it earlier though." He glanced out at the yard. "Look there's more money." He dashed down the steps and across the lawn with Hershey bounding alongside him.

Lightning lit the horizon and thunder boomed again as another gust of wind sent the tree limbs swaying violently.

"Ben, come back. Now! Just leave it," Anne called and Ben ran back with another twenty-dollar bill in his hand. She looked at the pile of money, noting that while there were several one-dollar bills, most were of larger denominations.

Wendy came down the stairs with an armload of towels. "Here you go." She handed the bath towels to Ben and Anne and they dried themselves off. Liddie was dry enough not to need one, but she dabbed at the mud Hershey had shared with her.

Anne gathered up the bills in the last towel and carried it to the checkout desk. Ben had Hershey by the collar again, and he dragged him through the library to the back door that led to the fenced yard and the doghouse.

"That's a lot of money," Wendy said as she briskly dabbed the bills with a towel and sorted them by denomination. "Who on earth left it?"

"I have no idea." Anne examined the sodden brown paper but couldn't find an address or name anywhere on it, which meant a delivery service hadn't left it. "Could one of our patrons have dropped it?"

"I didn't see anyone with a package like that," Wendy said.

Anne swiped back a soggy strand of hair that had escaped her ponytail as Ben joined them. "I fed Hershey. He wanted to come back inside."

With the storm raging outside, Anne couldn't blame the dog, but he was safe out there for now. The forecast hadn't predicted tornado weather, but if it did worsen, they'd get the dog and go to the basement.

"Ben, did you see anyone outside while you were playing?"

"I saw Miss Warring and Mrs. Brown leave. They asked if I like cookies."

"And did you tell them you didn't like cookies?" Anne teased.

"No," Ben said emphatically. "I told them I especially like chocolate chip. They said they'd bring me some homemade cookies one of these days."

"That was nice of them," Anne said. "Did you see anyone else?"

Ben shook his head. "I was in the backyard part of the time, but I did see Pastor Tom drive by in Bessie right before I saw Hershey with the package."

"I'll give Pastor Tom a call later. Thanks, Ben." Anne knew Rev. Tom Sloan owned a black 1948 Packard with heavy chrome grill and whitewall tires. His grandfather gave the sedan to him when he was twenty years old and he'd christened it Bessie. Everyone knew how Pastor Tom babied that car. So if Ben said he'd seen the car, she was pretty sure he wasn't mistaken.

Anne turned her attention to the growing stacks of bills.

"One thousand." Wendy set a stack of hundreds to the side. Anne grabbed another stack of twenties and counted them into one-hundred-dollar piles as Liddie and Ben watched.

Wendy jotted down the amounts as they methodically went through all the money. When they finished counting, she added the numbers.

"Eighteen thousand, five hundred, and forty-three dollars. Wow!" Wendy said. "This is a serious amount of money. Someone has got be looking for it."

"We better call the police," Anne said, feeling a little breathless. She reached for the library phone directory and turned to the community services page to get the station number. "I'm sure they'll want us to turn it in."

"But what if the money was meant for you or the library?" Wendy asked. "After all, it was on the porch."

"But I'm not sure it was on the porch," Ben piped up. "I only saw Hershey run across the porch. I just thought he could've picked it up there."

"Well, regardless, this looks like an answer to prayer," Wendy said. "Maybe someone heard about the literacy program and wanted to donate. Or maybe they were here earlier today and saw that the elevator was broken and wanted to help. You said yourself that the repair will be expensive." She looked down at the money. "What if this is a gift?"

Anne's hand rested on the phone. Indeed, the found money did feel like an answer to prayer, but what if it wasn't? She looked outside at the storm and wondered if they'd missed something. Was the money really meant for the library? But why not just leave a check instead of a bundle of cash on the front porch?

"Can we keep it, Mommy?" Liddie asked.

"I wish we could," Anne said with a smile. It would really help their situation. So tempting. "But, we have to make sure we know that it was intended for us. If not, it would be stealing. The money could've been dropped by someone visiting the library, or maybe it fell out of a car and Hershey got it on the side of the road." Anne had a hard time believing anyone would be so careless with that much cash, though. "I wouldn't feel right using it, even for a good cause, unless we make absolutely sure that it was meant for us."

Wendy sighed deeply. "You're right. I guess I just got carried away by the sight of all that money. It needs to be turned in. Call the police."

Anne turned to her children. "Ben, please go up and take a shower and then finish your homework. Liddie you need to get out of those muddy pants. I'll be up to make supper in a little while."

"Can I watch TV?" Liddie asked as she followed Ben to the stairs.

"Only until supper." Anne waited until they'd gone up the first flight and then called the police station. She asked for Officer Michael Banks. Michael and his wife, Jennifer, had been two of her high school buddies, and she felt comfortable seeking his help.

After several minutes, Michael's deep voice came on the line. "Hey Anna Banana, how's it going?"

Anne smiled at his old nickname for her. "Well, something interesting has happened. It seems someone dropped a large amount of cash in my yard. Eighteen thousand, five hundred, forty-three dollars to be exact."

"Whoa! Say that again!"

Anne explained about Hershey and the ripped package. "I'm not sure we even got all of it with the storm blowing in."

"And you have no clue whose money it is?" Michael asked even though Anne had already said so.

"No. The package wasn't addressed, and there are no markings on it."

Michael was silent for a long moment. "All right. I'm going to check with the front desk to see if anyone has reported missing money, and I'll get back to you. Meanwhile, who else knows about this?"

Anne glanced over at her friend who was slipping rubber bands around the money stacks. "Just Wendy and my kids."

"Well, I wouldn't tell anyone that you don't absolutely trust about how much money there is or where you found it unless you want all kinds of unscrupulous people suddenly appearing on your doorstep to claim it's theirs, or worse, trying to take it by force."

"Oh my. Do you think we may be in any danger with it here?" Anne's mind suddenly filled with the new possibility that this could be drug or other crime-related money. She glanced up at Wendy, who hurried to the door and drew the deadbolt.

"You're probably fine unless word gets out," Michael said. "But, if it makes you feel better, you can drop the money by the station, or better yet, I can come by in a little while to take the report and pick it up then. I have some other paperwork that has to be finished first, and then I'll head out."

Anne looked outside at the ominous storm. "It's pretty nasty out right now. You may want to wait."

"Neither rain nor sleet nor dark of night—"

"Isn't that the post office oath?" Anne interrupted with a giggle.

"Hey, can't it be applied to us other lowly public servants too?"

"It does apply, and we do appreciate you. Don't ever forget it." Anne hung up the phone and turned back to Wendy. "Michael is coming by in a little while.

"That's good. I'm glad you called. It was the right thing to do," Wendy said as if still trying to convince herself. She grinned at Anne. "For a moment there, it felt like we had won the lottery. Even if the police take the money and then we find out later that the money is a gift, the library will still end up getting the money eventually."

"I agree. Michael said not to mention the money to anyone unless we trust them absolutely."

"I won't tell anyone except Chad. I have a hard time keeping secrets from him," Wendy said, referring to her husband. "This is incredible." She picked up a stack of hundreds. "Do you think we should lock it up in a file drawer?"

"I was just thinking the same thing," Anne said as she gathered up the bills and stuffed them in the cabinet against the wall.

"I better head home and fix supper." Wendy slipped on her raincoat. "If you need me, you'll call, right?"

"Right," Anne said. "And thanks." She was so grateful to have found a friend in Wendy. When Anne and the kids had arrived in Blue Hill, Wendy hadn't let Anne's reserved nature keep her from befriending Anne. Wendy's boundless energy and enthusiasm for the library coupled with Anne's level-headedness made them a great complementary team.

Anne locked the door after Wendy dashed out into the rain, then checked the back door. Hershey lay in his doghouse and shot her a woeful look. Anne gave in and let him inside. The chocolate Lab loved to sleep in Ben's room. And no matter what mischief the sweet dog seemed to get himself into, Anne never could stay upset with him for very long. "Be a good boy."

She bolted the door, and as she trudged up the stairs, Anne glanced at the stuck elevator. Not only did the broken elevator inconvenience her when it came to taking laundry to the basement and moving carts of books around, but she frequently had elderly patrons, as well as mothers with young children who used the elevator. The second floor housed the Children's, Reference, and Fiction Rooms. Plus, she wanted the library to pass the county inspection with flying colors. She prayed that Alex would be able to find the right parts and determine the elevator could be repaired to meet safety codes at a reasonable cost.

She strolled around the second floor, turning off lights, and then unlocked the door to their private living area. She hurried up the next flight of stairs to her bedroom and changed into a dry pair of jeans and a cozy, soft blue turtleneck. She draped the wet things on top of the clothes hamper. She longed for a long hot shower, but her children must be really hungry by now.

When she'd filled a Crock-Pot with beef stew that morning, she had no idea how drastically her day would change. The stew aroma filled the kitchen, making Anne's stomach grumble as she checked on the kids. Ben must still be in the shower upstairs, but Liddie had changed into her pink sweatpants and top and was sitting in front of the television in the living room.

Anne quickly made up a pan of cornbread and, as she slid it in the oven, she thought about what Ben had said about seeing Pastor Tom's car drive by. Maybe Pastor Tom had noticed something. It couldn't hurt to ask.

Anne picked up the kitchen phone and dialed the pastor's home.

A pleasant, melodic female voice answered. "Good evening."

"Hi, Maggie. This is Anne Gibson."

"Anne, it's so good to hear from you," the pastor's wife said. "I've been meaning to call you. I have someone who could benefit from your literacy class. Silvia Morgan. I gave her your phone number, but she's worried that she may not be able to start for a week or so. Is that a problem?"

"Not at all. The program is designed for students to progress at their own pace. We like to start off with a class schedule, but the program is very adaptable."

"Excellent. I'll let her know and encourage her to call. Now, was there something I can do for you? I didn't mean to take over the conversation. I'm always doing that. Tom calls me a stealth conversationalist." Maggie's merry laugh was infectious, and Anne laughed too.

"Oh, it's fine. Actually I need to talk to Pastor Tom about something. Is he home?"

"Oh dear, I'm afraid not. There's been an emergency, and Tom is at the hospital with the Hewitts, whose little girl is having surgery. It doesn't look good right now, and I'm not expecting him back for hours. I've notified our prayer team."

"How scary for the Hewitts." Anne's hand gripped the phone tighter. Her biggest fear was that something bad would happen to her children. "I've seen them at church, but I don't know them well. I'll pray for them."

"That's much appreciated. I don't know when Tom will be available, but you can try his cell phone if it's urgent. He has to keep it off in the hospital, but he will be checking his messages."

"It's not an emergency. I can talk to him later."

"Okay, dear. Is there something I can do?"

Anne hesitated as she thought how to word her request. "I'm trying to track down the owner of a package that was left here. Would you know anything about a donation to the library?"

"Not that I know of, at least Tom hasn't mentioned anything to me. I'll keep my ears open."

Anne thanked Maggie and hung up the phone. Ben must have seen the pastor driving to the hospital. Could Tom have dropped off the money on his way? Maybe he'd left it on the porch because he was in such a hurry to get to the hospital. But that didn't seem likely because Pastor Tom was much too responsible to leave a package of money without telling anyone about it. Or maybe it was a donation to the library from a parishioner who wanted to stay anonymous. In any case, perhaps Pastor Tom might have noticed someone unusual hanging around the front yard.

The possibilities swirled around her mind as she took the cornbread from the oven and dished up the stew. She called the kids and they came running.

"Cornbread!" Liddie exclaimed. "My favorite."

"Hungry?" Anne asked with a smile.

"I'm starving." Ben plopped down in his chair. He'd changed into fresh jeans and a striped shirt after his shower and had combed back his damp brown hair, which still smelled faintly of shampoo.

Liddie offered the blessing with Anne adding a request for divine intervention for the family in the hospital.

"So how was school?" Anne asked her children, and the conversation flowed pleasantly through supper as each remarked on their day.

After they cleared the table, Liddie scampered off to play in her room and Ben hauled out his math book. He really didn't need much help with problems, but Anne kept him company. She opened up the latest *Blue Hill Gazette* and checked the Lost and Found section. As she expected, there was nothing listed about missing money, but that could just mean that the money was lost today and there hadn't been time to place an ad.

If Michael didn't have any leads on where the money could have come from, maybe she should place an ad in the Lost and Found. She'd feel better if she knew she'd done everything possible to locate the owner. But, however would she word it? Michael had said to be cautious. She'd have to ask his advice when he arrived.

As she flipped the paper to the back page, she spied Wendy's ad for the literacy class.

> *Need help with reading?*
> *Free Adult Literacy Class*
> *Tuesdays and Thursdays 7:00 PM*
> *Blue Hill Library*
> *Call for more information.*

Anne wondered again if the money was somehow related to the classes. Maybe someone had a passion for literacy like her aunt Edie had.

She glanced at the clock. It was only seven thirty, but it seemed much later. Where was Michael Banks?

"I'm going to run downstairs for a while. You okay for now?" Anne said.

Ben looked up from his math problem and nodded. "I'm almost done."

Anne walked down the stairs to the main floor. She looked out the front window. No sign of a police car in the street. She returned to the checkout desk and glanced at the filing cabinet, a little worried about all that cash being there. What if it had been a criminal who had lost the money and he came looking for it?

Oh, Lord, please protect us.

She shelved a couple of books that were in the return basket and then sat at her desk. She pulled out a notebook and pencil. Sometimes it helped to think on paper. Where had the money come from? She started making a list of possibilities.

Someone might have dropped the package by accident, possibly a patron. She made a note to pull up the list of people who had checked out books that day.

Maybe someone who had been walking on the sidewalk had dropped it, or the package had somehow fallen out of a passing car. It was a remote possibility, but she remembered when Liddie had been two years old and threw her shoe out the window. Maybe something similar had happened.

The money could have been stolen from a store or a bank. Suppose the criminal was on the run and dropped the package or had hidden it on her property?

She paused and then quickly added the possibility that the money could have been for a criminal-type transaction. She didn't like to think about that, though, and moved on to the next possibility. Perhaps someone wanted to anonymously give the money to the library.

Now, who would leave the library such a gift? There were several wealthy people in town who had been friends of Aunt

Edie's and had expressed support of the library in the past. Mr. Barker and Mrs. Crenshaw came to mind. They had been involved with Aunt Edie in various fund-raisers for as long as Anne could remember. Maybe one of them had heard about the literacy class or her elevator problem and decided to help. Or maybe someone owed Aunt Edie money and wanted to finally repay it. But again, why leave it outside? The whole situation seemed bizarre to Anne. Maybe Aunt Edie's close friend Mildred might have some ideas, but unfortunately she was off on a vacation at the moment.

The doorbell pealed, causing Anne to drop her pen. She hurried to the window to see who was on the porch.

The police had finally arrived.

CHAPTER THREE

Officer Michael Banks stood on the porch, rain dripping off his hat. "Hi, Anne, sorry it took me so long. The captain called a late meeting. He said it was going to be short. Well, you know how it goes when everyone has to give their opinion."

Anne smiled. "No problem. I've been to many such meetings and I certainly understand. I'm just glad you're here."

Anne stepped back, pushing the door open farther so Michael could enter the library. Michael had been a star football player when they both went to Blue Hill High. He was still tall and broad with a muscular, youthful build. The only hint of aging was that his once full head of curly hair was now receding.

Michael shrugged off his raincoat and hung it on the coat rack that Anne kept by the door. "Jen mentioned how excited she is about volunteering for the literacy classes."

"I'm glad. I wasn't sure she'd have time, but she jumped at the chance." Anne smiled. Her vivacious friend hadn't changed much. Jennifer and Michael had dated in their senior year and were living proof that opposites attract.

Michael glanced around the room with his sharp, assessing gaze. "So where is this huge pile of money you found?"

"Over here behind the counter," Anne said, leading the way back to the checkout desk. "We locked it in the filing cabinet. It's making me nervous to have this much cash around." She unlocked the drawer and set the damp bundles on the counter.

"That's a lot of cash to lose." Michael pulled a small spiral notebook out of his pocket. "You sure it wasn't meant for you or the library?"

"I don't know. That's the big problem. I've been trying to think of people who could've donated such a large sum of money. I suppose there are some wealthy friends of Aunt Edie's who may want to help out, but why cash? Why not just write a check?"

"Good point. Most people don't walk around with this much cash unless they're up to no good."

"Here's the package . . . or what's left of it. Our dog managed to shred it with his teeth."

Michael examined the paper. "No identifying marks. It has a soft wrinkled texture like it's been used before."

Anne picked up a stack of tens. "The money looks aged too. Of course, it *was* out in the rain."

"I agree. These aren't freshly printed anyway. They don't look counterfeit either, but I'll double-check that back at the station. There wasn't a letter or anything with the package?"

"Not that I saw," Anne said. "But the wind was blowing pretty hard. We did our best, but some of the contents could've blown away, I guess."

Michael stroked his chin. "This is what I advise: I'll take the money into custody until an owner is determined, if that's okay with you. If no one claims the cash in thirty days, it will be returned."

"Would it help if I ran a Lost and Found ad?" Anne asked. "I mean, what if this was someone's life savings that they were keeping under the mattress and they were finally taking it to the bank or going to buy a car or something . . . ? They emptied their piggy bank, so to speak."

"This is a lot of money for a piggy to swallow." Michael grinned. "An ad would be fine, but do not reveal the location, description of the package, or amount of money recovered. If anyone does come forward with the correct information or almost correct, considering you don't know if you collected all the money, then you can refer them to the police station and we'll take it from there. Don't have anyone who answers the ad come here to retrieve it, okay? They could be dangerous."

A shiver ran down Anne's back. "I won't. I'll use my cell phone number too, rather than the library or the house numbers."

"That would be wise. And leave off your full name on the voice mail," Michael said, still looking at the stacks of money. "We're going to have to count this again so I can give you a receipt. You know there are a lot of people who would've just kept it and not said a word."

"I couldn't do that, although I could use the money for repairs and the literacy program," Anne said. She related the elevator disaster to him.

Michael looked up at the elevator stuck between the first and second floors and snorted. "Looks like a mini jail cell."

"It felt like that," Anne said and told him about getting stuck. They both had a good laugh before proceeding to count the money.

Anne pulled the rubber band off a stack of hundreds and handed it to Michael. After Michael counted each stack, she bundled them back up. They were almost finished when Anne noticed something unusual. Stuck to the back of one of the bills was a small piece of torn white paper with handwriting on it.

"Look at this." She handed Michael the bill. "It's just two letters. An *e* and *n*, but there must've been something else in that envelope."

"As soon as we get done here, I want to see where you found the money."

They finished the counting, coming up with the same total that Wendy and Anne had. Michael filled out a form and signed it to confirm he was taking the money into custody.

He pulled a flashlight off his utility belt. "Okay, let's see what we can find outside."

Anne grabbed a flashlight from the drawer and hurried out after him.

The night was pitch black with the clouds covering the moon. The rain had stopped, but droplets still plopped off the trees with the slightest breeze.

Anne pointed to the left side of the yard. "That's where Hershey tore the bag."

Michael marched across the yard, sweeping the beam of his flashlight back and forth. He reached the street and said, "I found a bill. Luckily it got snagged on a branch or it would've gone into the drainage system." He picked up the money and shook the mud off. "Another twenty."

"I hope there weren't any more that got washed away." Anne tramped along the sidewalk, searching the street, and then turned to go up the other side of the yard. The wet grass soaked her shoes and a chill shook her.

Lord, please, if there is anything else out here, let us find it soon.

Another ten minutes passed. "I think we've covered the area pretty well, but you might want to take a look in the morning." Michael flashed the flashlight beam around the yard once more.

"Okay. I'll do that," Anne said, trying not to let her teeth chatter. This was the second time today she'd gotten chilled. She just hoped she didn't catch a spring cold.

She followed Michael to the porch and, as she went up the steps, her flashlight beam skimmed over a nearby plant and illuminated something white. She stopped short and leaned over, nearly falling off the step as she tried to see what had gotten snagged in the rosebush.

"Michael, I think I found something!" Anne pulled the brambles aside.

Michael looked over the railing. "Let me get it. Don't hurt yourself." He used his long flashlight to part the bush and carefully extracted a wet sheet of paper. They hurried back into the library.

Michael gently unfolded the paper on the checkout desk. The corner was ripped off, and the piece Anne had found stuck to a bill matched perfectly. The rain had smudged the ink, but the words were legible. Michael read them out loud.

Gracious Lady,

When the little girl spied the mangy dog limping over the hill toward home, she ran and threw her arms around her pet. She never knew about the fire or the act of bravery her dog did. But in her eyes, her pet was a hero for returning home. The past was forgiven and a new life begun.

A kind deed is never forgotten.

"*Hmm.*" Michael stroked his chin. "What does this mean?"

Anne reread the note. Mangy dog? Little girl? She looked at Michael. "I have no idea what this means, and I don't get the feeling that the note is addressed to me."

Who was the gracious lady? She couldn't remember changing someone's life, other than her late husband's. They had changed their lives together when they got married. Her aunt, however, was always doing kind things for other people, and many, including Anne, would have certainly classified Aunt Edie as a gracious lady.

"At least we have something else that we can use as proof of ownership," Michael said.

Anne nodded. "Can I make a copy of it before you leave?"

"Sure. And let me have that receipt back and I'll add the twenty dollars to it."

While Michael fixed the evidence receipt, Anne blotted the note dry with tissue the best she could and then laid the damp page carefully on the scanner that doubled as their copier.

When she had finished, Anne got a file folder and laid the note inside and traded it for the receipt that he'd modified to $18,563.00 and made a notation about the note. "Thanks, Michael."

"Anytime. This is a strange one," Michael said. "And in my profession, that's saying something significant."

Anne walked him to the door, mulling over his words. *Strange indeed.* Anne wasn't going to be able to rest easy until she found the owner of the money and learned what that note meant.

* * *

"Read some more, Mommy," Liddie said and then yawned.

"Okay, just two more pages. It's getting late." Anne smoothed back Liddie's light brown hair as the child snuggled down farther in her bed. Anne stifled a yawn of her own and turned the page in one of Liddie's favorite storybooks about an owl who wanted to learn to read. After Michael left, Anne had jumped in the shower and stood under the steamy water until the chills left her body. Even though it was May, she put on her soft flannel pajamas that she usually reserved for the snowy winter nights.

By the time she finished the next two pages, Liddie's eyes had closed. Anne set the book down and turned off the lamp on the bed stand. She treasured the nightly prayer and reading time with Liddie. She was going to miss their ritual when Liddie grew older like Ben. Lately Ben read to himself before going to sleep. She thought about the father Liddie had mentioned who couldn't read to his daughter. So sad he had to miss out on that. She wished Eric could have had more precious time with the kids. She pressed her hand to her heart where she still carried the ache of missing him.

I miss you, Eric.

Fighting the now-familiar sense of loss, she stood and tugged the blanket up to Liddie's neck. She couldn't do anything about Eric, but maybe she and Wendy could help Luke Norris learn to read to his daughter. She would check with Wendy tomorrow to see if she had extended an invitation.

Anne crossed the hall and poked her head into Ben's room. "Fifteen more minutes, okay?"

Ben looked up from his adventure book. "Sure. Night, Mom."

"Good night, sweetheart." She picked up a pair of socks and tossed them into his laundry hamper before leaving the room. She sure hoped the elevator would be fixed soon. She didn't relish the idea of lugging all the clothes down three flights of stairs to the basement.

After checking to make sure the house was secure, Anne said a prayer with Ben and then retired to her bedroom. It was the same room she'd had as a child whenever she stayed with Aunt Edie, so it felt cozy and familiar. Her family had lived in a house four blocks away, but her mother's job as a nurse and her father's accounting career often kept them working late, leaving Aunt Edie to take care of her. Anne had needed the familiarity of this house badly when she had uprooted her life in New York to return here.

She picked up the fat blue binder containing the literacy volunteer instructors' guide that Wendy had provided her, along with other educational aids. Anne had gone through the process of teaching her children to read, but there were differences when teaching adults.

Wendy was leading tomorrow night. They were going to alternate classes, but Anne wanted to be prepared. Wendy enlisted the help of Ben's fourth-grade teacher, Mr. Layton, to oversee their program, so Anne hoped they had covered all their bases.

After reviewing the lesson plan, she opened a devotional book for mothers she'd just purchased and enjoyed the day's lesson on the stress of raising young children. She had memorized the lesson's accompanying verse before, but she repeated the words of Philippians chapter four, verses six and seven until they were fresh and foremost in her mind.

Do not be anxious about anything, but in every situation, by prayer and petition, with thanksgiving, present your requests to God. And the peace of God, which transcends all understanding, will guard your hearts and your minds in Christ Jesus.

The Scripture was a balm on her sorely stretched nerves. She said a prayer, remembering the Hewitts in the hospital, and then turned out the light. She lay listening to the old house creak under the onslaught of the wind that had kicked up again. Another storm must be on the way. They weren't expecting any severe weather like tornados, but the approaching storm made her a little nervous just the same. She turned on her side and snuggled against the pillow, but the mystery of the money kept popping into her thoughts.

She finally sat back up and turned on the lamp. She'd left the notes she'd started about the missing money in the kitchen, so she padded quietly downstairs. She put a mug of water in the microwave to heat water for herbal tea.

Outside, the horizon lit up with flashes of lightning, but the storm was still too far away to hear the thunder rumble. She tucked a bag of chamomile tea in her mug and carried it to the table. She opened her notebook and placed the copy of the note she'd found in the rosebush on the table. She read it over again.

Gracious Lady,

When the little girl spied the mangy dog limping over the hill toward home, she ran and threw her arms around her pet. She never knew about the fire or the act of bravery her dog did. But in her eyes, her pet was a hero for just returning home. The past was forgiven and a new life begun.

A kind deed is never forgotten.

A kind deed is never forgotten. She mulled the phrase over as she sipped her tea. Was the money a gift to repay a kindness? And what about the mangy dog and the little girl? It had to be a message that only the recipient of the money would understand, and, since Anne couldn't make a connection, then obviously the note and the money were intended for someone else. But who? Aunt Edie was the most logical choice if the package had been left for her or maybe her legacy of the library. In that case, then Anne could use the money for the library projects. But then . . .

Anne sighed deeply. Her thoughts were whirling like the wind outside, and it was getting harder and harder to focus. But she knew she was going to have to try hard to find the owner of that package. With her usual routine with the kids and their school, the literacy class, and now the broken elevator, she didn't have a lot of time to track down mysterious note writers. But, she was going to give it her best shot.

She drained the teacup and set it in the sink. Chances were, Michael would call in the morning and tell her that the poor person who'd lost the package had picked it up at the police station. Problem solved.

A flash lit up the kitchen followed by a loud bang that shook the house.

"Mommy!" Liddie yelled.

"It's okay, sweetie. I'm coming." Anne hurried up the stairs and was met by Liddie in the hall. She flung her arms around Anne.

"Hey, it's just a storm. You're safe in the house." She patted Liddie's back. "You need to get back in bed or you won't be able to get up in time for school."

Another rumble vibrated the walls of the old mansion. Liddie's arms tightened around Anne's waist.

"Do you want to stay with me for a little while?"

Liddie nodded, her face still pressing into Anne's stomach.

She gently peeled Liddie off of her and, taking her hand, walked over to Ben's room and peeked inside. Ben's peaceful face and even breathing indicated the storm hadn't disturbed him at all. His father had been able to sleep through almost anything as well.

Thunder expanded the air again, but it sounded farther away as Anne returned to her bedroom. Liddie climbed on the bed as Anne turned on her radio and dialed through the channels until she came to one broadcasting the local news. The weather forecaster declared that the worst of the storm was already beyond Blue Hill.

"The storm will be gone soon, sweetie." Anne turned off the radio and slid onto the bed beside Liddie. She hummed some of Liddie's favorite Sunday school songs, but every time Liddie's eyelids started to droop thunder would rumble and they popped open again.

Anne picked up her Bible from the nightstand. "Would you like me to read to you?"

Liddie nodded and snuggled closer as Anne opened to the book of Psalms.

"The Lord is my shepherd, I shall not want," she began and by the time she was into the next psalm, Liddie was breathing softly and evenly.

Anne finished reading the chapter silently and set the Bible back on the nightstand. She glanced at her daughter. If she tried to move Liddie back to her bed, she'd most likely wake up. Anne tucked the quilt around the little girl and moved to the far side of the bed. She reached over and turned off the light.

Outside, the wind howled and splatters of rain smacked the windows, but the old house remained solid as an oak. Anne thanked God again that, after all she'd gone through with Eric's passing and being laid off from her library work in New York, she had ended up back here in Blue Hill, safe and sound. Home. Now it was her job to take care of the gifts that she'd been given.

Chapter Four

A nne yawned as she poured her second cup of coffee for the morning. She gazed out the window at the soggy, dripping trees down Bluebell Lane. Liddie had tossed and turned all night, preventing Anne from ever falling into a deep sleep. Liddie seemed fine this morning and full of energy. Ben, too, seemed rested. He had awakened Anne and Liddie when the alarms didn't go off.

The electricity must have bleeped off during the night since all the appliance clocks were blinking, including Anne's alarm clock. They had to rush through breakfast, but they managed to get to school on time.

The rain had finally stopped. She hoped the forecasts were wrong and this would be the last of the storms for a while. Rain had swelled the area streams and rivers to near capacity and some low-lying areas had been barricaded with sandbags.

Anne sipped more coffee, hoping she'd feel more energetic soon. It was going to be a long work day. The literacy class was that night and with the elevator out of commission, they probably should set up the meeting area on the first floor. Usually they held meetings in the Reference Room on the second floor, but it would be better to be safe than sorry since they didn't know if anyone coming would have trouble with stairs.

The doorbell for their private entrance rang. She pushed the button on the intercom. "Hello."

"It's Alex," a deep voice responded.

"Come on up." She buzzed him in and heard Alex bounding up the back stairway.

He burst into the room radiating energy. He was dressed for work in jeans and an unbuttoned long-sleeved flannel shirt over a navy T-shirt. Sometimes he wore a uniform shirt with the name of his contracting business embroidered on it for meeting new clients, but he'd once told her that he preferred to be able move around without worrying about ruining his clothes.

"Good morning!" he said.

"Morning," Anne said with considerably less enthusiasm.

Alex's grin widened as he looked closer at her. "Uh-oh. Did you get up on the wrong side of the bed?"

"More like I needed a few more hours in it." Anne smiled at his teasing. "The storm kept Liddie up, which kept me up. I didn't get nearly enough sleep last night. Do you have time for some coffee?"

"Sure." Alex plopped down in a chair, and Anne handed him a mug. "That was some storm," he said. "It flooded several of our construction sites. While we're waiting for them to dry out some, I thought I'd work on your elevator problem."

He handed her a file. "These are brochures of newer elevators with motors and wiring similar to yours. I could take out the old one completely and replace it if you wish. But before you consider those, I'm still trying to get contact information on the company that installed your elevator."

"Didn't Aunt Edie's folks buy it from D & P?" Anne asked. She'd seen the company name engraved on the elevator button plate.

"It appears the D & P Company has been sold to another company. The Diamond Brothers. I tried calling them this morning, but their phone has been disconnected. They may have moved or gone out of business. I'm still checking."

"I appreciate your trying. Here's a reward." Anne placed a bag of blueberry muffins on the table in front of Alex. He opened the bag and inhaled deeply. "Boy, do you know a way to a man's heart or what?"

"Correction. Wendy knows a way to a man's heart." Anne smiled. "She made these this morning and brought them by. They're samples of the batch she made for the literacy class tonight."

Alex took out a golden brown muffin filled with plump blueberries. "If our teachers had muffins waiting for us, no one would've been tardy."

"You were never tardy," Anne said. Alex had been an honor student and president of the student body in high school. He'd also been a close friend and they had casually dated. Alex had hinted that he wanted more of a relationship during their senior year, but Anne had resisted, knowing she was going off to college. There she met Eric, the love of her life.

She watched Alex pick a blueberry out of the muffin and pop it in his mouth. When she'd first moved back, things between Alex and her had been a little awkward, but over time they were rebuilding their friendship. She'd also been able to connect with some of the others in their little friendship gang, and tonight

Jennifer Banks and Heather Stafford were coming to the class as literacy volunteers.

Alex glanced up and caught Anne watching him. He grinned. "I still say that if they'd offered muffins and doughnuts before class, it would've made getting there on time much more enjoyable."

Anne bit into a muffin and almost moaned. "Okay, I can see your point." These were even better than the delectable muffins they served at Coffee Joe's, a small downtown coffee bar. She was going to have to ask Wendy for the recipe.

As Alex helped himself to another muffin, Anne checked out the brochures on elevators. The cost of replacing the elevator would be a huge, unexpected expense. "That money sure would come in handy," she murmured.

"What money?" Alex asked.

Anne looked up. "Wait until I tell you about yesterday. You're not going to believe it." She told him about finding the package of money.

Alex chuckled when she mentioned how Hershey had evaded them and suddenly there was a cloud of money all over the yard. "Sorry. I realize that it must've been stressful, but I wish I could've seen that."

"It's not something I'll likely ever forget." They must have looked ridiculous tearing around the yard in the pouring rain. "Then there was the note, which hasn't helped." She got up and retrieved the notebook from the counter. She pulled out the copy and handed to Alex.

His eyebrows furrowed as he read it through. "Interesting, but what does it mean?"

"I don't know. Yet. I'm just hoping we find the owner of the money. I'm going to run an ad in the paper. Michael cautioned me to be careful and not reveal any details. People can get very strange over large sums of money."

"Even small sums," Alex said. "How much are we talking about here?"

"Eighteen thousand, five hundred, and forty-three dollars. Correction. Eighteen thousand five hundred, and *sixty*-three dollars. Michael found another twenty."

Alex let out a low whistle. "He's right. You need to be extra careful."

"Don't worry. I will be. Anyway, that's why I said the money would come in handy around here. The library needs funding for the elevator and the literacy class."

Alex nodded with understanding. "I wish I had that kind of money to donate, but even if I did, I wouldn't have left it where Hershey could get at it. That is just so irresponsible."

"I know, which is why I wonder if whoever left the package didn't consider it a lot of money. Does that make sense?"

"I suppose. If they are really rich and this is pocket change, I guess they wouldn't care how they delivered it. If this was someone's life savings, you'd think they'd be pounding down your door."

"The day is still young." Anne smiled again.

"True," Alex said. "Do you have any ideas of who might've lost or left the money?"

"I started a list." Anne opened her notebook. "So far my list is pathetically short in terms of people who might've left money to the library. I have Mrs. Patsy Crenshaw and Randolph Barker. They've been instrumental in fund-raising over the years and also donated funds to the town."

"Mr. Barker is now in a nursing home. He had a stroke. I ran into his son at the market a couple months ago. I've done work for him. He says his father will be in the home permanently."

"That's sad." Anne made a checkmark by Mr. Barker's name. He had much bigger problems right now than to think about donating money to the library.

"I don't know Mrs. Crenshaw, only what I read in the paper about the activities she has been involved in." Alex stared at Anne's list. "What about Theresa Henderson?"

"The name sounds familiar."

"You may have read about her in the newspaper. She won the lottery."

"Oh yeah, and she's been donating to some charities." Anne jotted her name down.

Alex was silent for several moments. "But she hasn't been secret about her donations."

"And why would she write a note like that?"

They fell silent again, both thinking. Anne took a sip of coffee and then nearly choked when Alex said, "Maybe you have a secret admirer."

He handed her a paper napkin and she wiped her mouth after she quit coughing. "I seriously doubt that. But . . . maybe Aunt Edie did." Her aunt had been a unique lady with a bubbling, enthusiastic personality and an energetic lifestyle. Anne could imagine she had lots of admirers.

She looked down at the note. "But you have a good point there. The way this is written, the message has special meaning for someone. Like a secret message between the two of them."

Alex got up to help himself to more coffee and refill Anne's mug. "Did your aunt mention any special male friends?"

Anne thought back over the years. "Aunt Edie had many friends and at least one love of her life, but I wouldn't really know about her dating. I can ask my mother if there was anyone special."

Alex drank more coffee and then snapped his fingers. "What about Mr. Bartholomew? Remember him?"

Anne had to think for a moment. "Was he the one who secretly put in the sod on the school ball field?"

"That's him. Remember he was always leaving gifts to the town and wanted to remain anonymous. I haven't seen him in years. I heard he rarely leaves his estate these days."

Anne jotted his name down on her list and put a star beside it. The memories came flooding back. Mr. Bartholomew, a rich eccentric who liked to dress in old-fashioned suits and a top hat, was embedded in Blue Hill history. He'd been active on various committees, but purportedly did more than the average volunteer. If Aunt Edie's legacy was the library, then Mr. Bartholomew's legacy was his custom of donating secret gifts to the town.

One day when she and Alex were in grade school, they arrived Monday morning to find badly needed fresh sod laid over the entire baseball field. He'd had it clandestinely done overnight as a surprise for the school, and it had taken weeks for the school officials to find out who was ultimately responsible. And even then he didn't want any acknowledgment. There had been rumors of his other gifts, such as the marble benches that suddenly appeared around Rosehill Park pond and the truckload of brand-new clothing and toys that had arrived at the local shelter on Christmas.

"Mr. Bartholomew must've known Aunt Edie since they were both involved in many projects improving the town," Anne said.

"Maybe he holds a soft spot for her memory and he wants to support her library."

"Could be. But why the cryptic note?" Anne said more to herself.

Alex lifted a shoulder in a shrug. "He's done stranger things before."

"So true. I'm going to see what I can find out about him." Anne glanced at the kitchen clock and pushed back her chair. It was time for the library to open. "Thanks for the help with this and for the brochures."

"I'm going to take another look and see if I can get the elevator going at least temporarily. I can't promise anything though."

"I just appreciate your trying," Anne said sincerely. She walked with Alex down the stairs to the main floor and he continued down to the basement. Anne followed the sound of clicking computer keys to find Wendy working on literacy class handouts.

"Your muffins are fantastic," Anne said.

Wendy looked up, her frown lifting to a smile. "So you think they're okay for serving tonight?"

"Perfect, especially if it rains. Coffee and muffins will be appreciated. I have some frozen cookie dough too. I think I'll bake some before the class."

"That sounds great. I just hope the rain doesn't keep our students away." Wendy clicked the print button and stood.

Anne unlocked the front door and, since Wendy was finished with the computer, she reviewed the previous day's checkouts to see if there might be a clue of who might have left the money. Except for some of the students who needed reference material, mothers who came for Story Time, and patrons who liked to stop by to read the newspaper or magazines, most of the patrons only came in every one to two weeks. None of yesterday's visitors struck her as people who could or would carry around a large sum of money, but it wouldn't hurt to ask if any of them saw a package outside.

She printed out a list of the patrons and jotted down their phone numbers from their library card information.

"Do you think these handouts are adequate?" Wendy placed three colored sheets on the counter. "I copied them from the administration manual and then added our contact information. I also put a border. It looked too plain."

Anne set her list aside and examined the handouts. "These look great. I like the borders. I just read last night in the material you gave me that they recommend when starting literacy classes to make things look attractive and inviting."

"Good. I'll print out six copies of each with hopes that we get at least that number tonight," Wendy said. "No one else has signed up, but maybe we'll get some walk-ins."

A whirling sound drew their attention. The elevator shuddered and then lowered to the first floor and kept going to the basement. A few moments later it came back up with Alex inside.

Alex held up a hand as Anne and Wendy rushed over. "Before you get too excited, I only patched the motor. The wiring could go any minute. Don't put any people on it until I get the replacement parts. It could get stuck again."

Anne looked at Wendy. "We better have the class downstairs tonight."

"I agree." Wendy chewed on her lower lip as she looked around the first floor. "We could set up a couple tables over in the History Room.

"I can get the tables down for you," Alex offered.

"Thanks. We can use two portable tables from the Reference Room," Anne said and Alex headed up the stairs. A few moments later the elevator shuddered and ascended to the second floor.

Wendy walked back to the checkout desk with Anne. "Anything new on the money?"

"It's still safely at the police station, but there is something new. Last night, when Michael and I searched the yard, we found a note that must've been in the package. Do you want to see it?"

"Of course," Wendy said. Anne handed her the note and when she'd finished reading it, she had the same incredulous expression Alex had earlier. "Who is 'Gracious Lady'? You?"

Anne shook her head. "Most likely it would be Aunt Edie *if* the money was meant for her. I can't think of a kind deed I ever did to warrant someone leaving me that much money. Does the reference to the dog mean anything to you?"

Wendy tucked a lock of her dark hair behind her ear, her expression thoughtful. "It sounds like a story I've heard."

"It's vaguely familiar to me too, but which one and how does it pertain to the money?" Anne asked as Alex came down the stairs. He pushed the elevator call button and the elevator lowered carrying the two tables.

"Where do you want these?" Alex asked as he opened the elevator's metal gate.

"History Room," Wendy said as they went over to assist him. Alex carried the portable tables into the room, and they decided to lean them up against the wall for the time being.

"Anything else you need?" Alex asked.

"If there is, Wendy and I can handle it. Thanks again, Alex," Anne said.

"No problem. I'll get back with you on the elevator repair." He gave them a wave and went out the door.

"Where were we?" Wendy asked she helped Anne move the room's study table and chairs over to later accommodate the other tables. "Oh yeah, the note."

"Alex suggested that maybe the note writer was a secret admirer of Aunt Edie who wanted to leave a gift. Maybe in her memory."

"That sounds so romantic, but . . . why not just say what the money was for or even address it to someone? Any ideas?"

"Maybe. Do you know Mr. Bartholomew?" Anne asked as she carried another chair to the side of the room. "He has done loads of good for the town."

"Is that the same guy they mentioned on the news the other night who funded the remodel of the Senior Center?"

"I didn't see that report," Anne said with regret. "What did they say?"

"They just thanked him for his generosity. Supposedly he was a silent partner in the project, but someone wanted to put up a plaque in appreciation. They showed a photo, an old one. He had a mustache and was wearing a top hat."

"That sounds like him."

Anne and Wendy decided they'd done all they could to prepare for the class in the History Room, and Anne went back to her library work. The rest of the morning flew by as Wendy worked on the class and Anne checked books in and out and ran upstairs for books for some of their elderly patrons who didn't want to attempt the stairs.

After lunch, Anne methodically went through the list of library patrons who had come in the day before, marking each name off with a highlighter as she contacted them. Since the package most likely appeared in the afternoon, she worked backward through the list. The page was almost solid yellow by the time she finished. She still had three more to call who weren't home, but so far no one was missing a package or had seen one out front. Trying not to feel discouraged, Anne put the list away as Remi Miller, one of her part-time helpers arrived and helped Anne set up the portable tables for the class. Remi manned the desk as Anne drove over to the elementary school to pick up her kids.

Liddie flew out the school door, just bursting at the seams with information about the visitor who had come to the school. All the grades had met in the auditorium for a science program.

"Mr. Rigsby had all kinds of frogs!" Liddie exclaimed.

"Frogs?" Anne asked as she secured Liddie in her car seat.

"Big ones and little ones. Some were a pretty green, but there were ugly ones too with warts on them."

"Those were toads," Ben said as he scooted onto the seat next to Liddie. "He had snakes too. He showed us some of the snakes that live around here."

"Really?" Anne said with a little shudder as she remembered thinking how they'd pushed through the bushes and tall grass at the edge of the yard looking for the dollar bills. She closed the back door and got into the driver's seat.

"But they are good snakes," Liddie said.

"Not all of them," Ben added. "There are poisonous ones too. He showed us how to tell the difference. The poisonous ones have a flat head shaped kind of like a triangle. The harmless ones have round heads."

"Mr. Rigsby told us to just leave all snakes alone 'specially if we aren't sure what kind they are," Liddie said, her voice rising. "They all can bite."

"That's good advice. Let's just leave them all alone." Anne put her blinker on and merged into the line of cars leaving the school. She wasn't necessarily afraid of the reptiles but preferred that she and the snakes just ignore each other's existence. She imagined that since they had Hershey around, the snakes weren't keen on entering the backyard or coming around the house.

She glanced at Ben through the rearview mirror. "And no, you can't have a snake for a pet."

"I didn't ask."

"But you were thinking about it."

Ben grinned.

Anne chuckled. Did she know her son or what? Too bad she couldn't figure out other people as easily, like the author of the Gracious Lady note. What secret was he or she trying to convey?

CHAPTER FIVE

By the time Anne fixed dinner and baked some frozen cookie dough, it was a half hour until their first literacy class began. She left Ben in charge of cleaning up the kitchen and watching Liddie. She hurried downstairs with her plate of cookies and started a pot of coffee on the machine in the office area.

Wendy placed a platter of muffins on the small table in the History Room. "You'd think we were throwing a party." She'd added a bowl of mints and another of nuts.

"It looks great, Wendy. Very inviting." Another guideline for establishing a successful literacy program was to make the students as comfortable as possible. Anne hoped a table laden with goodies and the homey smell of the baked goods would help accomplish that.

The world had darkened outside the windows. More foreboding storm clouds were rolling in.

Anne checked over tables. Wendy had already placed notebooks and pencils on one of the tables with the day's current lesson and handouts. They were ready except for the arrival of the other volunteers and the students.

The door opened and Jennifer Banks rushed in. She pushed back the hood on her purple rain cape revealing her short, spiky red hair as she headed straight to Anne. She gripped Anne's hands in hers and her green eyes narrowed with concern. "Are you okay?"

"Y-yes I'm fine," Anne said, startled. "Why?"

"I know Michael made a stop here last night. Something about a package, but he wouldn't give me any details. He said everything was fine, but I can read that man. He's very concerned about something."

"Oh, that," Anne said. "I found some money in the front yard and we're trying to track down the owner. That's all there is to it."

"That's it? Oh, that man!" Jennifer said with a stamp of her foot. She released Anne's hands. "He got me frantic for nothing. I know he can't discuss his cases with me sometimes, but this was about *you!*"

Anne suppressed a giggle at Jennifer's outrage. "He did say that I was fine."

"Yeah, but he always says everything is fine, even when Tim broke his arm. Sure, he was fine in that he wasn't dead, but I wouldn't classify a broken arm as *fine*. Nothing seems to ruffle that man on the surface. It's like trying to read a wall and looking for the cracks."

"And you never, ever overreact," Anne teased. Jennifer was easily excitable, as well as fun-loving, creative, and flamboyant compared to Michael's calmer, no-fuss demeanor. Even in high school their relationship was fraught with misunderstandings, but they loved each other dearly and now had three adorable children, Jed, Tim, and Mia, to prove it.

"Okay, maybe I do overreact at times." Jennifer giggled as she shed her cape and smoothed her bright green sweater over her black jeans. Her black platform shoes added a few inches to her height.

"I think Michael is more worried that the package might have been dropped by someone doing something illegal." Anne explained about Hershey and the money. "I plan to place an ad and hopefully the owner will come forward soon."

"I hope you get to keep the money. Isn't there a saying about being dumb and losing money?"

"A fool and his money are soon parted?"

"That's it," Jennifer said with a laugh.

"I think that quote refers to spending it."

"I could spend the money real quick, which in that case would make me a fool." Jennifer grinned. "Anyway, I don't mean to sound greedy and insensitive. I'd do the same thing as you."

"I know you would," Anne said.

"Michael would make me."

They giggled so loudly that Wendy lifted her finger to her lips. "Sh!"

Anne and Jennifer almost erupted into more laughter about Anne being shushed in her own library, but at that moment Heather Stafford walked in.

"What are you laughing about?" Heather placed an umbrella in the stand by the door.

"We're just being silly, as usual," Jennifer said with a wink at Anne.

Anne nodded. Normally she was composed and more on the quiet side in everyday life, but when she got together with her high school friends, it was like being transported back to her teen years before life got so serious.

"Some things never change," Heather said with affection as she hugged them both. She'd dressed in a fitted black-and-white-striped knit dress and black tights that looked both stylish and comfortable. Her long, curly dark hair hung down her back. A talented flutist, she had been employed by several symphonies before love brought her back to Blue Hill. She still played the occasional concert with different musical groups, but most of her focus these days was on being a teacher at the Blue Hill High School and her students.

"Am I too early?" Heather asked, looking around.

"No, right on time. The students haven't arrived yet."

"I just hope they do." Wendy strolled up behind them. "That storm could get nasty."

"Well, if they don't show, we can have a little party ourselves," Jennifer said looking at the refreshment table. She was joking but Wendy didn't appear amused, which wasn't like her. Anne realized that Wendy was a little nervous. She had put so much of her time and heart in launching this program, and Anne hated to see her disappointed. It would be such a shame if no one took advantage of the free public service.

Anne looked out the window for any sign of approaching cars.

Lord, please let the students show up. And please protect everyone from the storm.

Jennifer poured a cup of coffee and added extra cream and sugar. Heather settled for a bottle of water before they sat in the chairs that lined the bookshelf. From there they could observe the class without appearing intrusive.

To Anne's relief, at five minutes to seven, an elderly man arrived. He walked with a wooden cane gripped in his hand, although he didn't seem to need it much as he marched up the steps to the porch and then inside.

"Is this where the reading class is?" His snowy hair contrasted with his dark skin and his lively brown eyes twinkled as if he was secretly laughing at something. He stopped in front of Wendy, cracked a huge smile, and saluted. "William Harris. All present and accounted for, ma'am."

Wendy appeared slightly taken aback but then smiled warmly. "Good evening. Mr. Harris. So nice to meet you."

"Call me 'Willy.' Everyone else does, except my son. He calls me 'sir.'" He chuckled deep in his chest. "He lives in Philly now with my seven-year-old granddaughter, one of the sweetest children that God ever created. Not that I'm biased or anything."

Anne smiled, immediately liking his sense of humor. "Welcome, Willy. I'm Anne Gibson and this is Wendy Pyle. We're volunteer literacy coaches and class instructors. The class will be meeting in the History Room tonight."

"My, I didn't expect such pretty young things to be my teachers." He gave Anne a wink. "I might have to arrange for lots of private tutoring."

"Well, we can arrange that if you like," Wendy said as she looked up from her clipboard. She hadn't caught the wink. "In fact you will spend time each week with a tutor during the program, but if you want to practice more than twice a week, we can schedule you with someone."

"Perhaps we should see how tonight goes before you decide," Anne said. "We have coffee, muffins, and cookies if you'd like to help yourself while we wait for the others to come."

"Ah, the way to a man's heart is through his stomach," Willy said, patting his slightly rounded belly. "Bring on the feed." He headed for the refreshment table.

Anne shook her head with amusement. Alex had said the same thing that morning. Were men that easy to please? The two other women who had called and preregistered were listed as Trisha Corwin and Sandy Benson. Wendy waited by the front door and kept making little fussing remarks about the storm keeping them away, but the two women dashed in just before the sky opened up and poured buckets of rain.

Wendy greeted them enthusiastically and then asked everyone to take their seats around the long table in the History Room. Anne lingered in the doorway so she could keep an eye on the checkout desk. The library was open until eight on Thursday evenings.

"Welcome, everyone," Wendy said. "We are glad you're here. For the next six weeks, we're going to be learning and reviewing the necessary skills needed to read. Everyone will go at their own pace, so if you don't finish by the end of the six weeks, you can just continue on as the session repeats. Before we begin, let's make introductions. These are our volunteer tutors, Jennifer Banks and Heather Stafford. We will add more volunteers as we go along."

Willy let out a low whistle. "More pretty girls," he whispered loudly.

"We will also have a teacher, Mr. Layton, who will be joining us next week," Wendy said with a stern look for Willy. "He's busy with the school year coming to a close, but he will be reviewing everything that we do." She gestured toward Anne. "And this is Anne Gibson, the codirector of the program and librarian here. She will be teaching some of the classes and will be available for tutoring."

Anne smiled and gave a little wave.

"Now, let's go around the table and get acquainted," Wendy said. "Willy, can you start? Just tell us a little bit about yourself and what your reading goals are."

"I'm seventy-seven years old and proud of it," Willy proclaimed with a puffed-out chest. "I had to drop out of school in the third grade to help my folks on the farm. I bet you young'uns don't even remember the days when this was mostly farm land around here. Anywho, I could read a little and cipher a little and that's all I needed. My wife Thelma, God rest her soul, could read just dandy. But now that my old legs can't get me to places much anymore, I figure I should improve my mind. I want to learn to read the Bible for myself" — he thumped his fist on the table — "so I can know if my preacher is on the up-and-up, if you know what I mean."

"That's a wonderful goal, Willy," Wendy said as Anne turned aside so they couldn't see her lips twitch from trying not to laugh. Jennifer caught her eye and covered her mouth with her hand. Anne wondered if Pastor Tom received questions about if he was on the up-and-up. Thinking of the pastor reminded her that he had never called her back. She sent a quick prayer for the poor family in the hospital that everything would be okay.

Trisha Corwin, a petite twenty-something redhead, dressed in a T-shirt and shorts frayed at the ends, spoke next. "I was just dumb, you know? School was boring so I blew off my classes. Figured I'd just get married or something and get by just fine, but that didn't work out. I'm divorced and getting tired of waiting on tables at the diner, you know? I don't want to do that for the rest of my life so I want to go back to school."

"What do you want to study?" Anne asked.

Trisha shrugged. "I'm thinking business or maybe social work. I'm not sure. I just need to be able to get a good score on my ACT so I can get into college. And I want to improve my reading so I won't struggle so hard this time."

Wendy made a note. "That's something really important to work for. We can make sure to get you the right ACT material to study when we get to that stage." Wendy turned toward the next student. "Sandy, how about you?"

Sandy Benson, a pretty woman with short, dark hair streaked with silver, let out a big sigh. "Reading never really clicked with me. I graduated with poor grades eons ago and reading has never been fun. I see other people enjoying reading books or a magazine, but for me it just seems like work."

She looked around at the library shelves. "I want to be able to come into a library or a bookstore and have fun. Some of my friends practically live in libraries in the winter."

"Anne can relate to that. She lives here at the library, literally, on the top floors if you didn't know," Wendy said with a chuckle, and everyone laughed.

Anne smiled. "I obviously love libraries, and I hope you'll feel the same way when you finish here. They can open up your whole world."

Wendy reached for a file on the table. "The first thing we need to do is have everyone take an assessment exam to see at what level you're reading."

Willy groaned. "A test? We just walked in the door and you want to give us a test?"

"Sort of," Wendy said with a reassuring smile. "But no worries. You can't fail it. A tutor will listen to what you can read on the page, and that will give us some idea where we can assist you the most." She paired up each student to a literacy volunteer, and they fanned out across the library so they could talk privately.

Wendy had assigned Willy to Anne. He didn't look so sure about Wendy's assurance regarding not failing, but he attempted to identify letters and read the paragraphs of increasing difficulty to Anne. She marked the sentences and words he repeated correctly. Anne would have to look more carefully at the assessment chart when they finished tonight, but at first glance it appeared Willy could read at about a second-grade level.

After the initial assessments were taken, Wendy taught the first lesson on basic phonics, and all but Sara did really well.

By the time the class ended, everyone seemed to feel comfortable with each other. All three students said they would be back on Tuesday. Wendy offered that if any of them would like a tutoring session on the weekend to let her know. They finished the evening by enjoying the refreshments and chatting with each other.

Anne stood to the side watching the students and her friends interact, thinking how much Aunt Edie would have enjoyed this evening. The class was off to a good start despite the low enrollment.

Anne turned to Jennifer and Heather after Willy ambled out the door. "Thanks for coming. I know how busy you both are."

Jennifer slung her purple rain cape over her shoulders and pulled up the cap. "No problem. This was awesome."

"Yes, it was." Heather picked up her umbrella. "Thanks for getting a program going. I'll help out as much as I can. I might even get Mark to volunteer. Make it a family project."

After Heather went out the door, Jennifer said to Anne, "I'm going to go home and give Michael a piece of my mind for making me worry about you." She laughed. "Just kidding, but keep me updated, okay?" She dashed out into the rain without waiting for an answer.

Anne shut the door and helped Wendy clean up the History Room. "I think that went really well. You did a great job."

"Thanks. I think we're off to a good start and Mr. Layton should be pleased. I'll write up the report for him tonight and turn it in. I just wish we had more people. Surely there are others out there who need these classes."

"What about Luke Norris? Were you able to get ahold of him?" Anne asked as she folded up the metal chairs and stacked them by the elevator.

"I called and left a message, but he never called back. Maybe I'll see him at church this Sunday, and I can find out if he's interested," Wendy said.

"Good idea," Anne said. Luke Norris might not want lessons, and they didn't want to hound him. Liddie could have misunderstood and maybe Beth's father could read just fine but just didn't like to read bedtime stories.

They folded the legs on the tables and placed them by the elevator. The room looked back to normal, and Anne walked Wendy to the door. The rain had become a drizzle and a wet earthy smell greeted them.

"See you tomorrow," Anne called as Wendy hurried to her car. After Wendy turned on her engine, Anne locked the library and turned off the lights.

Her steps felt like lead on the stairs as she climbed to the second floor. It had been a very busy day, successful too—other than she still didn't know who left the package of money. The police had the money now, so it literally was out of her hands—but was Jennifer correct in assuming Michael was concerned about something? Her instincts had always been good. Did Michael suspect something sinister was going on? Anne hoped not. Surely Michael would tell her if there was any danger. But she couldn't shake the feeling of apprehension as she hurried into her apartment and locked the door.

Chapter Six

G ood morning, Anne," Michael said over the phone. "Just wanted you to know that no one has inquired about the missing money yet, and there are no recent reports of area bank robberies and crimes involving cash in that large of an amount."

"Jennifer got after you last night about not calling sooner, didn't she?"

"Yep," Michael chuckled. "But I was waiting to hear back on some feelers I put out. So far nothing."

"Well, it's a relief that we may not be dealing with a crime." She'd gotten in bed last night with a slightly uneasy feeling, despite her efforts to put her worry and trust totally at the Lord's feet. Luckily she'd been so exhausted from the previous night and all the energy spent on the class, she had fallen asleep right away.

"I wouldn't go that far," Michael said. "A crime may not have been reported. We can't rule out that possibility, even though there was that note."

He had a point. Until they determined where the money came from, they shouldn't rule out any possibility. The money could have been stolen. Maybe the note was a code for an exchange of merchandise or something.

Michael's voice broke through her thoughts. "Have you placed an ad yet?"

"No, we were really busy yesterday, and I was waiting to hear if anyone had come forward."

"If you still want to place one, let me tell you how I think you should word it, if you don't mind my saying."

"Not at all." Anne picked up a pencil and jotted down the simple ad Michael suggested word for word. She thanked Michael and hung up just as her two morning workers walked through the door.

"Good morning!" Remi said with a bright smile and bouncy step. Her twin, Bella, trailed after her.

"Morning, Remi. Hi, Bella." Anne took a closer look at the two. The twins were a study in contrast this morning. Remi was dressed in a cute polka dot skirt and white blouse and black Converse tennis shoes. She'd pulled her thick brown hair into a sleek ponytail. Bella wore the same black shoes, but the laces were untied and her rumpled jeans and T-shirt looked like she'd slept in them. Her light brown wavy hair was tousled as if she'd combed the locks with her fingers.

"Bella stayed up most of the night studying for a final this morning," Remi said. "She's wiped out."

"You poor girl. What subject?" Anne asked.

"World Lit. It rocked, although I hated the multiple-choice questions on the test. I do better with essays." A yawn stretched Bella's pretty face. She blinked several times and looked around the library and then down at her clothes as if suddenly aware of where she was. She tucked her shirt in and then tied her shoelaces.

"I'll get you started on some things, and then I need to run over to the newspaper office," Anne said.

"No problemo." Remi scooted around to the back of the checkout desk. Remi wanted to be a librarian someday and enjoyed working the desk and helping people find reference material.

"Do you mind updating our Web site with more summer events?" Anne asked Bella, who had been instrumental in setting up a page for the library on all media sites. She picked up the calendar she used for planning and was amazed to realize that they were approaching mid-May. Liddie and Ben would be off for the summer soon. "And Bella, if you're too tired, it's fine with me if you want to take off early."

"Thanks. I think I'll do that after I input these dates into the system." Bella tapped the calendar and yawned again.

Anne handed Remi a stack of paperwork to file and two new best sellers to cover with plastic. She explained to both of them about the elevator and to be prepared to run upstairs to retrieve books if necessary.

"I'll be back in a couple hours." Anne grabbed her raincoat and went out the back door. She was thrilled to see the sun peeking through scattered clouds and took a deep breath of the damp, earthy air. She tossed a fallen branch for Hershey and as she waited for him to bring it back, she took a quick look around the yard. No more dollar bills were visible. Hopefully they'd gathered them all.

She threw the stick for Hershey again and then hopped into her silver Impala. She drove down Bluebell Lane and turned onto Main Street. Anne loved the downtown with many of the businesses housed in buildings with charming Victorian architecture. Anne found a parking spot in front of the *Blue Hill Gazette*. The two-story, red building was close to the curb and had a quaint covered porch, which she crossed over to open the door under the triangular gable.

Anne was delighted to find Grace Hawkins, editor of the newspaper, behind the counter. The pretty blonde woman with blue eyes smiled when she saw Anne. From the moment she met

Grace, Anne had been impressed with her warmth and her ability to draw people to her. She and Anne had become good friends.

"Anne!" Grace said. "I was just thinking about you this morning and wondering how the literacy class went last night."

"The class went really well, thanks. We only have three students to begin with, but I think the class will grow over time. Wendy suggested that we may need to take out a bigger ad next time we start a new session and run it a few weeks earlier than we did this time."

"Just let me know when," Grace said. "I think what you're doing is wonderful. We've needed classes like yours in Blue Hill for a long time. If you even help just one struggling person, then it's totally worthwhile."

"Thank you for the encouragement," Anne said, touched by Grace's caring and ability to get to the heart of the matter. Numbers weren't necessarily a measure of success.

"Don't worry, word of mouth works really well in this town," she said with smile.

"That's what I'm hoping too. She handed Grace the piece of paper where she had written down Michael's suggestion. I have another personal ad I need to place in the Lost and Found section."

"Package found near Bluebell Lane. Please call to identify," Grace read. "Simple enough but effective." She got out an order form and wrote it up. "There you go," Grace said, pushing the form over so Anne could add her phone number.

After Anne had paid, she lingered by the counter, knowing she should get back to work, but since she was here . . . "Grace, would it be okay if I checked some back issues of the *Gazette*. I'm doing a little research."

"Sure. Come on around to the back." Grace walked with Anne back to the large storage room, which housed two microfiche machines. Stopping in front of a shelf with large binders, Grace tapped the spine. "Just in case you don't remember from last time, the years the newspaper covered are noted here." She pulled out one of the binders and opened to the front page. "Each month has its own page, with the four issues broken down into headline, byline, and a one-sentence summary of each article. The microfiche reels are labeled by year and month." A phone rang in the distance, and Grace headed for the door. "I need to get that," she said over her shoulder. "Our receptionist is out sick today."

"Thanks, Grace." Anne turned on the machine and selected the binder, searching for any photos and any articles that Mr. Bartholomew, Mrs. Crenshaw, or Aunt Edie might be mentioned in. She would make copies of those she found.

This kind of research could get tedious for some, but Anne loved scanning through the back issues and reading about times gone by. When she had more spare time, she'd linger over interesting articles, but today she swiftly scrolled through the newspapers, scanning the headlines and photos, starting twenty years back when Anne had started high school. When she reached June 1998, she spied a group photo with Aunt Edie and her garden club. The article featured Rosehill Park, a pet project of Aunt Edie's. It had been a favorite place of Anne's when she was a young girl, and now Anne took her own children there.

She looked closely at the photo and the people standing in front of the entrance to the park. A fellow dressed in an old-fashioned suit and top hat glared into the camera, very solemn in contrast to the smiles of the others. An old-fashioned handlebar mustache adorned his lip, and he carried a cane with a silver handle. The caption listed him as Marcus Bartholomew, but Anne had recognized him before that. He was a unique character in Blue Hill history, and her past life had crossed his a couple times. The caption also indicated that Mrs. Crenshaw and Mr. Barker were also there, along with Mrs. Frank Davis, Mrs. Geoffrey Clark, and Mr. Garfield Whitesburg. These were people Aunt Edie had worked and socialized with over the years. Could any of these people have made a contribution to the library? Anne made a copy of the page to read later and continued her hunt.

She continued to scan through the articles, printing out anything containing Aunt Edie and her associates. Being an active citizen of the town, Aunt Edie was mentioned in many news articles.

Anne glanced at her watch. It was nearing noon and Remi and Bella would be off work soon. She looked at her stack of articles and photos, pleased with her progress. Her research might not yield anything useful to finding the owner of the missing money, but it would be fun to read about what her aunt had been up to.

She paid for her copies, chatted with Grace for a few minutes, and then headed out. Feeling hungry, she stopped by Coffee Joe's, the coffee shop situated across from the police station, and ordered a tuna sandwich for herself and a dozen cookies for Bella and Remi to take home. They deserved a treat after a week of finals.

As she was coming out of the café, she spotted Michael Banks outside the police station. He saw her too and crossed the road.

"Hi, Anne, how's it going?"

"Great. I just placed an ad with the *Gazette* using the wording you suggested."

"Good," he said. "At least we're covering all the bases. I e-mailed a report to the stations in neighboring towns, and so far no one has inquired about missing money, other than one guy's wallet that had been pickpocketed."

"I appreciate your keeping me informed," Anne said. "This whole incident has been surreal. Just so you know, I've been doing some research on who might've left Aunt Edie some money. Acquaintances of hers. I know it's a long shot, but some of them have been generous to other causes around town."

Michael stroked his chin. "Hey, anything is possible at this point."

* * *

Anne had just gotten out of the shower and put on her bathrobe when the phone rang. She raced for the bedroom phone. Sure enough, it was her mother.

"Hi, sweetheart, sorry it took me so long to get back to you," Charlene Summers said.

"No problem." Anne grabbed a towel for her hair. She'd called her mother when she returned from the newspaper office but had to leave a message when no one answered. "It wasn't an emergency. How was your trip?"

"Perfectly wonderful until your dad insisted on driving straight back from Key West with only stops to get gas. Once he decides it's time to go home, that's what we do. I was hoping to stop along the way to shop and sightsee. Oh well, I guess I wore him out traipsing all over Key West. Poor dear," she said with affection in her voice.

"I'm sure Dad had a great time," Anne said. After all their years of being married, Anne's parents still acted like they were in love and best of friends. Just like Anne had felt with Eric. A day didn't go by that she didn't wish that they had more time together. He had been far too young to have a heart attack. Anne wondered if she'd ever get over the emptiness in her heart. She was so grateful for Liddie and Ben. Eric would live on through them and they would always be her greatest comfort and joy.

"I found two great books that I thought Liddie and Ben would like. They are about the Florida Reef and the Everglade birds. I also bought copies for the library. I'll send them to you on Monday along with a couple shirts I bought for my little darlings."

"That's terrific," Anne said. Her mother had such great taste in books and clothes. "Thanks, Mom."

"So now, what's going on?"

"Something weird happened." Anne explained about finding the money yet again. She was getting good at condensing the facts by now.

Her mother gasped when Anne mentioned the amount. "Imagine leaving that much money lying around!"

"There was also a note. Listen to this." She read the letter to her mother.

"That's sweet. 'A kind deed is never forgotten' makes it sound like the money was a gift."

"I had that thought too, but not for me. Maybe Aunt Edie. She was most certainly gracious."

"I can see someone leaving a donation for the library in memory of Aunt Edie. But why not just knock on the door and say so?" her mother asked.

"And why now?"

"The note sounds a bit old-fashioned. Could the package have been there for a while?" her mother suggested. "Maybe Hershey had dug it up from someplace nearby or found it under the porch."

The package paper had been muddy. Could it have been tucked away somewhere? Alex and his crew had done a thorough job with the remodeling and checking over the house, including the foundation and the porch. So if someone had hidden the package, it couldn't have been too long ago.

But why intend to give someone a gift and then hide it? Suppose Hershey found it on the porch awhile back and buried it. The dog wasn't intentionally left unattended outside the yard, although occasionally he did scamper away when they weren't watching carefully.

"Okay, let's assume that the package was for Aunt Edie or the library, who would donate that much money in cash? Was there anyone special in her life?"

"Like a boyfriend?" asked her mother.

"Or maybe just a close male friend. The handwriting on the note is somewhat bold, suggesting a man could've written it, but it could've been anyone."

"Well, your aunt did know a lot of people," her mom said thoughtfully. "She was active with the church and on many committees over the years. Of course some of her friends may have passed away by now."

Anne consulted the list of names she'd compiled that afternoon from the news articles. "I saw some photos in old issues of the *Blue Hill Gazette* and made a list of some of Aunt Edie's acquaintances. Mrs. Davis, Mrs. Crenshaw, Mrs. Clark, and Mr. Whitesburg? Do you know anything about these people?"

"If I recall correctly, Mrs. Davis went to live with her daughter Jenny in Arizona about two years ago. Jenny is a friend of mine. Mrs. Clark had a falling out with your aunt. I'm not sure what it was all about, but I doubt she'd leave Edie or the library any money."

"What about Mr. Whitesburg?" Anne asked as she made notes.

"I don't know what happened to him. He could still be living in Blue Hill. Now, he was quite wealthy. I believe he may have had a crush on your aunt at one point, although nothing came of it." There was a pause and the sound of a hand muffling the phone. "He did too. Remember he asked her to the Auxiliary dance that one year?"

She came back on the line. "Sorry. Your father is eavesdropping."

Anne circled Mr. Whitesburg's name. She couldn't remember Aunt Edie ever going out on a date when Anne lived in Blue Hill. She certainly attended a lot of the events in town, but it was usually with her female friends. "How about Mrs. Crenshaw?"

"The name is familiar, but I don't know her."

"Okay, I'll see if she is still listed in the phone book." Anne made a note. She'd saved the man on the top of her list last. "Did you know Mr. Bartholomew?"

"Who in Blue Hill doesn't? What a character. I remember when he replaced the steeple at the Baptist church after the storm damaged it."

"I didn't hear about that, but he's been known to do a lot of good deeds around town. Alex and I were discussing how he once donated sod for the baseball field. He didn't want anyone to know he'd done it. He was on a garden club committee with Aunt Edie for years. Alex said that he heard Mr. Bartholomew rarely leaves his house these days."

"He is a strange man, but he has a good heart. I don't believe I ever met him in person. I used to see him driving about in some of his old cars. You know one of those old Fords? Hold on." The connection sounded muffled again for a few seconds. "Your father says it was a Model T, but Mr. Bartholomew had a large collection of vintage cars at one point. He was always old-fashioned, which was refreshing in a way, and I believe he and Aunt Edie were on several committees together besides the garden one, but I never saw them together alone, like on a date. Of course, I wasn't around your aunt all the time. Let's see, Mr. Bartholomew would have to be in his nineties by now. Do you think he may have something to do with the money?"

"'Gracious lady' is an old-fashioned expression like Mr. Bartholomew might use," Anne said. "But surely he would know that Aunt Edie passed away."

"Unless he is forgetful or has dementia by now. Unfortunately, that happens to a lot of people. I know I'm always laying things down and forgetting where I put them. And just last Sunday I went totally blank on Myrna Holster's name when I was about to introduce her to a visitor. Of course I remember now, but how embarrassing."

"You're not that old, Mom," Anne said with a grin. "It happens to everyone." But her mother had a good point. Maybe Mr. Bartholomew forgot that Aunt Edie had passed away and left the money for one of her projects. Or maybe the package had been misplaced years ago somewhere nearby and Hershey found it. It was common knowledge that Aunt Edie wanted the town to have a library. Maybe he was up to his old tricks and wanted to leave money for the library or Aunt Edie, a gracious lady, without anyone knowing it was him.

She chatted with her mom for a few more minutes and after they hung up, Anne grabbed the phone book. She flipped through the pages to the B section, but there was no Marcus Bartholomew listed. She tried calling information but still no listing. The man had lived in the town for his entire life, surely there had to be a listing somewhere.

Liddie appeared in the kitchen dressed in her pink pajamas with kittens on them. "Mommy, are you going to read to me?"

"Sure thing, honey. I'm coming." Anne put the phone book away and followed her daughter up to her bedroom. Tomorrow she'd do some more research on Mr. Bartholomew, Mr. Whitesburg, and Mrs. Crenshaw. And if someone called about the money in response to the ad too, the problem could be solved.

She set aside thoughts of the money and Mr. Bartholomew as she settled into her favorite time of the evening and started to read. "There once was a little fox named Red who lived in the big meadow behind the barn . . ."

CHAPTER SEVEN

Anne leaned back against the pew in the Blue Hill Community Church, enjoying the closing words of Pastor Tom's sermon. The topic of his sermon was Ask, Seek, and Knock. His key text, Matthew 7:7, had always been one of her favorites. *"Ask, and it shall be given you; seek, and ye shall find; knock, and it shall be opened unto you."*

She bowed her head as the pastor offered a closing prayer and then waited in her seat for the crowd to thin in the aisle. Many of her library patrons attended the church, and she smiled and chatted with some as they passed by her. Ben and Liddie had attended children's church today. She was so thankful for a day of fellowship and rest after the busy week.

Yesterday had been extra hectic. The library was only open until one on Saturday afternoons, so she'd anticipated time with the kids and getting some housework done before squeezing in more research on Mr. Bartholomew and other friends of Aunt Edie.

But just as she had closed the library she received a frantic call from Wendy who was at the high school. Two of the mothers assigned to help with a fund-raising bake sale for new gym equipment had not shown up, and Wendy needed to take two of her five children to ball practice because her husband was gone for the day. Could Anne help out? She was stuck.

Anne and the kids had rushed over to the high school, and they'd manned the table for a couple hours. After arriving back home, the rest of the day flew by while Anne tried to catch up on cleaning their living quarters, folding a couple loads of laundry, helping Ben finish a science project due on Monday, and washing the car.

Anne brought her thoughts back to the present. The aisle had cleared some, so she picked up her Bible and purse and walked to the door. She waited for her turn to shake hands with the pastor and his wife, Maggie.

Rev. Tom Sloan had a slim, lanky build, graying hair, and kind brown eyes. He always had a ready smile and was totally trustworthy as a confidante. Anne knew she could always discuss her problems with him.

Tom grasped her hand. "Anne, I'm so sorry I didn't get back to you last week. I tried calling you yesterday."

"That's okay. I totally understand you were in a serious situation," Anne said. Pastor Tom had reported to the congregation that the Hewitts' daughter was going to recover, but it was going to take some time. "Yesterday was so hectic I didn't check my phone messages until late."

"Can you wait a few minutes so we can talk?"

"Sure. I'm not in a hurry. It will give the kids a chance to visit."

He gave her hand a squeeze, and Anne joined the flow of people exiting the foyer. She stopped on the steps, enjoying the sunshine that lit up the huge stained glass window above the front entrance. The church, a red brick building constructed in the late nineteenth century, was located on Church Street. The original church bell still hung above the steeple, and Anne loved to hear it ring on Sunday mornings. She had grown up in this church and it held many happy memories.

Anne smiled at Alex as he came out the door with his nephew, Ryan, and Liddie and Ben. The children ran down the steps and joined their friends on the sidewalk, and Alex stepped down next to her.

Alex gazed up at the blue sky. "Nice day."

"It sure is," Anne said with a contented sigh. "Makes up for all those days of rain."

"I meant to call you yesterday. I may have located a motor for the elevator. And I'm still trying to track down the original manufacturer of your elevator to see if they have a button plate that would match your damaged one."

"I almost called you too. I sent several loads of laundry on the elevator to the basement." A soft giggle, sounding a little hysterical to her, escaped.

"Did it get stuck?"

"Not on the way down, but when I tried to send the clean clothes back up the elevator stopped between the first and second floor."

"I was afraid of that," Alex said with a groan.

"Not only was the elevator holding the kids' school clothes captive, but anyone visiting the library could see our laundry hanging overhead." She giggled again, although it hadn't been funny at the time. "I had Wendy push the button on the first floor while I pushed the button on the second. We alternated doing that a couple times and it finally started up."

"Sounds like a short somewhere in the internal wiring, and I may have to rewire the whole thing. I'll check it again. Sorry."

"It's okay. You warned me that it could happen, and all that got stuck were clothes. It's not like Betty Warring or her sister got trapped in the elevator."

"Now that's a scary thought," Alex said with a twinkle in his eye. "Betty would probably give my ear a good tug like she did when she caught me snitching a handful of olives off the reception table during prayer."

"When did that happen?" Anne asked.

"My family was attending a wedding when I was nine or so. I knew better, but I loved olives and figured by the time my turn came in the line they may be gone. So I grabbed a bunch during prayer. Next thing I knew someone had ahold of my ear. It was Betty. I nearly dropped the olives all the over the floor. She didn't hurt me, of course, but I got the point and never did it again." Alex grinned and affection warmed his tone. "Well, at least not when Betty was around."

Anne laughed. She knew Alex liked and respected the elderly sisters. "Shame on you," she teased.

"Shame on Alex?" Pastor Tom stood behind them on the steps. He raised his eyebrows in mock surprise. "Are you in trouble again?"

"Trouble seems to follow me around," Alex said as someone called his name. He looked over his shoulder. "See? It looks like Mrs. Cratchet needs a word with me. Excuse me." He trotted back up the steps.

"Now, what can I do for you, Anne?" Tom asked. "Maggie said something about a package you found?"

Anne briefly explained about finding the money and Ben seeing Tom drive by in his Packard. "I was wondering if you might have seen anything unusual or . . ."

"Dropped off the package?" Tom asked intuitively.

"I know I'm grasping at straws, but I was thinking that maybe one of our church members wanted to help out the library and donate money anonymously."

"Wouldn't that be a nice gesture? But I'm sorry to say that wasn't me driving by," Tom said. "Bessie was in the shop for repairs, so I used Maggie's car all week."

"I just thought I'd ask," Anne said.

"Do you have any other ideas of who left it?"

"There was a rather cryptic note that seemed to indicate someone may have been thanking Aunt Edie for a kindness."

Tom smiled. "I'm not surprised if it was. Your aunt was a kind and gracious woman."

There was that word *gracious* again, Anne mused. "She was indeed gracious and kind, and I owe her a great deal. So do many others. I'm checking to see if any of Aunt Edie's acquaintances might've wanted to leave something in her memory. So far I haven't had much luck."

"Maybe I can help. Who are you trying to talk to?"

"Do you know Mrs. Crenshaw or Mr. Whitesburg? They spent time with Aunt Edie at various functions."

"No, I don't recall ever meeting them. Were they ever members here?"

"I'm not sure," Anne said. "What about Marcus Bartholomew?"

"That's a name I've heard around town, but I don't know him personally. When I started here, I was told he'd once made a large contribution to the church about twenty years ago when they needed a new organ."

"Oh, so that's where the money came from for the organ," Anne said. She'd been young, but she could still remember the excitement and relief at the arrival of a new organ after the previous one died during a service. There had been much speculation as to who the anonymous donor could be.

"The name of the donor didn't come out until years later, and still only a few people knew. It was Mr. Bartholomew's wish to stay anonymous."

"It appears he did that a lot in the past. I'm wondering if he was up to his old tricks and left the money for the library."

"Mildred Farley should know some of your aunt's acquaintances, including Mr. Bartholomew." He nodded toward the parking lot. "There she goes now. Better hurry if you're going to catch her."

"I didn't realize she was back in town," Anne said as she caught sight of Mildred striding in between the parked cars. "Thanks, Pastor Tom. I'll see what she knows."

"Have a blessed day." Pastor Tom started back up the steps but then turned back to Anne. "I just thought of something. Maybe Shaun was out test-driving Bessie and that's who Ben saw driving by the library."

"Shaun Milhouse? Who owns Fowler Auto Repair?"

"Yes. Do you know him?"

"Shaun and I were in high school together."

Tom smiled. "Nice young man. He's the best mechanic in town when it comes to working on old cars. He normally just does body work, but he's great with engines too, especially vintage. Wish I could convince him to attend church here again. Shaun says he works so hard during the week that he likes to sleep on Sundays. But anyway, maybe he noticed something unusual while driving by the library."

"I'll talk to Shaun then. Thanks again."

As Anne hurried down the steps and across the sidewalk to the parking lot, she glanced over at her youngsters. Liddie was still talking to a young girl with a sweet face framed by cascading brown curls. Was that Beth Norris? Anne had seen her about the church but hadn't officially met her yet.

Mildred was unlocking the door to her compact silver car and Anne picked up her pace.

"Mildred," she called and waved when Mildred turned.

"Oh, there you are, dear," Mildred said with a big smile as Anne reached the car.

Mildred had befriended Anne when she'd moved back to town, and now Anne liked to think of her as her surrogate aunt. She and Anne would often share their memories of Aunt Edie. Mildred also occasionally helped out at the library.

"I waved at you earlier, but you didn't see me," Mildred said. "I would've waited, but I have company coming for lunch and need to get the lasagna in the oven to warm.

"I won't keep you then. Something odd happened, and I want your advice. But it can wait."

"Something odd?" Mildred's gray eyes took on a curious gleam. She placed her hand on Anne's arm. "Why don't you and the kids come over for lunch? I'm sure we can find time for a nice chat."

"That would be fun, but I don't want to impose at the last minute."

"Oh, you're not," Mildred said. "In fact, you'd be doing me a favor. I'm one of the hospitality hosts today and so I have a visiting family coming over. They have three children around the ages of yours. It would be wonderful if they had someone to play with." She slid into her car. "Now, I won't take no for an answer. I should have lunch ready in about forty-five minutes."

"Okay, then yes. We'll be over after I pop by the house to change," Anne said, knowing better than to argue once Mildred had made up her mind. She shut Mildred's door and stepped back so Mildred could maneuver her car out of the parking spot.

She gave Mildred a wave and hurried back to the church to collect Ben and Liddie. She noted that Alex had detached himself from Mrs. Cratchet and stood near Wendy, who was talking to a man with very short dark hair who looked to be in his late twenties. He shook his head, seeming a little agitated, and stepped away from Wendy. He went down the steps, and the little girl whom Liddie was playing with followed closely behind. He must be Luke Norris, Beth's father. He took Beth's hand and they crossed the street and turned down the sidewalk.

Wendy noticed Anne and hurried over to meet her. "Oh dear, I'm afraid I handled that badly. That was Luke Norris. I asked him if he was interested in the literacy class, and he acted like I'd asked to do a tax audit or something. He said he didn't know what I was talking about and he was just fine. I think I may have embarrassed him. I didn't mean to."

"Of course you didn't," Anne said. Wendy tended to throw herself enthusiastically into projects, and although she got a little too driven at times, her heart was in the right place.

Alex moved closer. "Didn't mean to eavesdrop, but are you talking about Luke?"

Wendy nodded and blinked as if ready to cry. "I get over enthusiastic sometimes."

"You do?" Alex asked and winked at Anne. "I never would've guessed. I remember the library camp you put on when the mansion wasn't even finished being renovated. Now *that's* enthusiasm."

"And despite my moments of doubt, you pulled the program off magnificently," Anne added with a smile. "Who else but you could have done that?"

To Anne's relief, Wendy sniffed and then smiled at their lighthearted teasing. Trust Alex to be able to smooth over an uncomfortable situation.

"Besides, I wouldn't worry about offending Luke. He's a great guy with a sense of humor," Alex continued. "I use him quite a bit on my crews. He's a competent carpenter. I just don't understand why you were you talking to him about the literacy class. I never noticed him having any difficulties."

"Well, that's my fault," Anne said. "Liddie said that his daughter Beth had mentioned that Luke wasn't able to read her bedtime stories. Maybe she got it wrong and he's just too busy being a single parent."

"The next time I see him, I'll apologize," Wendy said.

"If you'd like me to, I can convey your apology when I see him at work tomorrow," Alex said. "Since we spend time together on the job, he may be more willing to talk to me if there is a problem."

"That would be great if there's an opportunity," Wendy said with relief in her tone. "We started these classes to help people feel better about themselves, and I'd hate to think I made someone feel bad. Sometimes I just don't know what is the right thing to say or do."

* * *

"That was a wonderful lunch, Mildred," Anne said with a deep sigh after waving a final good-bye to the Fosters. She sank into one of the two cushioned rockers on Mildred's porch. She was grateful for a friend like Mildred and liked to visit her, but making small talk with strangers wasn't one of Anne's gifts. She tended to be too quiet, but the meal had been delightful and full of conversation thanks to Mildred's hospitality. Liddie and Ben were playing a board game in the living room, so for the moment all was peaceful.

Mildred carried out a tray with the cookies Anne had brought from home and glasses of ice-cold lemonade. Anne sipped the tart drink but didn't have room for dessert after enjoying a second helping of lasagna.

"I'm glad you could come over. I've missed you," Mildred said.

"I've missed you too," Anne said. "It seemed like you were gone forever, but I'm glad you had a great trip."

"It was fun. My travel group made it all the way to New Orleans and it was steamy hot. They are having a heat wave and it's not even June yet."

"My mother mentioned last week that it was unusually hot and humid in Florida too," Anne said, wondering what her folks were doing now. She missed them especially on Sundays, which were always family days when she was growing up. "My dad didn't even want to play golf, and you know it has to be seriously miserable weather if he won't get out his clubs."

"I'm not sorry I missed all the rain here though."

"It came down pretty hard at times. In fact it was during a bad storm last Wednesday when we found a package. That's what I wanted to talk to you about."

Mildred leaned forward, giving Anne all her attention. "So what's going on?"

Anne summarized the story for Mildred and her quest for finding the owner of the money. She pulled the note out of her purse and handed it to Mildred. "I'm thinking 'Gracious Lady' may be Aunt Edie. What do you think?"

Mildred looked up from reading the note. "I would certainly call your aunt gracious. She was a wonderful woman."

"Let's assume someone did write the note to Aunt Edie. Do you have ideas who it might be? Alex mentioned that maybe it was a secret admirer."

Mildred smiled and leaned back in her chair. "I'll have to think about it, but Edie did have a few admirers. No one serious but with a little encouragement from Edie they could've been."

"My mother mentioned that Mr. Whitesburg had a crush on Aunt Edie."

"Garfield and Edie?" Mildred laughed. "He was a short little guy, really cute if you liked bald men, and quite a character. He was always flirting with the ladies, which may have explained why his wife left him early in their marriage. He was a diehard bachelor until the end. Anyway, I could see him donating to the library for Edie's sake, but sadly, he passed away a couple years ago.

"Then there was a Jonathan White who fancied your aunt for a while. He's still around here, but I can't see him writing a note like that. He was very smart but a bit on the stuffy side and no imagination. I also heard recently that he got married for the third time." She looked over at Anne. "Sorry I'm not being much help."

"That's okay," Anne said. "What about Marcus Bartholomew? He has been known for giving gifts to the town, some anonymously, before he was found out. He was on committees with Aunt Edie."

Mildred's chair stopped rocking. "Marcus! Now there's a strong possibility. I've known him since we went to high school together. He is . . . interesting, to say the least." Mildred jumped up. "I'll be right back."

Anne leaned her head back against the chair and listened to the birds chirping in the trees. She thought again about Pastor Tom's sermon. "*Ask, and it shall be given you.*" Well, she was asking now.

Lord, please help us find out who wrote that note and left the money. And guide us into doing the right thing.

The screen door squeaked open. Mildred handed Anne a wide scrapbook and dragged her chair closer. "There are some high school photos in there of Marcus."

Anne opened the book and examined the black-and-white photos with delight. She paused over a group shot of young ladies all clad in light-colored dresses.

"You'd hardly recognize me now," Mildred said.

"Not true." Anne studied the image of a sweet-faced young woman with long dark hair. "You haven't changed that much."

Mildred laughed. "You inherited your aunt's kindness, although she'd point out my nose has gotten bigger. We were always teasing each other."

Anne smiled and turned the page.

"There's Marcus." Mildred pointed to a tall, skinny gentleman standing in the background by the high school front steps. "And there he is in that one too."

"Mr. Bartholomew wore a hat in every photo I've seen of him," Anne noted.

"Oh, that's quintessential Marcus. He loved to dress well, and even if his style froze in the 1940s, he always remained dapper. It suited him. He was like a breath of fresh air, at least to me, even though he's still very old-fashioned . . . if that makes sense." Mildred's soft expression and faraway look in her eyes made Anne wonder if she had fancied him at some point in her life.

"It does," Anne said. When she lived in New York, she had enjoyed the variety of personalities and different cultures the big city offered.

Mildred gave herself a little shake. "Sorry, I'm getting caught up in memories. But back to your situation. I can imagine Marcus donating money in Edie's memory, even dropping it off on the porch like you found it."

"I'd like to talk to him, but I can't find a phone listing."

"That's because he doesn't have a phone, another one of his quirks. He's been mostly housebound for several years now, although I think it's more by choice than poor health. His daughter lives with him now and she has a cell phone. Her name is Carol Davis."

"Does her family live here too?" Anne asked.

"No. It's a sad story. She's had a bit of a rough time. She married a scoundrel of a husband who eventually ran out on her. Marcus used to growl about him marrying Carol for her inheritance. She's his only child and of course he's very protective, especially since her mother died when she was still in her teens."

"It's terrible to lose a parent," Anne said, remembering how devastating the loss of Eric had been for her own children. Over time the pain had lessened, but they would always miss their father.

"But the good Lord makes everything work out for the best. Marcus is getting up there in age, and Carol moved back home to help him out. They seem content together. I still visit him occasionally. How about I set up a visit with him sometime this week? All this talk has me wanting to see him."

"That sounds great," Anne said.

"I think this may be very productive." Mildred nodded. "Marcus knows everything about this town, and he used to know almost everybody. We can ask him about the note. Even if he didn't write it, he might know who did."

CHAPTER EIGHT

"Fetch, Hershey!" Ben threw a stick across the backyard.

Anne sat on the back steps and watched the dog race after the stick. Since Hershey's mischief might be a sign he needed more attention, Anne had suggested that they play with the dog for a while after they got home from Mildred's. Hershey happily retrieved the stick, dropped it at Ben's feet, and sat on his haunches.

"Good boy, Hershey," Anne called. Now, why couldn't Hershey have obeyed so well with the package of money the other night?

"Yes, you are a good boy." Ben rubbed Hershey's ears and threw the stick again.

"My turn," Liddie said as the dog bounded after it.

Ben shook his head. "You can't throw the stick far enough."

"I can too!" Liddie said hotly as Hershey carried the stick back to Ben. "Give it to me."

Ben ignored his little sister and threw the stick again.

"Mom!" Liddie yelled. "Ben's not being fair."

"Liddie, I'm right here. You don't have to shout," Anne said. "Let Ben have a few more throws, and then you can play with Hershey for a while."

Liddie stuck her lower lip out in a pout and plopped down under a tree. Hershey dropped the stick and bounded over to her. He licked her face until she squealed with laughter.

Anne pulled her cell phone out of her back pocket. She usually turned the ringer off during church and sometimes forgot to turn it back on. Sure enough, the screen indicated she had missed two calls. She didn't recognize the numbers. Maybe they were about her ad in the paper.

She dialed back the first number and no one answered. She tried the second and this time it connected.

"Yo," a male voice answered.

"Hi! I'm A—" Anne almost forgot she wasn't supposed to give her name. "I'm the person who placed the ad about the package. Were you calling about that?"

"Oh yeah, yeah. I can come and get it."

"Well, can you describe it?" Anne asked.

"It was package, you know? A box."

"I'm sorry, but I don't have what you're looking for. Thank you for calling," Anne said as she moved her thumb to sever the connection.

"Yo, don't hang up," the man said. "I'll come over there and look to make sure it's not mine."

"No, it wouldn't do any good. The contents are with the police."

The phone clicked off.

Anne pulled the phone away from her ear. Obviously the calls from unscrupulous people that Michael warned her about were beginning.

The phone buzzed in her hand and Anne recognized the caller ID as the other number she had tried to call earlier.

"I lost a package and I'm in deep trouble," a woman said. "I was on Bluebell Lane, and I don't know when it fell out of the car. Maybe when I stopped at the library."

Anne's heart nearly stopped. Maybe she'd found the owner. "Can you describe the package?"

"I don't know what was in it. I never even looked at it that closely. It was just there in my car." Her voice went high into a wail. "It was my *husband's*." A sob tugged at the woman's voice.

"It's okay," Anne said gently. "Everything will be okay. I sent the contents over to the police station."

"Oh dear, that won't work. Not at all. I can't get involved with the police. My husband will kill me if he knew I lost it. Can you go get it for me? I'll pay you a reward."

Anne's radar went up. The woman was willing to pay a reward for a package that she didn't even know the contents of? Anne didn't think so.

"Don't worry, I know the police officer who's in charge of this case, and he will be very discreet. I can meet you at the station in an about an hour."

The woman swore at her and hung up. Anne sighed. What was it about the idea of getting something for free that brought out the worst in some folks?

Maybe the ad hadn't been a good idea, but there was still the chance the rightful owner would see the ad and call. She'd just have to be cautious. Meanwhile she would try to find other ways to identify the author of the Gracious Lady note.

* * *

On Monday morning as Anne waved good-bye to Liddie, her daughter turned in the school doorway and blew her a kiss. Anne laughed and put her hand over her lips and blew her one back. The previous evening they'd watched a children's movie where a young princess blew a kiss to a knight. Liddie had been blowing dramatic kisses ever since. Ben hadn't found the gesture quite so amusing. He rolled his eyes when Liddie sent one off to him as he trudged up the school stairs.

As Anne drove away from the school, her mind shifted back to the dilemma of the missing money. The calls yesterday had yielded no results. So far neither Anne nor the police had identified any witnesses who might have seen someone drop the package except for whoever had been driving Pastor Tom's car. Ben said it had gone by shortly before Hershey had appeared with the package clenched in his jaws.

Tom had mentioned that Shaun Milhouse had been working on his car. She couldn't imagine Shaun carrying around that much cash or writing a cryptic note like that. He was a pretty straightforward guy. But, if he had driven by, maybe he saw something unusual along the street or someone lingering in her yard. It was a slim chance, but worth a visit to Shaun's.

She turned off on a side street and headed to Fowler's Auto Repair. Tall, ancient oak trees shadowed the street, and the water droplets on the leaves shone like tiny diamonds under the morning sun.

The business was housed in an ancient stone building with narrow windows. Anne always thought that the building must have had some historical significance since it had never been replaced with something more modern. Mr. Fowler had owned the shop for four decades before turning it over to Shaun.

Cars lined the front of the building. Anne did a U-turn and parallel parked across the street. She stepped out onto the asphalt and waited for a car to pass before cutting across to the parking lot, sidestepping puddles.

Two of the three large garage doors were rolled up and inside were several cars in various stages of repair. A loud machine noise greeted her as she strolled into the bay.

"Hello!" she called.

A short, wiry man dressed in paint-spattered overalls leaned over the hood of a pickup truck, a sander in his hand. Anne waited until the sander stopped whirling and then said hello again.

Shaun Milhouse lifted the protective goggles off his face and smiled. "Hi, Anne! What brings you down here? Did something happen to your car?"

Anne smiled at the deep concern in Shaun's voice. He had loved cars since he was a kid. "No, my car is fine. Thanks. But you'd be the first person I'd come to if I needed repair work done."

"You know who the best in town is." Shaun grinned and set the sander down. "So what's shaking?"

"I have kind of an odd question for you and —"

Shaun held up a gloved hand. "How about a cup of coffee first? I could use an excuse for a break. I just brewed a fresh pot and I promise it's good. Really."

"Really?" Anne teased as she followed him to a side room. "I assume you've had complaints."

Shaun's grin widened as he shoved open the door to his office crammed with a desk and filing cabinets. "You could say that.

"Have a seat."

Anne chose one of the two chairs and sat as he sauntered over to one of the filing cabinets where a fancy-looking coffee machine rested on top. He poured her a mug of dark, fragrant coffee.

"Cream? Sugar?" he asked.

"Just black. Thanks."

He handed the mug to her, and Anne took a cautious sip of the rich brew. "This is really good."

"See? I told you. I can also make espresso or cappuccino. My new office manager insisted we upgrade to a better machine and gourmet coffee or she threatened to quit."

"That's right. I did." A tall, slender woman with lots of wavy dark hair stood in the office doorway. "Someone had to do something about the sludge he was brewing. Ugh." She slid the purse strap off her shoulder and tucked the bag into the filing cabinet.

"Lily Thompson, this is Anne Gibson. We went to high school together," Shaun said. "I hired Lily about a month ago and she's transformed the office. I actually can find things now."

Anne smiled. "It's nice to meet you, Lily."

"Nice to meet you too," Lily said to Anne and then waved a hand at Shaun. "Don't get up. I have to go back out to my car in a sec to get some things."

"I've been meeting a lot of Shaun's schoolmates and people he grew up with," Lily said. "I'm from Boston and still getting used to small-town living. It's a different world in Blue Hill. Much slower, but I like it."

"Anne lived in New York for a while," Shaun said.

Lily's green eyes widened. "You did? I've always wanted to visit there. That must've been exciting."

"It was. I enjoyed the big city, but Blue Hill is a wonderful place too. This is home to me."

"Hopefully I'll feel that way soon too." Lily glanced at Shaun and then sidestepped to the door. "Excuse me, I'll be right back."

The way Shaun watched Lily leave gave Anne the distinct impression that Shaun cared for the woman more than as just an employee. At least she hoped so. Shaun had been a bit of a loner in school and he'd never married. He'd worked in the body shop even back then, and judging from the amount of cars waiting out front, he continued to be successful.

Shaun shifted in his seat. "Okay, so what's this odd question you have?"

"It has to do with Pastor Tom's car. He said you'd been working on it."

Shaun leaned back in his chair and propped a foot up on his desk. "Yes, I worked on dear old Bessie. Tom picked up his baby early this morning. I don't think he could stand another day without it. Got to love a man who has great taste in cars."

"My son said that he saw Bessie pass by the library on Wednesday afternoon."

"That was me. I test-drove Tom's car several times that day. His wheel well was slightly dented and causing a vibration." He grinned. "And frankly, I like driving it."

"When you passed by the library, did you see anything unusual? Someone dropped a brown package either in the yard or on the front porch. I'm trying to find the owner."

Shaun tilted his head back and stared at the ceiling. "I'm trying to think. Lily was with me, and I must've gone past the library at least three times. I wasn't really paying attention to anything but how the car was driving."

"Wasn't that where we saw the Porsche?" Lily marched back into the room with a thick folder tucked under arm. Shaun took his foot off the desk and sat up straighter.

"Oh yes! *The Porsche.* That was in front of the library. Good memory, Lily." He smiled at her.

"So you saw a Porsche?" Anne asked, drawing his attention back to her. She had never noticed any of her library patrons driving such a fancy car.

"Yep. This year's model," Shaun said.

"Porsche Cayenne. Black. 4.5 liters. V8," Lily added and earned another admiring look from Shaun. "She pulled out right in front of us. Shaun had to swerve."

"I'm glad you were okay," Anne said. "Did the car come out of the driveway?"

"No, it was parked along the street. I didn't recognize it," Shaun said. "And I usually notice those types of cars around town."

"So you wouldn't know who was driving it then," Anne said, disappointed.

Shaun shook his head but Lily said, "It was a woman. She seemed youngish, but it was hard to tell since she was wearing sunglasses. I think she had blonde hair. She wore a scarf over her head so I can't be sure. She went by pretty quickly."

"Was there anyone else in the car?" Anne asked.

"I don't think so. I was just relieved we didn't collide," Shaun said. "But then if we had, I might've gotten to work on it."

"Oh, don't even joke about that," Lily said with a slight giggle and poked Shaun in the arm. "Now I need my chair so I can get some work done. Isn't Mr. Fuller coming by to get his car at ten?"

Shaun popped to his feet. "Yeah, he is. Break time is over."

Anne said good-bye to Lily and walked with Shaun back into the garage.

"Did you learn anything helpful?" Shaun asked, donning his goggles again.

Anne smiled. "Maybe. At least I'll be on the lookout for the black Porsche. Take care, Shaun. Oh, Pastor Tom mentioned he would love to see you back at church."

"I may start going again." Shaun glanced at the office. "See you later."

As Anne walked back to her car, she thought about the Porsche. Her mother had mentioned that Mr. Bartholomew had a car collection, and Mildred had said that his daughter was living with him now. She wondered if Carol drove a Porsche. Perhaps she'd driven by the library for her father and dropped off the package of cash.

Anne shook her head as she unlocked the Impala door. Okay, so maybe that was just a wishful notion, but it was still worth checking into. Hopefully Mildred could set up a visit with Marcus Bartholomew soon.

CHAPTER NINE

Remi Miller leaned forward and studied the library's computer screen. "I can't find the book *Conquering Procrastination* on the shelf. The computer says it's not checked out."

Anne hurried over to the desk and looked over Remi's shoulder. The book had been checked back in over a month ago. "It may have gotten shelved in the wrong place."

The young woman who'd been waiting patiently by the counter said, "I guess I can come back later. Or would that be procrastinating again?" She let out a little giggle.

Anne smiled, noting the other two books she carried were on time management and organization. "If you have a few minutes, I can take another look, or I can call you when we locate it."

The woman looked at her silver wristwatch and gave a little shrug. "I can wait a few minutes."

"I'm Anne, by the way. We've never had a chance to meet."

"I'm Bonnie, and I just love what you've done with this old house."

Anne smiled. "Thanks. It was remodeled by Alex Ochs. If you ever need a contractor, he's excellent."

"I'll have to remember that. Adding another bedroom has been on my husband's to-do list for eight years now. Procrastination runs in the family. I'm hoping these books will help me at least."

"I'll see what I can do. Maybe Remi can help you find a similar book just in case," Anne said as she jotted down the reference number. She hurried over to the Nonfiction Room and checked the stacks. The book was indeed missing from the place it should have been shelved. She discovered another book out of place too. Her volunteer team was good at shelving books where they needed to be, but she knew from long experience that little mistakes could happen, especially if the person shelving the books was tired. She would have to start checking the stacks—a boring but necessary job sometimes, even in small libraries.

She ran her finger across the whole row with no luck. She studied the reference number again. She reversed the reference number and checked that shelf. Bingo! There, tucked between two books on world spies and airplanes, was the book on procrastination. She tucked it under her arm and returned to the front desk, where Remi and Bonnie were in deep discussion about a new shop opening in the mall in nearby Deshler.

"Here it is." Anne handed the book to Bonnie. "Sorry about the wait."

"Oh no, it's fine." She flashed Anne a smile. "Guess I have no excuses not to get things done now."

As Remi processed the book, Anne turned and surveyed the area. Two middle-aged women wandered around the nonfiction stacks, and a gentleman was seated in one of the big comfy reading chairs across from the checkout desk, leafing through a sports magazine.

"Remi, I'm going to run up and grab some lunch before you go. You okay here by yourself?"

"Sure," Remi said. "I can even stay longer if you'd like. I don't have anything this afternoon with classes being over."

"I think I'll take you up on your offer. I could use the extra help this afternoon," Anne added, thinking about the task of checking the stacks for misplaced books. She also didn't like to leave the front desk unmanned for long if she had to run up to the second floor to get a book for a patron who didn't want to take the stairs.

"Awesome. I'll stick around then," Remi said and smiled at an approaching patron.

"Okay, I'll be back soon," Anne said. "Call me if you need anything."

Anne trotted up the stairs to the second floor, casting a glance at the elevator where she'd put an out-of-order sign on the gate. Alex had said he'd stop by today. She hoped he'd find a way to get it running again—and soon. The inspection time would be here before they knew it. She let herself into their apartment and hurried to the kitchen.

She spied her cell phone on the table. She had forgotten to take it downstairs with her after she had gotten back from talking to Shaun Milhouse. She checked the call log and noticed there had been two calls from numbers she didn't recognize and one voice mail.

She pushed the button to connect her with her messages. Sallie Token, a young library patron, had called about the ad and said she'd lost a small box of video games that she'd picked up at the post office. She thought maybe it had fallen out of her backpack. Anne called her back and left a message that the package she'd found didn't contain video games, but Anne would check the library's Lost and Found box just in case it was there.

Since Anne already had the phone in her hand, she decided to call Mrs. Crenshaw, who was on Anne's list of Aunt Edie's acquaintances who might have donated money to the library. She looked up the number in the phone directory and placed the call.

"Hello?" a woman answered in a loud, raspy voice.

"Mrs. Crenshaw?"

"Yes. Speak up, please."

Anne raised her voice. "This is Anne Gibson at the Blue Hill Library. I was wondering if you had left a package here."

"Say what? Who are you?"

The poor woman was obviously very hard of hearing. "This is Anne Gibson. Edie Summers's great-niece. I'm calling from the library about a package that was left here."

"What package?" Mrs. Crenshaw asked and then coughed several times. "Where are you calling from again?"

"The library. Did you lose some money?" Anne asked, growing frustrated and breaking her rule about discussing the package contents.

"Money? Are calling for a donation? I already gave one to the Library Guild a few months ago. Two hundred dollars. Please make note of that. Thank you for calling."

Anne set the phone down. That had been exhausting, but at least she could cross Mrs. Crenshaw off the list.

Anne fixed a turkey and Swiss cheese sandwich and stood looking out the window as she ate it. The bright sun highlighted the brilliant green hues of the rolling hills. Such a glorious spring day. Unfortunately, the forecasters were predicting more rain tomorrow.

A barking rose from the backyard. Hershey bounded after a squirrel. She rapped on the window. "Hershey, leave the squirrel alone."

The dog didn't hear her, but luckily the squirrel leapt to the back fence where it scolded the Lab before scampering away. Hershey balanced on his hind legs, tongue hanging out, not looking at all disappointed, and dashed away after a leaf rolling in the breeze.

Anne laughed at the dog's antics. The squirrel reappeared on the fence, and something behind it caught her eye. A construction scrap pile lay beyond the fence. Was that a dollar bill stuck on the one of the planks?

Anne hurried down the back stairs and out the door. Hershey loped up to her, and she patted his head before she let herself out the back gate.

The debris pile consisted of wood, plaster, and pieces of pipes. Not all of it was from the remodel of the house. It had been a burn pile back in the days when it was more common to dispose of trash that way. Grass and brush had overgrown most of it so it resembled a small hill.

She circled the pile until she found the spot she'd seen from the window. A ten-dollar bill had snagged on a slivered board. She plucked it off and spied another one caught in a small bush farther up the hill. Her shoes sunk in the mud as she climbed higher and the cold wetness seeped in the fabric of her tennis shoes. As she parted branches and shoved over a block of wood to get closer to the money, her knee bumped into something hard.

"Ouch!" Anne rubbed her knee and examined what she'd hit. A partially covered pipe was sticking up out of the ground. A curved piece, shaped like a candy cane was lying beside it. She picked up the broken shard. She'd seen similar pipes like these sticking out of the ground from people's storm shelters. She peered down into the upright pipe but of course could see nothing but darkness. She tried tugging on it, but the pipe was apparently buried deep.

This was weird. Could it be possible that there was a storm shelter down there? If so, where was the entrance? She climbed off the mound and rounded the debris pile again. If an entryway was down there, then it was under the dirt.

She pulled her cell phone out of her pocket and called Alex.

"Hey, Anne," he said before she even spoke. "I was just on my way over to check the wiring on the elevator."

"I appreciate that Alex, but could you meet me behind the house?"

"Sure. What's up?"

"You'll have to see for yourself," Anne said, hoping that she wasn't just letting her imagination run wild. He'd probably tease her if it turned out to be nothing. She pulled some weeds along the fence to keep busy until Alex's truck rolled up the driveway. He jumped out of the cab and strode over to her.

She showed him where she'd found the strange pipe. "Isn't this the type of pipe they use in storm shelters to provide ventilation?"

"Could be." Alex squatted in front of the pipe. He tapped it and then went back to his truck for a shovel.

He dug down around the base of the pipe "Looks like it's set in concrete. I think you may be right about something being down there, but this is news to me. I never saw anything on the blueprints of the property to indicate your aunt had a storm shelter."

"If she did, where do you think the door is?" Anne asked looking around.

Alex took several steps back and studied the area with a thoughtful expression. He glanced over at the detached garage that stood about twenty feet away. "I was working on a house last year and it had a passageway to a storm shelter from their garage."

"Let's take a look." Anne headed for the garage door.

She had used the garage frequently since they moved in but had never seen anything unusual. She had sorted through some of the old lawn equipment stored in the main area, but there was a back closet, which was on her to-do list to clean out someday.

She opened the door and stepped inside the crowded closet. "Could the entryway be in here?"

"It's in the right place if it is," Alex said coming in beside her. "Let me move some of this stuff."

He stepped around her and shoved an old lawnmower out the door and then grabbed a stack of lawn chairs.

Anne picked up some clay pots and noticed that a tarp lined the entire floor. It took them another ten minutes of clearing items away before they could both stand easily in the center of the small room.

Alex used an old rake handle to bang on the floor. The dull thudding sounds turned to a ping. "There's something metal under here." He tugged on the tarp and it tore in his hands. "Sorry about that. It's old."

"No problem," Anne said as Alex's efforts revealed a metal trapdoor.

"This has got to be it," Alex pulled on the handle, but it didn't budge. "I'm afraid it might be rusted shut. Hold on, I'll get some lubricant from the truck."

The door had been painted a deep blue, but big flakes revealed steel underneath. Alex returned, carrying a can and a long flashlight. He squirted oil into the trapdoor hinges. He gave a mighty tug and the door creaked open.

They stared down into the dark hole and then looked at each other in amazement. Alex clicked on his flashlight and the beam revealed a concrete floor.

"That's deep," Anne said.

"It's a good fifteen feet down." The flashlight beam traveled over a metal ladder attached to the wall and there appeared to be a passageway on the opposite side.

"I didn't realize that they buried storm shelters that far down."

"They don't usually," Alex said.

"Let's go down and see what's there," Anne said feeling like a kid again when she used to explore Aunt Edie's big house.

Alex tugged on the ladder rung. "Seems safe, but let me go first." Alex swung his long legs down onto the ladder and slowly lowered himself. When he reached the bottom, he looked up at her. "It's solid. Come on down."

Anne gripped the cold metal in her hands and lowered herself until she was standing by Alex. Alex shone his light down a narrow passageway lined with concrete and steel. A closed door blocked the other end.

Anne swiped cobwebs off her face and hair as they ventured forward. The metal door was actually cracked open. Alex pushed on it and then stopped short. "Well, look here! This couldn't have been built just for storms. This was built for a war."

"A fallout shelter?" Anne tried to see around him. In school she'd read about the bomb shelters that Americans had built during the Cold War. Why hadn't Aunt Edie ever told her about this?

Alex felt along the wall and clicked something. "There's a switch for that bulb up there, but it may be burned out or the wiring has been disconnected."

Anne used the flashlight app on her phone and shined it along the walls. She gasped as she caught sight of the shelves stocked with canned goods, boxes of food, paper products, cooking utensils and pots, a propane stove, matches, glasses, and a stack of melamine dishes.

Alex circled the room examining the walls and the ceiling. "The room is reinforced with steel beams. I'm impressed. Whoever built this made it to last."

Anne spied a 1963 calendar hanging on the wall. "I feel like I've stepped into a 1960s time capsule." She stopped in front of a big cylinder with a crank on its side. "What's this?"

"I think it's some sort of filter. There's the other end of the air pipe you found." He pointed to the ceiling.

"There's another door behind you," Anne said.

"I think it's the other entrance." He grabbed hold of the handle and pulled hard. The door opened with a screech and revealed metal stairs. "There's another door at the top of the stairs. We must be directly under the debris pile."

Anne suddenly realized how much time had passed. "Remi probably needs me. I hate to go, but I better. I can't wait to show the kids. This is fascinating."

Alex followed her back to the ladder. "People are going to want to see this place once they hear about it."

Anne stopped at the base of the ladder and looked at Alex. "I hadn't thought of that. Maybe we should only share this discovery with close friends and the kids, at least for a little while."

"I agree. This could become a liability if anyone got hurt going down the ladder. "I can try digging out the other entrance."

"Good idea. I'll see about getting a padlock for the trapdoor," Anne said. It would be a good deterrent for her adventurous daughter, who would likely try going down there on her own.

"I may have a lock in the truck," Alex said. "I'll take care of it."

Anne climbed back into the garage. She dusted off her slacks and headed back to the library.

Remi was at the checkout desk. "What's that in your hair?" she asked with a giggle.

Anne ran her hand over her hair. "Cobwebs."

"Where have you been?"

"In the garage." Anne steeled herself against telling Remi about the bomb shelter. She stepped back into the office area and brushed the filmy strands away.

"Better?" she asked Remi.

"Much," Remi said. "I'm glad you're back. A guy stopped by and was asking about some money he'd lost around here. I didn't know what he was talking about. I told him you'd be back in a few minutes, but he didn't want to wait. Said he'd be back in an hour."

"Did he leave a name?"

"Nope. I asked, but he seemed a little anxious to get going."

Anne bit her lower lip. Could he be the owner of the package? "What did he look like?"

"Young guy, but older than me, I think. I've never seen him before." Remi pushed back her chair. "Also Bella called and wants me to go get her some chicken soup. She's home sick with a cold."

"You better go then," Anne said. "Give her my best wishes for a speedy recovery."

"I will." Remi reached under the counter and pulled out her backpack. "Just so you know, I put away all the books that came in except for a couple of children's books that need to go upstairs. I can put them away now if you want."

"Thanks, Remi, but I'll take care of it later. Bella's waiting for you."

After Remi departed, Anne straightened up the counter, thinking that maybe the mystery of the lost money had been solved. She should be relieved, but something didn't feel right. If she lost over eighteen thousand dollars, she wouldn't just leave. She'd stick around until she had her money back.

Feeling uneasy, she distracted herself by running an Internet search on fallout shelters. In the early 1960s, the threat of nuclear war was very real and had many people building fallout shelters. The government got involved, and shelters were made available for the public in cities and towns. Anne remembered her old high school used to have a sign by the basement door identifying it as a shelter.

She discovered several articles on people finding forgotten shelters. So she wasn't the only one who'd discovered a time capsule in her backyard. She read about two similar incidences, one in California and another in Wisconsin, where homeowners found forgotten stocked bomb shelters on their property. One of the families had donated the items to a historical society so people could see what life was like in the 1960s. The other decided to leave their shelter as it was so generations to come could see it. Anne wondered what course she should take. Right now the discovery was so new, and she wanted to get back there and explore.

Time seemed to creep by. She looked up to see Alex crossing the room with a box that had electrodes hanging from it. He gave her a smile as he headed for the elevator.

She glanced around the first floor. The man in the easy chair was still there. He was reading another magazine but appeared to be nodding off. His eyes closed and his chin dropped for a few moments and then he jerked his head back up. He caught Anne's eye and smiled. He sat up straighter and flipped the magazine page.

Anne turned back to her research on the computer screen. Since the radiation fallout purportedly could last a couple of weeks, many shelters were stocked with food to last that period of time. From the quick survey she'd done of the shelter, Aunt Edie had been well prepared to spend time down there.

Thank You, Lord, that she never had to use it.

Just as Anne was thinking about checking with patrons on the second floor, the front door opened and a man dressed in black jeans and a blue polo shirt sauntered in. He slid his sunglasses up onto his head as he walked to the counter.

"Are you Mrs. Gibson?"

Anne scooted out from behind the computer and stood. "Yes, I am. How may I help you?"

"I'm Steve Jones. I was here earlier and talked to your assistant." He gave her a friendly smile. "I'm here to pick up the package I lost."

"I see," Anne said. "Can you identify the contents?"

"Sure, it was a package with money in it."

Anne's heart skipped a beat. "How much?"

"Actually, this may sound weird, but I'm not sure how much was in it. It's my grandmother's. I was supposed to be taking it to the bank. I had a flat tire. Right out front there. It must've fallen out of my car, only I didn't realize where I'd lost it until I saw your ad in the paper. My grandmother will kill me if she knew."

His story sounded like the woman on the phone who said she'd lost her husband's package. But then, she hadn't come into the library either. He looked nice enough. Friendly. She supposed it was plausible that Hershey had picked the package up out of the ditch by the street. And Steve Jones knew there was money in the package.

"There was a note inside too," she said, watching him carefully.

He raised her eyebrows. "Really? What did it say?"

When Anne hesitated, he gave a little shrug. "Like I said, I only glanced inside the package. Granny hasn't been all there lately if you know what I mean." He made a twirling motion with his finger around his ear.

Anne did know what he meant, but she still wasn't sure he was telling the truth. "I'll be happy to talk with your grandmother and make sure she gets the package back."

Steve shook his head. "That would just upset her. She's a sweet old thing. I'd prefer you just let me take it to the bank."

"The money isn't here. You can pick it up at the police station."

"Seriously, lady?" The smile left his face and his voice rose. The patron with the magazine looked over them. "Why don't I believe you? Are you trying to steal from my grandmother and keep the money for yourself?"

"You don't have to believe me, but it's true," Anne said firmly, but her knees felt rubbery. "The money's not here. The police have it and you can go down there. In fact, I'll call Officer Banks and let him know you're on your way." She reached for the phone.

"I wouldn't do that if I were you." His tone had dropped low with an edge of menace.

Alex walked up to the counter. "Problem here?"

Steve looked Alex over and stepped back. "Don't bother." He turned and headed for the door.

"You okay?" Alex asked, not taking his eyes off the man until he went outside.

Anne took several deep breaths and nodded.

"What was all that about?" he asked.

Anne explained about Steve's claim to the package, "But obviously he was lying. I just don't understand how he knew about the money. That wasn't in the ad. Neither was my address except for Bluebell Lane. *And* I just gave out my cell phone number, and I changed my voice mail to the generic auto-answer. The only people who know that package contained money are the kids, you, Mildred, Wendy, Officer Banks, and Pastor Tom." And she supposed Mrs. Crenshaw, although she probably didn't hear her.

"I haven't told anyone, but the word must've got out somehow. If the guy was telling the truth, he would've gone to the police station."

Anne agreed. "I better report this." She picked up the phone. If Steve, or whatever his name really was, could come here and try to trick the money away from her, then there may be others out there who knew about it. Her fingers trembled as she punched in the number for the police station. She wasn't going to feel safe until she found the real owner of that money.

Chapter Ten

M om, are there bats down here?" Ben asked as he waited in the dark passageway to the fallout shelter. He scanned the ceiling with his flashlight beam.

Anne watched Liddie climb down into the shelter. She'd decided after supper to provide a living history lesson for the kids. Plus she was anxious to see what else Aunt Edie had stored down there.

"No. No bats." Anne glanced around her. At least she hoped not. It hadn't occurred to her that there might be other creatures living down in the hole.

"Bummer. I've never seen a bat."

"Are there spiders?" Liddie hopped off the ladder.

"There are probably spiders," Anne said. Cobwebs hung all over the walls." Just don't put your hands down on anything without looking first."

"What about snakes?" Liddie asked. "I know about snakes now."

Anne shuddered. "Liddie, let's just be careful, okay?"

Alex smiled at Anne from above. She'd invited Alex and Ryan to join them in their little adventure. Alex had mentioned that he wanted to see if the electricity worked down in the shelter. "If you make enough noise any critters down there will go into hiding."

"Well, that won't be a problem," Anne said as Liddie let out shriek.

"Mom, Ben touched me on the neck and scared me."

"Ben, don't scare your sister," Anne said automatically. She held up her hand to spot Ryan just in case he slipped, although it was highly unlikely. All the kids were nimble as monkeys.

Anne stepped back to give Ryan more room and brushed up against something cold. She lurched forward, her heart pounding, and then realized it was just a rivet in the steel beam. She took a deep breath. She was still a little unnerved about the visit from Steve Jones. Michael had taken a report and then tried to reassure her that obviously the guy was a con man and since she'd seen through him, he probably wouldn't be back. Michael still cautioned her to keep the doors locked when the library wasn't open and to report any suspicious people.

"Let me go into the room first and try a new lightbulb." Alex squeezed past Anne and the children.

"This is so awesome!" Ryan said. "Like a cave."

"Liddie, quit shining the light in my eyes," Ben said. They were all manned with flashlights so Anne didn't have a problem making her way down the passageway. She kept a sharp lookout for any unwelcome creatures.

"Here goes," Alex said. A click sounded and light flooded the shelter.

"Wow!" Liddie said, shining her flashlight around the room although there was no need for it now.

Wow was right. The light from the bulb hanging in the middle of the room allowed Anne to see the entire layout.

Two bunks hung from the wall on one corner. Blankets and pillows were stacked on the upper one. Shelves lined two of the other walls with cans, boxes and other supplies all neatly lined up. A small table and chairs occupied the center of the room. An easy chair rested by a shelf containing books and magazines.

"Cornflakes!" Liddie pointed to a box.

"Those are very old cornflakes. Don't eat anything from down here, okay?" Anne realized some of the food was probably still safe to consume, but she didn't want to chance it after over fifty years.

"What is that?" Ben stood in front of the big cylinder with the pipe rising to the ceiling.

"It's an air purifier," Alex said. "I did some research on it this afternoon. You turn the crank to make it work. That way if you don't have electricity you could still filter the air."

"Why would you need to do that?" Ryan asked and, as Alex explained hazards of radiation, Anne did a quick inventory. Aunt Edie must have put a lot of time and thought into the stocking of the shelter. Not only had she provided for physical needs but also things to occupy the mind.

The kids had gathered around a stack of old games. "And to think those don't require electricity," Anne teased.

Alex shot her a grin.

Anne wandered over to a wooden trunk tucked in the corner. She lifted the lid and a whiff of cedar greeted her.

A Bible lay on top of some neatly folded clothing. Aunt Edie had filled in the page that contained a family tree, but it was empty after Anne's father was born. She turned back to the chest and lifted out some slacks and brightly colored shirts, which portrayed the sixties era. Time had set folds in the fabric, but there were no moth holes thanks to the cedar paneling. Underneath the clothing she discovered a pair of sturdy boots and a small brown backpack. Curious, Anne opened the flap and pulled out a pocketknife, iodine pills to purify water, a wallet with no identification that contained forty dollars and some coins, all dated prior to 1963.

She was setting the backpack to the side when she felt something hard and square-shaped in the lining. She examined the seams. There appeared to be a loose seam. She tugged gently at the fabric and it gave way. Tucked between the lining and the outer fabric was a small leather-bound notebook. She leafed through the pages, which were filled with rows of tiny letters and numbers in Aunt Edie's handwriting. It didn't make sense to Anne.

"What's that, Mommy?" Lizzie looked up from the game the boys were playing.

"I'm not sure. It's a book, but I can't read it.

Ben sidled over. "Can I see?"

Anne passed the book to him. "Be careful. The pages feel a little thin."

Ben studied the page. "Oh! Do you know what it looks like?"

"What?" Liddie asked.

"Secret codes. This is a codebook," Ben said.

"What's this?" Alex crossed the room.

"Mr. Layton told us about secret codes that spies used during war," Ben told Alex.

"We played a game where we made up codes and the other person had to try to figure them out," Ryan added with a big grin. "It was fun."

"May I see the book?" Alex asked and Ben handed it over.

Alex examined the pages under the light. "Maybe they are account or stock numbers."

Anne agreed that seemed more logical than secret codes. But she could tell by Alex's expression he was as puzzled by the sequence of numbers and letters as she was.

There had to be a logical explanation. What would Aunt Edie be doing with a codebook? And why hide it in the backpack? She set it on the table and decided to take the book back to the house with her. Ben asked if he could take some of the magazines, and Anne agreed as long as he didn't lose them. They explored the contents of the room a bit more while Anne took photos with her cell phone before they called it an evening and climbed back up the steps.

Alex went out to his truck and returned with a chain and padlock. "I found these in my garage so you can secure the trapdoor if you want to. That way people can't get in there without your knowing."

"Thank you. I think that's a wise decision." Anne glanced at the kids. They were already calling the shelter their clubhouse. She didn't want them going up and down the ladder and playing inside without supervision. She also needed to figure out what to do about this momentous discovery.

Alex ran the chain though the trapdoor handles and snapped the lock shut. He gave the ring of two little keys to Anne.

They trooped back to the house and gathered around the kitchen table while Anne heated up hot cocoa on the stove. She counted out the minimarshmallows as she dropped them into mugs so Ben and Liddie wouldn't argue over who got more. She sent the kids off to wash their hands and set a plate of cookies on the table.

Alex returned from washing his hands and said, "I was wondering if you knew where the paperwork on the elevator was. I was talking to someone familiar with elevator installation and he said that sometimes companies issued lifetime guarantees. I'm not sure how much they'd cover in this case, since it was caused by lightning, but it would be worth checking."

"That would be terrific. The paperwork should be around here someplace. I thought I saw some for the elevator when we first moved in," Anne said, trying to remember. "I'll make it a priority to look tomorrow."

The three children ran back into the room and helped themselves to cookies and sipped their cocoa. As Anne had predicted, Liddie and Ben eyed each other's mugs to see how many marshmallows each received.

"Meanwhile, do you want me to go ahead and order a new motor and see if we can adapt it? We're running out of time before the library inspection."

Anne nodded. "Please see if they have a payment plan. The Library Guild meets at the end of the month, and I'll have to resolve the budget with them."

"Okay, it's a plan then." Alex set his mug down and turned to his nephew, who was in deep discussion with Ben about a video game that was releasing soon. "Ryan, please finish your cocoa. We need to go home. Tomorrow is a school day."

All three kids groaned. They were all anxious for summer vacation to start.

"I'm risking sounding like an overprotective parent here, but you did lock up downstairs, right?" Alex asked.

Anne smiled. "I double-checked the locks when I closed the library."

"I figured you did, but I don't like what happened today with that Steve Jones," Alex said. "Call if you need me."

"Thanks, I will." Anne locked the door behind them, grateful for having friends she could count on. Alex wasn't a substitute for Eric, but it was nice to have him around to make her feel safe.

Eric would have been intrigued about the storm shelter, and Anne wished she could share the discovery with him. It was in remarkably good shape.

The shelter hadn't been all that dusty—especially considering it may have been over fifty years since Aunt Edie stocked it, but Anne still felt grimy. She sent Ben off to take a shower first. Once he was done and tackling the one assignment he had for English class, Anne drew a bath for Liddie, planning to take a long, relaxing one herself after the kids were in bed. She shampooed her daughter's hair and helped her get into her pajamas.

After they finished their bedtime story, Liddie knelt down to pray. "Dear Lord, thank You for this day and thank You that Mommy found a secret room under the ground. Thank You for keeping us safe from snakes and spiders too. Please help me to do good tomorrow in school. Amen."

"Amen," Anne repeated and then said a prayer too before getting up. Liddie blew her a kiss as Anne turned off the light.

"Good night, sweetie," Anne cracked the door open so she could hear Liddie if she needed her in the night. Anne had checked the weather while she was getting supper ready that night and yet another storm was headed their way. The forecasters didn't think it would last long or be severe. Still, what they didn't consider severe could be mighty scary to a five-year-old.

Ben sat cross-legged on his bed, his hair still damp from his recent shower. "Ben, is everything okay? Do you have your assignment done?"

He nodded, looking up from the *Science Life* magazine that Anne had let him take from the shelter. "This is cool stuff!"

Anne sat on the edge of his bed so she could see what he was reading. The article was entitled "Will Man Walk on the Moon?" There were several diagrams of spacesuits, some looking like they were right out of an old science-fiction movie, but one or two resembled something that real astronauts eventually wore during flights into space.

"It's interesting how far science has advanced, isn't it?" Anne said. "Even since I was a girl. Who would've thought we'd have a space station up there?"

"They did." Ben pointed to a paragraph in the article. "The scientists back then were talking about living in space. Maybe on the moon. How come we didn't build a space station there?"

"I don't know," Anne said. "That's a good question you could ask your teacher." She looked down at the other magazines on the bed that Ben had brought and picked up one titled *Survivor*. She flipped through it. Some of the articles were dog-eared with the corners folded down. Most likely Aunt Edie had been marking pages she wanted to go back to. She turned to a page with a column on making beef jerky. There was another on using wild plants for medicine.

"Can we go down to the shelter tomorrow?" Ben asked.

"Maybe. We'll see how the day goes," Anne said. "Can you do me a favor, Ben? Don't talk about the fallout shelter at school yet. Tell Ryan not to mention it either. I know it's really cool, but we need to decide how we want to share this discovery with everyone."

His forehead wrinkled. "What do you mean?"

"Well, I was thinking we might donate some of the items to the historical society or —"

"We can't give that stuff away," he said, aghast. "It belonged to Aunt Edie. She wanted to keep it a secret."

"Possibly," Anne said, wondering why Aunt Edie hadn't ever shared the place with her. Or maybe she'd just put it out of her mind. Those were scary times. "Anyway, just think how interested people will be to see all that stuff from the 1960s. Like people come here to see the historic items we sometimes have in the library."

"So why don't we display them here?"

"Well, that's an idea," Anne said. They could display some of the items in the History Room. Or maybe if they could clear the debris pile around the outside door, they could open the shelter to the public. "Let's think about it for a little while and maybe we can do something fun with it."

"Better tell Liddie then. She can't keep secrets very well. She was telling everyone about all the money we found. I told her we weren't supposed to talk about it."

Oh dear. Anne sighed. The gossip chain in Blue Hill flowed swiftly, even at the schools. That could explain how Steve Jones may have heard about the package of money. He could have a child or relative who went to the elementary school. Anne didn't recall any of Liddie's classmates with the last name of Jones, but Steve could have been lying about his name.

Well, what was done was done. Anne put her worries out of her mind as she took a long soothing bath and got ready for bed. She picked up Aunt Edie's little leather book and examined it again. She didn't think the contents were account numbers. The letters and numerals were too mixed up. And she still couldn't accept the idea that it was full of codes. But what else could they be?

She remembered the books on World War II she'd seen on the shelf when she was looking for the book on procrastination. Perhaps there was something about codes in them.

She padded downstairs, pausing at the stairwell to listen. The creaks and groans of the old house were familiar ones. She flipped on the lights. Nothing seemed amiss. She found the books on the war and then checked the library catalog for books on codes. Nothing else came up, so she searched the Internet for information on secret codes. A multitude of articles popped up and she printed off the most informative ones. After a half hour passed, she figured she had enough materials and headed back upstairs.

Once Anne settled into bed, she eagerly read over the information. The more she learned about codes, the more excited and perplexed she became. So the numbers and letters in Aunt Edie's little codebook might be codes after all. But why did Aunt Edie have such a book? And why did she hide it in the bomb shelter?

CHAPTER ELEVEN

A nne awoke an hour before the alarm clock sounded, much to her dismay. The forecasted storm had rolled over Blue Hill not long after she'd fallen asleep, but thankfully Liddie had slept through it this time. Although the lightning show only lasted for about fifteen minutes, Anne had been restless the remainder of the night, plagued with hazy dreams that she could not fully remember, but Aunt Edie had been the lead character.

Anne sat up and realized the articles on secret codes were still fanned out on the quilt, and the World War II books lay on the other pillow. That could explain why she had a vague recollection of dreaming about Aunt Edie in a trench coat ducking around buildings like a spy. What a thought!

She slid out from under the warm quilt and padded across the room to the large, leaded glass window that looked out over the valley. Except for a few puddles on the road, there were no lingering effects of last night's thunderstorm.

Cooper's Pond lay in the distance, reflecting the pink of the pretty sunrise. The pond, named for the family that had farmed the land a century ago, had been a favorite spot of Aunt Edie's. Anne had wonderful memories of her great-aunt taking her for picnics and fishing on the pond's shore. It still puzzled Anne that in all the time they'd spent together, Aunt Edie had never mentioned the room under the garage.

Anne pulled her rocker close to the window and picked up her Bible and devotional book. The day's lesson was on teaching kids about truth. She turned to the Scripture reference and read through John 8, lingering over verse 32.

"And ye shall know the truth, and the truth shall make you free."

Anne smiled, drawing strength from the promise. She had accepted the truth about the gospel when she was a child, and she knew that Liddie and Ben were also developing a strong relationship with God. She thanked the Lord for having Him in their lives, guiding and protecting them. As for today, she prayed that she could find out the truth behind the mysterious note and the money and Aunt Edie's little leather book.

Anne dressed in jeans and a scoop-collared pink blouse and walked down the stairs to the kitchen. Since she'd gotten up earlier than usual, she decided to make pancakes, something they usually saved for the weekend. She whipped up the batter and had a stack ready to eat by the time Ben and Liddie arrived ready for school. They were apparently arguing about something, judging from Liddie's pout.

"The club will be for boys only," Ben said to Liddie as he sat in his chair.

Liddie shook her head. "That's not fair. Mom, tell Ben he has to have girls in the club too."

"What club?" Anne asked as she scooped up the last pancake and moved the griddle off the burner.

"The one we're going to have in the shelter," Ben said. "Ryan and I want to start a club."

"It's not fair," Liddie said again.

Anne set the plate of pancakes on the table. "Let's stop arguing. We don't even know what we are going to do with the shelter yet." She sat next to Liddie. "I mentioned to Ben last night that maybe we shouldn't tell people about the shelter for a little while, unless I say it's okay."

Liddie's eyes grew round. "So it really is a secret room!"

Anne smiled. "For the time being. I'd like to get the other door cleared and the stairwell uncovered before inviting your friends to see it." She didn't want to chance any of the kids falling off the ladder, and until Anne figured out what Aunt Edie's little book meant, she didn't want the contents of the room disturbed.

Liddie smothered her pancake with syrup. "Can I tell Cindy? She's my best friend."

"Aren't you listening, Liddie?" Ben said. "Don't talk about it to *anyone*."

Liddie stuck her tongue out at her brother.

"Hurry up and finish breakfast," Anne said. "And Liddie stop sticking your tongue out at your brother."

They finished breakfast and, as Anne helped Liddie find her shoes, Anne noted the laundry hamper was already filling up. She dropped Liddie's pajamas into the basket, thinking she could throw a load in the washer later today.

She retrieved Aunt Edie's book and stuck it in her purse. She needed help figuring out what the sequences of numbers and letters meant, and she knew just the man who might help her.

They managed to leave the house on time and Anne drove the kids to their school. Like yesterday, Liddie turned in the doorway, blew Anne a kiss, and waved. She looked for Ben but he'd already sprinted inside with Ryan.

Franklin's Antiques had been located at the far end of Main Street since before Anne was born. She'd been in the shop a couple times since she moved back looking for a particular reading lamp for the History Room. She'd been delighted to discover that Mr. Franklin had a whole bookcase full of old books, some of them first editions.

She parked in front of the brick building. The closed sign was still on the door, but the overhead lights were on behind the large storefront window. Anne grabbed her purse and walked to the door.

Mr. Franklin was running a feather duster over a stately china cabinet. She knocked gently on the glass door. He squinted at her behind his thick round spectacles, and then a smile let up his wrinkled face. He set the duster down and hurried to open the front door.

"Well, hello, Anne!" Mr. Franklin said. "Come on in." He stepped back and let Anne enter.

"Hi, Mr. Franklin, I'm sorry to get here before you open, but I was hoping to be able to show you something before I have to get back to the library."

"Well, come on back to the office. I have a teakettle on the hot plate, and I was just going to fix myself a cup of tea. My wife picked up a nice Cinnamon Orange Spice in Philadelphia last week when she was visiting her sister. I find the brew energizing. Would you like a cup?"

"That sounds good. I could use something energizing," Anne said, still feeling the dregs of the restless night. She followed him through the store, which specialized in early American antiques, to a large storage room crammed with furniture. A rolltop desk hugged one corner. Steam rose from the curved ceramic spout of a pretty kettle on top of a single burner hot plate.

"Do you take milk with your tea?" Mr. Franklin asked, pausing by a small refrigerator beside the desk.

"No, thank you."

"Well, have a seat and I'll be just a minute." He pulled a dining room chair, the pad upholstered with a rich burgundy fabric, closer to the desk.

"Here you go." Mr. Franklin handed her a delicate blue china teacup and saucer. Anne inhaled the sweet cinnamon and orange flavors and took an appreciative sip.

Mr. Franklin tasted his tea and then let out an audible sigh. "Perfect." He set his cup down. "Now, what's this something you want to show me?"

Anne pulled out the leather book from her purse and handed it to him. "I believe this was my great-aunt Edie's. I found it in a trunk that I don't think has been disturbed since the 1960s."

"Is it a journal?" Mr. Franklin turned the book gently over in his hands, treating it as he would a rare artifact.

"I'm not sure what it is. My son thinks it's a codebook," Anne said with a little laugh. "But after some research I did last night, I'm starting to think so too."

"A codebook. How intriguing." He opened the front cover and then reached for a large magnifying glass on the desk. Anne waited quietly as he examined page after page.

He finally set the magnifying glass down. "You say this was your aunt's?"

"It's her handwriting."

"I see." He turned the book over in his hands again "Well, I'm not sure exactly what we're looking at, but I know someone who might. He's an old friend of mine and a cryptologist."

"A cryptologist? Here in Blue Hill?" Anne knew from her research last night that cryptologists were code makers and breakers, but she'd never met one.

"Not in Blue Hill, but close enough. He lives in Deshler now when he's not traveling." He flipped through an old Rolodex on his desk. "Dr. Emmett Stone. A retired history professor now. We met in college and he dated my wife's younger sister briefly. We became good friends. He's done a lot of research about military ciphers and even wrote a book on the Cold War code breakers. Would it be okay if I contacted him?"

"Sure," Anne said. "I'm really curious about what he might say."

Mr. Franklin picked up the receiver of an old rotary phone and dialed. "Emmett! George here. I think I have something you might want to see." He explained about the book and then covered the talk piece with his hand. "He'd love to meet up with you. How about tomorrow?"

"Here? Oh, I don't want to inconvenience him," Anne said.

"Believe me, it's not. He lives for stuff like this."

"Okay, I guess that would be fine. I'm free at lunch tomorrow."

Mr. Franklin relayed the information and then said, "He asks if you know the pizza place down by the high school."

"Stella's? Sure, I used to go there a lot," Anne said. Stella's Pizza had been a favorite restaurant of hers since she was a youngster, and it became a teen hangout during high school.

Mr. Franklin confirmed the restaurant, and they decided on twelve thirty. He handed Aunt Edie's book back to Anne. "I know this may be forward, but do you mind if I sit in on your meeting? I'd really like to know what he has to say."

"Oh, sure, I just assumed you would come. Please do." Anne glanced at her watch and rose from the chair. "I better get back to the library."

"Here's my number in case you need to reach me to cancel." He gave Anne his business card and walked to the front of the store with her. "See you tomorrow."

As she stepped outside, her cell phone rang. It was Officer Michael Banks.

"Hi, Anne," he said in his deep booming voice. Any chance you can stop by the police station this morning? I really need to talk to you."

* * *

Anne shifted impatiently on her chair in the small, stuffy interrogation room, her fingers tapping a soft rhythm on the scarred tabletop. They'd just started their conversation in which Anne told him about Liddie mentioning the found money at school when he was called away for a phone call.

The door finally opened and Michael walked back in carrying a heavy-looking binder. "I appreciate your waiting. I didn't know when I'd get a chance to see you today."

"No problem. But I've only got twenty-five minutes until I have to be back to open the library."

"This won't take long. I did a records search on Steve Jones. As you can imagine, Jones is a popular name. I had to cross search for extortion crimes. Unfortunately those types of crimes are fairly common, even around here, especially against our elderly population."

"Seriously? In Blue Hill?"

"Seriously." Michael grimaced. "Most of the perps are from the outside though. You'd be amazed how many people can be conned by phone calls from these scum-bums lying to them that they've just won the lottery or a car or some other enticing item. They only have to pay a fee to have the item transferred. They also pose as bank managers or investors promising to ease all their retirement worries about money. They take them for large sums."

Anne shook her head. "That's terrible. So Steve Jones is a con artist?"

"Looks that way." Michael pulled out sheets from the notebook and placed them in front of her. "Do any of these faces look familiar?"

Anne looked at the rows of facial photos of men with similar coloring and features as Steve Jones. She realized Michael was conducting a miniversion of a lineup.

Her gaze landed on the photo on the far left. A scraggly beard covered the man's jaw and dirty blond hair hung over his eyes, but there was no doubt that this was the young man who'd come to the library insisting he'd lost the money.

Anne tapped the photo. "That's Steve Jones. Except he didn't have a beard and he had a haircut."

Michael separated the photo from the others. "His legal name is Mark Reynolds. He hasn't been around Blue Hill for a while, or at least he hasn't been in trouble. His rap sheet makes for interesting reading."

"Reynolds." Anne's stomach dropped. "I recognize the last name. Liddie has a classmate named Lenny Reynolds."

"Yes, that's Mark's nephew, and if Liddie had talked about the money at school, then that's how he got the details about the package."

"I've spoken to Lenny's mother. She seems so nice," Anne said.

"Well, her brother-in-law isn't. I'll track down his whereabouts and have a chat with Mark Reynolds—aka Steve Jones—and convince him it's in his best interest to stay far away from you. We can try to press charges, but it's your word against his about his intentions."

Anne shivered. "Do you think he's dangerous?"

"Not that we know of." He glanced down at the file. "Of course he'd cheat the coat off a homeless man's back if he thought he could turn a profit. There are no records of him assaulting anyone, but just continue to be careful. Call if you catch sight of him."

"I will," Anne said.

Michael frowned. "Have you made any progress on your own?"

"I have a couple of possibilities. Well . . . maybe one good one." Anne thought of Mr. Bartholomew. She hoped Mildred would call soon. "I'll let you know if I find out anything important."

Michael shoved back his chair. "I can't really stop you from poking around a little, but stay safe while doing it, okay?"

Anne stood and gave him a salute, trying to lighten the mood. "Yes, sir."

Michael wasn't amused. "Just be careful."

CHAPTER TWELVE

Anne shifted her gaze around the table of the Tuesday night literacy class. "It's time to go into our practice sessions now. If you have any questions about your homework assignments, please let us know," Anne said. "And remember to bring something that you have always wanted to read or that looks interesting to you for Thursday night."

The students pushed back their chairs. Attendance had swelled to six, filling the table. Wendy was thrilled. The newest members, Maria and Lucia Rodriquez, were sisters, transplanted from Puerto Rico. They had taken English-as-a-second-language classes and could speak English fairly well but had trouble reading the language. They thought they needed more practice since they were planning on opening a clothing store in a year.

Maria tossed back a lock of her long black hair and raised her hand. "Is there a phone number we can call if we have trouble?"

"Yes, there are several. You can find them on the yellow sheet in your packet." Anne reached into a folder and showed them a copy. "You'll find Wendy's and my phone numbers, as well as our teacher/adviser Mr. Layton's number. Mr. Layton will be joining us on Thursday night."

The students and volunteer tutors squeezed past each other as they made their way out the door to find private areas in the library.

Wendy drew Anne to the side. "Could you work with Sandy tonight? Heather told me that she met up with Sandy over the weekend for an additional session and thinks Sandy should be tested for a reading disorder. I agree, but see what you think the best approach might be. I'd hate for her to stop trying because of something we said. And I get the feeling she is looking for an excuse to quit. She's been resistant to the idea of more testing after her previous negative experiences."

"Sure. I'd be happy to. I'll give Mr. Layton the heads-up too, and we'll see what he suggests." Anne spied Sandy across the room. She looked like she wanted to bolt out the door.

Anne walked over to her. "Hi! Would you like to work with me tonight?"

Sandy gave her a shy smile. "Sure. But I have to warn you I'm very, very slow."

"That's perfectly okay. That's what we're here for."

Sandy blew out a breath. "I know, but it's embarrassing. I'm just dumb. I suppose it's useless being here."

Anne's heart went out to her. It must be terrible to be trying so hard and not making any progress. "You don't have to be embarrassed. No one else will hear but me." She looked around the first floor for a place to sit where Sandy would have privacy. All the tables were taken. Finally she suggested they go upstairs to the Reference Room.

They climbed the stairs and, as they passed the Children's Room, Sandy looked inside. "That is so cute. Can we go in there?"

"Sure." Anne grabbed two of the larger chairs placed in the room for parents and pulled them close together.

Sandy took a seat and sighed. "My parents never took me to the library when I was little. I went in school, but it wasn't a happy time for me. This looks like a happy place."

"It's one of my favorite rooms." Anne had such fun decorating the bright and colorful room with three walls painted yellow and another coated with chalkboard paint. Child-sized tables and chairs were placed around colorful throw rugs and short natural bookcases.

Sandy sat on the chair next to Anne and they went over the lesson. Sandy caught on quickly to the concepts and could pronounce the letter sounds correctly but had trouble with words longer than three letters. There definitely was a barrier, as if Sandy couldn't quite get through to the other side. And Anne didn't have the key to unlock it. This was beyond Anne's skills, but she didn't let Sandy see her concern. Anne kept the lesson light and fun. They were laughing over a funny picture in one of the books when Anne noticed they'd gone over time.

"On Thursday Mr. Layton will be here. He has training in reading problems, and he may be able to provide you with some fresh insight. I can set up some time with him for you."

"Well, I don't know. I'm starting to think that nothing will help. I'm just dumb."

"Please stop saying that. You are *not* dumb!" Anne said louder than she intended. "Sorry, I didn't mean to startle you, but please stop saying you're dumb. Look at all the great things you've done with your life. You are successfully raising kids, volunteering at the school and church, working a part-time job, all with a reading handicap. That takes guts and ingenuity. Now, you just need to give yourself a chance to do something you've always wanted. You have to believe in yourself."

Sandy blinked several times, her lips pressed tightly together, and Anne wondered if she had pushed too hard. But then Sandy smiled. "Thanks. I needed that. I'll come and talk to Mr. Layton."

Anne walked Sandy downstairs and saw her to the door. "See you Thursday."

"You bet. I'll be here."

Heather had already left, and Jennifer wrapped her arm around Anne's shoulders and squeezed. "Thanks again for including me in this. I get such a kick out of Willy Harris. I think I'm getting more of a blessing than he is."

"I know what you mean. Me too," Anne said, although she was feeling wrung out after teaching the class and her challenge with Sandy. As a librarian she enjoyed running Story Time and activities for the children and helping people with research, but she'd always been a bit shy and introverted. She'd never been very comfortable in large groups. She preferred socializing with a few close friends. Thankfully, teaching in this setting wasn't the same as having to make small talk and mingle with strangers. And if they could help people learn to read, then any discomfort or inconvenience was worth it.

Jennifer was out the door when she whirled and said, "Oh, and Michael said to call him tomorrow about Mark. Tootles." She gave them a fluttery wave. See you Thursday." She practically skipped down the stairs and down the sidewalk. As Anne had many times in the past, she wished she had just a portion of Jennifer's energy.

"Who's Mark?" Wendy asked as Anne shut the door.

"Steve Jones. That guy who came by saying the package of money was his. His real name is Mark Reynolds and he's a con artist. The police are onto him."

"I'm glad. Imagine coming in here and lying like that." Wendy followed Anne into the History Room and helped her move the tables.

"I think tonight went well," Wendy said. "How did Sandy do?"

"I think you're right that she has a bigger problem than you and I can handle without help. Hopefully Mr. Layton will be able to suggest a plan."

"Thanks for convincing her to see him. I was worried." Wendy carried the leftovers from the refreshment table to the counter. "Almost done here. I know it's late, but, um—"

"You want to go down and see the shelter." Anne smiled. That afternoon she'd confided in Wendy about discovering the fallout shelter and, as Anne had expected, her friend was eager to explore it.

"Oh yes, I do." Wendy laughed and then froze, staring at the window. "Anne, I think someone is out front on the porch."

A shadow passed the window. Anne's pulse raced. What if Mark Reynolds had come back? Was that why Michael had wanted her to call him? To warn her?

She went cautiously to the window. A man stood in front of the door and then turned back to the steps. He was halfway down, paused, and came back up the porch.

He stepped under the light and Anne recognized him. "It's Luke Norris."

Wendy opened the door. "Mr. Norris. Hello."

Luke stopped his pacing. "Er, hi. Sorry. I didn't mean to disturb you. I was just leaving."

"It's okay. Don't leave yet," Wendy said. "Did you come for the class tonight?"

"Well, I thought I'd just check it out, but I see that I'm too late." He started toward the steps again.

"The class just left. Please come on in for a few minutes," Anne said, trying to coax the nervous-looking man inside. "We have plenty of leftover refreshments. How about a cup of coffee or cocoa and some cookies?"

"They're homemade. My grandmother's recipe. Really good," Wendy added. "Old-fashioned oatmeal raisin and chocolate chip with walnuts. You won't find any better in Blue Hill."

Luke looked over his shoulder. "Well, I guess I can stay a few minutes." He walked inside and looked around the first floor of the library with sort of a lost expression on his face. "Alex told me he did the work here."

"Yes, he did an excellent job," Anne said. "He renovated the entire house and turned the first two floors into a library."

Wendy held out a plate of cookies and lifted the plastic wrap. "Care to have some?"

Luke selected a cookie, and Wendy said, "I'm sorry for ambushing you at church like I did. It really wasn't the place to ask you about the classes. Not that anyone should feel uncomfortable taking a literacy class, but it should be a private matter."

Luke's lips lifted briefly in a small smile. "Alex relayed your apology. I wasn't offended, just, er, you know, surprised."

He really did look uncomfortable, and Anne felt sorry for him. "Would you like coffee or cocoa?"

"Huh?" He looked startled at the change in topic. "I haven't had cocoa since . . ." The lost expression settled on his face again. "Well, it's been a long time."

"I'll have some too, please." Wendy hurried over to the History Room and grabbed some chairs so they could sit comfortably.

Anne poured three mugs of cocoa from the thermos and passed them around. "Liddie really likes playing with Beth. I'm glad they're in the same class."

"Beth talks about Liddie too. She thinks it's great that she and Liddie can outrun most of the boys. You'd think Liddie was an Olympic star the way Beth talks."

Anne laughed. That was her daughter. Determined to keep up with her big brother. "Sounds like they have fun together."

"My husband is the football coach over at the high school, and he says the PE coaches are always looking for new talent," Wendy said. "Perhaps Liddie and Beth will make the track team someday."

Luke grinned. "I'm not sure Beth will still be that interested in sports by then, but I'm all for it."

Luke seemed to loosen up some as he ate cookies, and they chatted a bit more about the children and the end of the school year. He grew quiet again and then said, "I'm glad Beth is making friends. She's had a hard time since losing her mother. It happened just after we moved here. Vickie just left one day. Left a note that she wanted a different life. And well, while I was dealing with feelings of betrayal and a smashed ego, Beth also had to adjust to a new home and school, as well as a mother who apparently went on a permanent vacation."

A lump rose in Anne's throat. "That must be so difficult. I'm sorry you both have to go through something so hard. How is Beth doing?" She knew what her kids went through losing Eric, but she couldn't imagine how hard it would be to know that your parent just left.

"She is coping with most things, but I feel like I'm failing her." He looked at Wendy. "After you came up to me at church, I realized that maybe God was giving me a nudge to quit feeling sorry for myself and do something to change the situation. Then Alex encouraged me to at least give the class a try. If not for me, then for Beth."

He took a deep breath. "I can't read well, especially out loud. I never really needed to. I got through school just scraping by. I hated being cooped up in a classroom. I knew I wanted to be a carpenter, so why work too hard at something I just wasn't good at? I met Vickie in high school and after we got married she took care of the bills and any paperwork. She read to Beth every night before bed."

"That must have put you in a tough place," Wendy said.

Luke nodded. "Well, I can figure out how to do the bills and things. It doesn't take a genius. The process just takes me longer. But then Beth keeps wanting me to read her bedtime stories like Vickie did. Someday she's going to want me to help her with her homework and she's going to figure out her old man is just a big dummy."

There was that word again. "You're not a dummy," Anne said. "Alex says you're a phenomenal carpenter. That takes skill and knowledge. I've seen Beth run up to you at church, and I can tell she adores you."

"She really does," Wendy said.

He nodded and let out a deep sigh. "I'm not sure how I'm going to manage it. It's hard for me to get away evenings since I have to get a sitter for Beth. That was why I was late tonight. I couldn't get someone in until it was late."

"If you have to bring Beth, we'd find a way to keep her entertained. My kids are upstairs," Anne said. "But what if you tried private tutoring?"

Wendy jumped up from her chair. "I think that's a marvelous idea and we can get started right now."

* * *

Anne looked up from a cardboard file box she was digging through in the kitchen in the hope that the elevator warranty was in there. Did she just hear Liddie?

She got up from her chair and went to the stairs. "Liddie?"

Liddie didn't answer, but Anne knew she couldn't concentrate unless she was certain her daughter was okay. She went up the stairs and heard the sound again. She pushed Liddie's door open and was greeted by a giggle. She crept closer to the bed. Her little girl was fast asleep and enjoying whatever dream world she was in.

Anne backed out, relieved, and then checked on Ben. He had fallen asleep with his lamp on. She went in and tugged the science magazine from his hand. It was another periodical from the shelter.

She trudged back downstairs and turned off the kitchen light. She decided she'd had enough of looking for the warranty for tonight. It bothered her that she thought she'd seen some contracts during the move and she couldn't remember where she'd put them.

She doubled-checked the door locks to their apartment, heeding Michael's advice of being careful. As she changed into her pajamas, she mulled over the evening. She felt good about the class and what happened after.

Thank You, Lord, that You brought Luke to class. Please let us help him in the best way possible.

Wendy had conducted the diagnostic assessment and then started on some reading exercises with him. Luke read in a halting voice, pausing to sound out words, which meant he remembered some phonics training.

As they worked together, Anne did a library search on Dr. Emmett Stone and located one of his articles in a history journal in the Reference Room.

She read over the short biography in the sidebar of the article, which contained a head shot of the professor. She liked being able to put a face to the name since she was meeting him tomorrow.

Silver streaked Dr. Stone's thick brown hair. His intense gaze and small smile at the camera suggested intelligence and confidence. If she had to guess his age, the experience on his handsome lined face put him in his late sixties

Dr. Stone had written a book called *Decoding the Wars* and dozens of articles on topics related to espionage. He was also credited with being one of the nation's leading experts on Soviet-era intelligence networks and their methods of communication, including secret codes. She was looking forward to hearing what the professor thought about Aunt Edie's little leather book. She also wondered if the meeting might provide her with insight about how she could go about "decoding" the note she'd found in the front yard. A note that had an eighteen thousand dollar prize.

CHAPTER THIRTEEN

The small parking lot in front of Stella's Pizza was jammed with cars, indicating the lunch crowd had arrived. She noted half a dozen bicycles locked in the bike rack out front. High school students, no doubt. She turned the corner and parked in the narrow alley behind the building.

For the meeting with the professor, Anne had traded her usual attire of jeans and T-shirt for a new pair of sky blue capri pants and a matching short-sleeved jacket over a sleeveless white cotton shirt. Her feet were slipped into comfortable white leather moccasins with a sturdy sole, which she appreciated especially since she had to traverse the pothole-riddled alley.

She reached the front of the restaurant, and a din of happy voices greeted her as she opened the door. Anne scanned the crowded room. Indeed, many of the customers appeared to be high school students. Backpacks littered the floor by the booths. Several textbooks lay open on the tables.

The aging decor of Stella's Pizza was forgivable when patrons discovered the low prices and delicious, high-quality pizza. Even now, many years later, when Anne visited, the smells of Italian spices, homemade pizza sauce, and baking cheese evoked a carefree feeling of being a kid again.

Lucy, a petite young woman with a long dark braid down her back, waved at her from the middle of the restaurant. "Hello, Anne!"

Anne waved back and made her way over to the waitress.

"There are two gentlemen waiting for you in the side room." Lucy gestured toward the room that the restaurant reserved for larger groups and parties. "I seated them in there because they mentioned you were having some sort of meeting and it's quieter. Can I get you a drink?"

"Thanks, Lucy. I'll have iced tea." Anne headed for the doorway into the next room. Mr. Franklin and Dr. Stone sat at one end of a long table with a red-and-white-checked tablecloth and six red vinyl seats. Mr. Franklin stood and waved her over. Dr. Stone politely rose too as she approached the table. He shook her hand with a pleasant smile after Mr. Franklin introduced them.

Dr. Stone pulled out her chair for Anne. "I can't tell you how pleased I was that you agreed to meet me here at Stella's. This used to be my favorite place to eat whenever our football team played Blue Hill High. I grew up in Deshler and decided to retire there."

"When he's not traveling the world or giving lectures," Mr. Franklin added.

"When I'm not traveling," Dr. Stone repeated with a smile. "My work has taken me to some interesting places."

"Were you on the Deshler football team?" Anne asked.

"Me?" Dr. Stone laughed good-naturedly. "I was a little twerp, but my brother was on the team. Big Jim Stone, the kids called him. I suppose that was before your time. Anyway, I was the towel boy, for want of a better name. It was an excuse to be able to travel around with my brother. And when we came to Blue Hill, our team would always eat here."

Lucy arrived with a glass of iced tea and set it by Anne. "Are you ready to order?" She pulled a pad out of the pocket of her faded red apron.

"You look familiar, but I haven't been in here in over thirty years."

"I'm Stella's daughter," Lucy said.

"Ah yes, I can see it now." He gave Lucy a big smile. "You look so much like your mother when she was younger."

"Thank you. I'll take that as a compliment."

"It is," Dr. Stone said. "Is Stella here?"

"Not today. She's semiretired now. My brother and I run the business most days. But don't worry. We still use all of my mother's recipes. I can say hello to her for you if you'd like."

"That would be nice, but I doubt she'd remember me. I was a little guy back then and hardly uttered a word. But if you can tell her that Emmett Stone from Deshler has fond memories of this place thanks to her, I'd appreciate it."

"I'll tell her." Lucy smiled and looked around the table. "Do you need a few more minutes?"

"For old time's sake, I'd like to order the Five Cheese Special. I know that sounds boring, but it was my favorite," Dr. Stone said.

"Actually that is one of my kids' favorites." Anne shut her menu. "I'll have the same."

"Sounds good to me too," Mr. Franklin said. "Why don't we split a large pizza then?"

They ordered salads as well and then Dr. Stone leaned toward Anne. "George says that you made an unusual discovery."

"I did." Anne reached into her purse and pulled out the tiny leather book. "Dr. Stone, I appreciate your taking the time to come all the way over here to take a look at this." She passed the book over to him.

"Don't think anything of it. I'm fascinated with anything to do with codes or ciphers. It's been my life's passion, and I'm just glad I can devote more time to it these days."

Dr. Stone turned the pages slowly. Mr. Franklin winked at Anne as the time ticked by, and Lucy brought their salads.

Dr. Stone finally looked up and set the book down on the table next to Anne. He waited until Lucy had refilled their glasses and then said, "Yes, this most certainly looks like a book of codes, but just so you know, there are also ciphers in there too."

Anne had heard the term *cipher* before, but hadn't given it much thought. "What's the difference between a cipher and code?"

Dr. Stone steepled his fingers together. "In the layman's world, the words *code* and *cipher* are used to describe any form of encryption, but actually they are quite different. Ciphers are individual letters or small groups of letters converted into something else."

"Like a decoder ring," Mr. Franklin said. "I got one out of a box of cereal once when I was a tyke and had great fun with it."

"Okay, so would a cipher be like the notes I passed in seventh-grade with my girlfriend Jennifer? The message just looked like lines of gibberish, but if you pulled out every third letter, it would spell out whatever our secret message was."

"You got it! That would be one way to cipher. Other methods are a cipher wheel, like George's decoder ring, which substitutes one letter for another. So a *B* might actually be a *T*. You can get much more complicated with ciphers too."

Lucy swept into the room holding up a pizza pan with one gloved hand. "Here you go. Pizza is served."

She moved the salt- and pepper-shakers to the side and set the pizza in the middle of the table. Anne breathed in the heady scent as Lucy gathered up the salad plates.

"So how are codes different?" Anne asked after everyone had helped themselves to mouth-watering slices.

"Codes are based more on whole words rather than numbers or letters," Dr. Stone explained. "Let's say you want to send a message to a coworker across town, but for some reason you don't want anyone else to be able to understand it. You would each have a list of words that can be substituted for something else. For example, say you want to meet at the park, but you would send a different message. The code for the 'meet at the park' could be something with the word *park* in it. Like 'I had to park my car in the garage and it took me twenty minutes to walk to work.' This could mean that you want to meet in the park in twenty minutes. Or the code could be totally unrelated to the message such as 'We need computer ink.' That phrase would only have special meaning to the coworker."

"Okay, that makes sense," Anne said. "I could say 'pass the salt' but I could really be conveying a secret message to Mr. Franklin that he needs to call his wife."

"Exactly." Dr. Stone beamed. "Some people think that codes are more secure than ciphers because you have to have a codebook to figure out the message. There is no pattern of transformation with code. Ciphers use a consistent transformation that is more easily discoverable, except in the case of a one-time pad."

"One-time pad?" Anne asked. "I assume that means it's used just once."

"That's correct. You get an A," Dr. Stone said in a pleased tone as if she were one of his students. "When I was doing research for my book, I studied how the Soviets would communicate with their spies in the United States. They would encode information using a one-time pad, which is an encryption in which plain ordinary text was combined with a key or pad. The pad was supposed to be used only one time and destroyed. This made the cipher unbreakable but very time-consuming for whoever was encoding them. They had to have a new pad every time they wanted to transmit information."

He reached for another pizza slice. "I'm sorry if I'm getting carried away and overtaking the conversation."

Mr. Franklin wiped his mouth with his napkin. "I find this fascinating."

"Me too." Anne glanced at the book. "So, obviously, my aunt wasn't using a one-time pad since she was carrying the book around with her. Unless she used it only once."

"But she didn't destroy it," Mr. Franklin pointed out.

Anne drank some iced tea while she processed what she'd learned. "So going back to what you were saying before, my aunt had both ciphers and codes in the book?"

Dr. Stone nodded. "From what I could deduce from my quick study of the book, the ciphers may actually be encrypting code words."

"A double layer of protection," Anne said.

"Right. It makes it more difficult to decode the message so not just anyone can understand what they are looking at in a glance."

"Protects the messages from people like me," Anne stated thoughtfully. Who else had Aunt Edie been trying to conceal the code from?

"So your aunt never mentioned this book before?" Dr. Stone asked.

Anne shook her head. "Not a word."

"Where did you find the book?"

"I actually stumbled across it in a fallout shelter that I recently discovered on the property. The book was hidden in a trunk, which I don't think has been opened since maybe the sixties."

Mr. Franklin stopped chewing and swallowed hard. "The sixties?"

"What was your aunt's name? If you don't mind my asking," Dr. Stone said.

"Edie Summers."

"She lived in that beautiful old Victorian on Bluebell Lane," Mr. Franklin said to Dr. Stone. "She left the mansion to the town for a library. Anne runs it."

"What a great use of an old landmark," Dr. Stone said. "I inherited my parents' place, which is a Victorian too. My wife started restoring it since we moved back two years ago. Fortunately, she thinks I'm all thumbs, which is mostly true, so I let her hire the workers she needs."

Anne smiled. "Aunt Edie's house was renovated into a library when we moved in. You should stop by sometime and see it. Bring your wife by for a tour if she'd like to come."

"I'd enjoy that, and I'd like to see that fallout shelter if you'd be kind enough to let me."

"So would I," Mr. Franklin said eagerly.

"You're welcome to, although right now the only access to it is down a ladder. We're eventually going to remove the pile of dirt that's covering the other entrance where there is a stairway," Anne said.

"I've climbed many a ladder in my day," Mr. Franklin said. "I'd be willing to come and appraise the value of whatever is down there."

"I'm sure you would, George. I can see dollar signs in your eyes," Dr. Stone said in a teasing tone. "Maybe Anne wants to preserve it as is. Like a museum. I can help with that."

"I'm sure you would," Mr. Franklin said to Dr. Stone. "But knowing the value of the items would help her consider the options."

Dr. Stone shook his head. "You can't always put a dollar value on historic significance—"

Anne cleared her throat, drawing their attention back to her. "Thank you both, I'll let you know what I decide."

The men smiled sheepishly. "Don't mind us," Dr. Stone said. "George and I have been friends a long time, and we enjoy our bickering."

Dr. Stone picked up the codebook again. "Let's get back to your aunt and her codebook. Did she travel out of the country a lot?"

"I think she took several trips to Europe, but that was before I was born. She was a travel writer for a while," Anne said. "Why? Do you think the trips have something to do with the book?"

"Maybe," Dr. Stone said. "If I'm not mistaken, the codes in the book are similar to those used forty to fifty years ago. That fits with the book being left in the shelter in the sixties when the Cold War was going strong. Today we have more sophisticated codes. Some computer generated." He pushed his plate to the side and wiped his hands on his napkin. "If you'd like me to, I could take the book with me and do a bit more research."

Anne looked at her aunt's book sitting between them on the table. She really didn't want to send it off, but maybe she would get more answers that way. "I suppose that will be all right."

"I promise to return it soon," Dr. Stone said. "And I'll be very careful with it."

"What are you expecting to find?" Mr. Franklin asked.

"Well, I can't be sure, but this type of book might be something a government courier would carry. They'd be given orders and use the book to decode them once they were on the road," Dr. Stone said.

Anne leaned back in her chair. "So you're saying my aunt could've been working for the government?"

Dr. Stone nodded. "If I had to guess by looking at that book, I'd say your aunt was somehow involved in covert operations. Possibly as a spy."

Chapter Fourteen

"M om, do you think Aunt Edie could have been a secret agent?" Anne asked as she leaned back on her living room couch with the phone propped against her ear. Ben and Liddie were in their rooms getting ready for bed, and Anne had grabbed the few minutes of quiet to call her mother.

"A secret agent?" Charlene Summers laughed. "That's a new one. Whatever gave you that idea?"

"It's kind of a longish story," Anne said, trying to decide where to start.

"I have the time if you do. Your father went out to the store to get ice cream. He has a hankering for a hot fudge sundae. So why do you think Aunt Edie might have been a secret agent? This has *got* to be interesting."

"It started with finding the fallout shelter under the garage and—"

"Hold on, honey," her mother interrupted. "Fallout shelter? You mean *bomb shelter*?"

"Yes and fully stocked for a nuclear war. Did you know she had one? From what Alex and I can figure, it hasn't been touched since the 1960s, or at least she hadn't added anything to it. The outside entrance had been buried by dirt and the construction debris."

"How fascinating. What does is it look like inside?"

"It's amazing, Mom. It's like stepping back fifty years in time. I'll e-mail some photos. But there's something else."

"More shocking than a hidden bomb shelter?"

"In the shelter I found this little book among her things." Anne went on to explain about meeting with Mr. Franklin and Dr. Stone.

"So this professor is suggesting she may have been a covert operator?"

"Possibly, although Dr. Stone may have been joking. She may have been a courier carrying or picking up secret documents. We can't be sure at this point."

"I suppose I shouldn't be surprised by anything Edie did, but I have to admit this one is a shocker. If it's true, of course."

"I'm having trouble believing it too," Anne said. Her sweet Aunt Edie, a secret courier? Her aunt had an interesting past, but a spy? Surely not. But then why would she hide the book in the shelter? Did she think she'd need it if there were a nuclear war? And how would Anne ever find out for sure? She couldn't just call up the CIA and ask if Aunt Edie was one of their agents.

"Dr. Stone asked if Aunt Edie had taken some overseas trips," Anne said.

"Actually she did. It was before you were born, probably in the sixties and seventies. She went to Europe at least twice."

"Do you know what countries she visited?"

"One time she showed me a few postcards she'd collected. I think she traveled to London and Paris, but I don't remember her talking much about the trips. Of course she was gone a lot back then."

"I was hoping I could find her old passport and see what visitation stamps she collected."

"I never saw her passport. I can ask your father if he ever saw it when he comes in. Wish I could be of more help, sweetie."

"Oh, it's okay, Mom. At least now I know for sure that she did go overseas. I'll take another look around the house for her passport and those postcards in case she saved them," Anne said, although she'd already been through a lot of Aunt Edie's things already. She didn't recall any European postcards or photos for that matter. Of course if Aunt Edie was a spy of some sort, she wouldn't want to document her trips, would she?

"Dr. Stone is supposed to get back with me at the end of the week, and maybe he'll be able to shed more light on what Aunt Edie was up to. I'll call you."

"You better." Her mother chuckled. "I'm dying of curiosity. Before you go, have you made any progress on locating the owner of that money you found?"

Anne debated about telling her mother about Mark Reynolds aka Steve Jones, but she didn't want to worry her needlessly. "The police haven't made any progress. And the phone calls I've gotten on the ad haven't panned out. But Mildred is going to set up a visit with Mr. Bartholomew this week. I'm holding out hope that he may be the one who left the money or has some idea who did."

Her mother sighed. "You've had such a busy week. I wish I were closer to help you."

"I know, Mom. But this is helping just to be able to talk to you."

"I'll keep praying that this all works out for the best."

Anne thanked her and hung up the phone. Usually she felt comforted with her talks with her mother. The comfort was still there today, but this time she had an overwhelming sense of longing to be in the same room with her mom. Maybe it was listening to

Luke Norris's story about coping with the abandonment of his wife that so reminded her of the early days after Eric died. Her mother had stayed with her for a little while, helping to take care of Liddie and Ben while Anne coped with everything else. She didn't know what she would have done without her mom's shoulder to cry on.

Anne shook off the melancholy feeling. She had lots of things she needed to do, such as look for the elevator warranty. Maybe it was in the secret room, a discovery Anne had made shortly after moving in.

She crossed the hall and entered a small sitting area. On the wall hung a star quilt, and behind it was a pocket door hidden in the wall. She pushed it open and walked into the tiny triangular room with no furniture but a small writing desk and a simple chair. During the day the light poured down on it from a strange skylight—a four-paned window set into the ceiling. As she came across any of Aunt Edie's important looking paperwork while exploring the house, Anne stored some of it in the desk. She opened a drawer and lifted out a stack of folders and miscellaneous documents and put them on the desk.

A navy blue book lay inside one of the folders. It was Aunt Edie's most current passport. Anne flipped through it, but there were no visas or visitation stamps in it. Expired passports were generally sent back to the owner after being renewed. There was a possibility that Aunt Edie had tossed her old passport, but somehow Anne thought that since traveling was so important to Aunt Edie, she would have wanted to keep it.

Anne stared at her aunt's passport photo. Edie had a quirky grin on her face, like she knew something everyone else didn't. "Aunt Edie, were you really a spy?"

Anne wanted to find the passport if it existed. Then she could determine where Aunt Edie had traveled, which might be related to why she had the codebook. Maybe the passport was in the attic somewhere. She quickly scanned through the rest of the documents and didn't see anything resembling an elevator warranty, so she stuffed them back in the desk drawer.

The kids were in the living room now. Ben had his history book open on his lap but seemed engrossed with a favorite TV show, and Liddie sat on the carpet playing with one of her dolls.

"I'm going to the attic to look for a few things."

"Can I come?" Liddie asked.

Anne hesitated. Liddie was already in her pajamas. "Only if you be careful not to get dirty, okay?"

Liddie nodded and jumped up. "Cleopatra wants to come too." She clutched her doll tightly as they trooped upstairs to the attic.

Anne flipped on the light and surveyed the room jammed with Aunt Edie's old things and items Anne had brought from New York. She had been through some of the trunks and boxes since she'd moved in, but there was still much to discover. Her goal was to go through everything and organize it all, but with raising kids and running the library, spare time was at a premium.

Liddie considered the attic a big playground, just as Anne had when she was that age. Anne and her friend Jennifer used to play dress-up on rainy afternoons or hide-and-seek among the boxes. One time they'd even built a fort with the trunks and leftover furniture. The fort had been great fun until part of if toppled and scared Aunt Edie when she came to call them to lunch. But, true to

Aunt Edie's adventurous nature, she had helped them rebuild a sturdier replacement.

Anne gazed around the attic. She wasn't sure where to begin. *Lord, if the passport is in here, please guide me to where it would be.*

"What are you looking for?" Liddie asked.

"Aunt Edie's passport."

"What is a passport?"

"It's a thin book about the size of my hand, and it tells people what country you're a citizen of. People use them to go visit other countries."

Liddie gazed around the room. "How are you going to find it?"

"That's a good question." Anne decided to start with the boxes and trunks on the far wall. She opened the first trunk she came to and lifted out a pile of tablecloths. Some of them had been embroidered by relatives, but stains spotted them. Anne wondered if she could find someone to restore them.

Next to the trunk was a box of magazines, which contained travel articles Aunt Edie had written. Anne had briefly looked through some of them before when she was exploring the attic. She didn't recall any of the articles being on Europe, but she hadn't read *all* the magazines. She picked up the box and set it by the door.

She returned to checking the trunks and then spied a battered metal filing box. Inside were several old appliance manuals, a couple of cooking magazines dated 1982, and a large green scrapbook. The binding creaked with stiffness as she opened it. Tucked between the pages were yellowed newspaper clippings and several photos. Whoever had been working on the book had never finished. But there might be something in it with historic significance.

She put it to the side and checked on Liddie, who'd found an ancient Easter bunny to introduce to Cleopatra the doll.

Anne tackled a large green plastic tub next and discovered an old red car cover, which Aunt Edie used to keep on her old convertible. Apparently she hadn't sold it with the car.

She turned to another trunk full of soft worn blankets and uncovered a small wooden chest on the bottom. Inside were a variety of postcards and some trinkets. She placed the chest and scrapbook on top of the box of magazines and glanced at her watch. It was fifteen minutes until Liddie's bedtime.

"Come, sweetie. Time to go back downstairs."

"Okay, Mommy." Liddie set the stuffed bunny down and turned around. A brown streak ran the length of Liddie's pajamas.

"How did you get a streak on just one side of your body?" Anne asked.

Liddie tried to brush off the dust. "I don't know. I'm sorry, Mommy."

"It's okay." Anne smiled. "Expecting to stay clean in this attic was an unrealistic expectation."

"Huh?"

"I mean I should've known better. Look at me. I'm worse than you." Anne pointed to the knees of her jeans, which had two circles of dust from where she had knelt in front of the trunk. "Now we both have to change."

Liddie giggled as she scampered down the stairs to her room.

Anne found a clean nightgown for Liddie and tossed the soiled pajamas on the laundry basket. She carried the box to the kitchen with Liddie trailing after her. "I want to see what's in the box."

"Okay, you can stay up a little bit longer. Let's see what surprises are in here." Anne set the box of magazines on the floor and moved the wooden chest and scrapbook to the table.

A pretty silver crest on the chest lid indicated it had been made in Austria. Inside were about a dozen unmarked postcards from Austria, Germany, Italy, France, Switzerland, and Holland. Liddie and Anne took turns taking out a trinket from the assortment on the bottom. There was a key ring from the Austrian Alps, a tiny metal Eiffel tower, a crystal light catcher, a bookmark cross-stitched with a castle, and polished river stones.

Ben wandered into the kitchen. "Whose are those?"

"Aunt Edie's," Liddie said, making a stack of the postcards.

"Well, we're assuming they are Aunt Edie's since they were in the attic," Anne said. Over the years, other relatives had sometimes stored things up there too. There was nothing in the box to indicate the postcards and souvenirs belonged to her aunt. No photographs. All the postcards were blank on the back.

Ben sat at the table and picked up the Eiffel tower. "I know where this is from. Paris."

"Very good, Ben." Anne reached for another postcard of a castle with garrets and spires surrounded by forested hills. "What about this one? Does it look familiar?"

"It looks like the castle in Disney World," Ben said.

"You're right. This is the castle used as a model for Disney World. Neuschwanstein Castle in Germany," Anne read from the back of the post card.

Liddie bounced on her chair. "Can we go there?"

"Wouldn't that be fun? Maybe someday we can travel and see all these places for ourselves," Anne said, thinking that maybe, if she saved enough money, they could go on a trip after Ben's high school graduation. It would be an awesome family trip to take before her chicks flew the coop. Looking at them now, she could hardly imagine them grown and living on their own, but if she did her job right, they'd be independent adults someday and building their own legacy like Aunt Edie had in this home and community.

The phone rang and Ben jumped up to answer it. "Gibson residence," he said as Anne had instructed him. "Yes, she is. May I ask who is calling?" He paused and then said, "Thank you."

He took the phone over to Anne. "It's Mrs. Farley."

"Thank you, Ben." Anne took the phone.

"Such a nice polite boy you have there," Mildred said with a chuckle. "Sounds so grown-up."

"He does," Anne agreed, feeling proud and a little wistful at the same time.

"I'm sorry I'm calling this late," Mildred said, "but Mr. Bartholomew's daughter, Carol, finally got back with me. She said her father can see us tomorrow morning at ten, if that works for you."

"That works out great. I've got coverage at the library," Anne said, mentally checking the schedule. Wendy would be in at nine thirty. She could manage the library alone for an hour or so.

"All right, I'll pick you up about nine forty-five," Mildred said. "See you in the morning, dear, and have a good night."

Anne hung up the phone, gently shooed the kids off to their bedrooms, and went upstairs to read Liddie her bedtime story. To Anne's delight, Ben joined them. He sat on the bed with Liddie, and when Anne had finished the story, they said their prayers together.

Anne kissed Liddie on the forehead and tucked her in as Ben headed to his bedroom.

"Are there going to be any bad booms tonight?" Liddie asked sleepily.

"No, we're not supposed to have any storms tonight. Just stars and the moon."

"Good," Liddie said with a sigh.

Anne went back to the kitchen and put the postcards and trinkets back in the box. She was pretty certain they were Aunt Edie's. It was too bad her passport hadn't been in there.

She turned to the old green scrapbook and pulled out the newspaper clippings. Most of them were articles on various activities and fund-raisers involving the garden club's beautification committee and the Rotary Club. Some of them were dated in the early eighties, but most were written when Anne was in high school and after she left for college.

She spied Aunt Edie and Mildred in some of the photos that were similar to the group shots that were in Mildred's scrapbook. Mr. Bartholomew appeared occasionally too, wearing his usual attire of old-fashioned suit and hat. She prayed that the visit with him tomorrow would result in determining if he was the one who'd left the money or at least provide some clues on where to look next.

CHAPTER FIFTEEN

Wendy burst in the library door with her usual exuberance.

"Good morning!"

Anne looked up from a list of overdue library books and smiled. She'd called Wendy at breakfast to explain that she needed to leave with Mildred that morning to go visit Mr. Bartholomew. Wendy had assured her that she'd be there at nine thirty and she was, on the dot.

Anne asked. "Did you need for me to pick up anything for the class tonight while I'm out?"

"Nope, I think I have everything," Wendy said. "I'm bringing banana bread and sliced apples and caramel dip for the refreshments tonight."

"That sounds so yummy. People are going to come just for the snacks," Anne teased. "Do you think Luke Norris is going to show up for tonight's class?"

"I don't know," Wendy said with a worried expression. "He said he'd call if he was. I'm not really expecting him. He's shy and uncomfortable about people knowing about his reading deficit, but I don't think he has a problem continuing with private tutoring."

"If that's what will work best for him, then we'll do the best we can to get Luke enough assistance," Anne said.

"I feel the same way." Wendy glanced at the clock. "I hope everything goes well with your visit with Mr. Bartholomew. I asked Chad if he knew him, and he said that he'd met him a couple times at some fund-raisers a long time ago. He said Mr. Bartholomew seemed a little stiff and strange but not crazy, as some people think."

"People think he's crazy?" Anne asked.

Wendy shrugged. "Apparently there have been rumors. Silly stuff that kids make up. Like he lets a pet tiger roam his property to keep people away. Another one is that he has a laboratory in his basement and is working on a time machine."

"A time machine like in H. G. Wells's novel?" Anne asked with a laugh.

"Or from one of those movies where the guy travels back to the fifties in a car," Wendy added. "At least the kids get credit for using their imaginations. In their eyes, Mr. Bartholomew is cool."

Anne glanced out the window as a car rolled up the driveway. "Mildred's here. I'll be back in an hour or two." She grabbed her purse from behind the counter.

"No problem," Wendy said. "When you get back, can we maybe check out the fallout shelter? I'm still dying to see it, and I've been keeping it a secret even from Chad."

Anne smiled. "You didn't have to be *that* careful, but I appreciate it. I just didn't want all the neighborhood children trying to play in it or attracting the history buffs in town before we're ready. We'll go down there when I get back. See you in a while." She hurried out to Mildred's car and slid into the passenger seat.

"Good morning," Mildred said. "Don't you look spiffy!"

Anne smoothed her skirt over her knees before she put on her seat belt. This was the second time this week she'd abandoned her jeans for meeting with people she didn't know.

"Thanks. I didn't know what was appropriate to wear since Mr. Bartholomew seems so old-fashioned." She'd chosen a casual but feminine soft-flowing blue skirt that fell mid-calf, topped with a white blouse. But she had decided against heels and wore her favorite navy flats.

"I think what you're wearing is just fine. Marcus used to have strong opinions that girls these days needed to dress more ladylike, but nobody pays him much mind, not even his daughter. If he had his way, everyone would be dressed like they did in the forties and fifties."

"I heard a rumor that Mr. Bartholomew has a laboratory in his basement and is building a time machine."

"What?" Mildred said with a laugh. "That's a new one. People have always speculated about Marcus because of his being independently wealthy and living for many years in that big house by himself."

Anne looked out the window at the downtown shops as Mildred drove down Main Street. They passed a travel shop with a huge poster of a cruise ship in the window. "Mildred, do you remember when Aunt Edie visited Europe?"

Mildred glanced at her. "I think she went two or three times. Maybe four. Your aunt caught the travel bug at a young age. She really enjoyed traipsing all over the place. She was a great writer too."

Anne nodded. "I brought a box of magazines with her articles in them downstairs last night. I only meant to skim through them to see where she had gone but found myself slowing down to read through most of them. She had me really wanting to visit those places. Anyway, I only found three articles so far on her travels to Europe. They were centered in Switzerland, London, and Paris, but I'm assuming she traveled to other countries too. I found postcards and souvenirs from Germany, Holland, and Italy. It could be I just haven't found anything she wrote about those places yet."

"Or maybe she just went over there for vacation," Mildred said.

"That could be. Do you know when her last trip to Europe was?"

"Oh, it must have been in the early to midsixties. I tried to convince her it was getting too dangerous to travel alone in foreign countries, but you know your aunt, she was determined to go."

"Maybe she wasn't alone. Maybe she was meeting someone over there," Anne said, thinking out loud. Perhaps someone whom Edie might have been exchanging information with."

"I suppose that's a possibility," Mildred said, "but why wouldn't she just say so?"

"I'm thinking that Aunt Edie had quite a few secrets." Anne explained how she'd found the shelter under the garage, hoping Aunt Edie's oldest friend might know about it. "I practically grew up in that house and didn't even know it was there."

"Mercy me. I forgot about that. Those days after the Bay of Pigs were pretty unnerving, and I remember Edie saying that she was trying to convince her parents, who still lived in the house, to hire someone to build a bomb shelter. She even offered to pay for it. I just assumed her parents had refused. What does the shelter look like?"

"It's a small room about fifteen feet underground with an entrance from the garage and another one leading to the outside. When you walk inside it's like stepping back to 1963," Anne said. "And this is going to sound even stranger, but I found a little book down there that an expert says may be a codebook. Did Aunt Edie ever mention working for the government as a secret courier, possibly during the Cold War?"

"Edie never shared anything like that with me." Mildred's lips lifted in a small smile, which confirmed to Anne that Mildred didn't find the idea of Edie being a spy a surprise.

"I've been trying to see if she saved her old passport. I'm curious where she traveled to. Do you think she ever visited Eastern Europe?"

Mildred shot her another glance. "You mean behind the Iron Curtain?"

"I know it was more difficult in those days, but I'm curious."

"I saw her passport once. It was full of stamps, just like she'd always wanted, but I didn't look too closely. Anyway, she quit traveling shortly after that."

"Did she ever say why?"

"No, but maybe she got too busy with taking care of her folks when they were getting on in years. Or maybe she had achieved those goals on her bucket list and moved on to other things like skydiving."

"Skydiving?" Anne's voice rose in a squeak. "Aunt Edie skydived?"

Mildred shot Anne a grin. "I'm teasing you, sweetie, although . . ." She lifted her shoulder in a shrug, "you just never know about your aunt. That's what I loved about Edie. Her ability to be a loyal friend, devoted contributor to the community, faithful church member, and yet she still had that spark of spontaneity and love of adventure." Her eyes grew moist. "I really miss her."

Anne's eyes stung, and she placed a hand on Mildred's shoulder. "Me too."

Mildred shook her head with a sigh. "And if she saw us now, she'd scold us for feeling sad, tell us to get off our duffs and go create some great new memories."

"Maybe that's what we're doing today." Anne wiped her eyes. How she wished Ben and Liddie had gotten to know Aunt Edie. But then, maybe they were. The house, the library were their aunt's legacy. You could still see her personality throughout the house even after the remodel. And look at the shelter that gave them a glimpse of their aunt's world in the 1960s. She wondered what else Aunt Edie would surprise her with next.

Mildred turned on her blinker and swung right onto a street, which actually was a long driveway. They came to a halt by a tall, black wrought-iron gate. Mildred pressed a button on the call box. When no one answered on the intercom, she looked at Anne. "They're expecting us. That must be why the gate is open."

She drove on and Anne leaned forward, eagerly taking in the vast estate. She'd only driven by the driveway and never been inside. Few people had, if the story about Mr. Bartholomew being such a recluse was true.

Mildred followed the curve around a large pond in which a variety of ducks and two swans floated. A rowboat was tied up to a dock. In the center of the pond was a small island and gazebo.

A sprawling mansion came into view, surrounded by luscious green lawns and flower gardens. The mansion's stone exterior and stately entryway reminded Anne of photos she'd seen of estates in England. Ivy climbed up the face to the bottom row of three levels of large multipaned windows.

"Impressive, isn't it?" Mildred said. "Marcus's grandfather built it after he made a fortune in the railroad."

The driveway forked, and Mildred turned to the left. The pavement turned to cobblestone and surrounded a marble fountain. Water shot into the air, sparkling in the sunlight, and splashed down into a shallow pool.

Mildred parked by the fountain and, as they walked to the door, Anne noticed that someone had thrown coins into the pool. The entryway dwarfed them. Mildred rang the doorbell, and the sound of distant chimes echoed throughout the building. After a minute of waiting, Mildred rang the bell again.

"Maybe they are out back," Mildred said. "There's a nice patio by the pool. Sometimes Marcus spends the entire day out there." She led the way around the house. Statues and marble benches were scattered about under the trees. No tiger in sight. *That rumor must be false*, Anne thought with amusement.

A vast oval blue pool came into view. White round tables with umbrellas were scattered around it. At the far end of the pool was a square, white structure. Large sliding doors were rolled open to one side and revealed a spacious room with a small kitchen, a breakfast bar, comfortable couches, and overstuffed chairs. There was even a large fireplace.

"Hello! Marcus? Carol?" Mildred called. She went up to the French doors of the main house and peered inside. She looked back at Anne and shrugged.

The sound of a drill drifted over from the large barnlike structure at the end of the driveway.

"Oh, good, someone's here." Mildred marched across the lawn. "This used to be the old stable that Marcus converted to a garage. He loves old cars."

A side door was open. A man with a shock of white hair and navy overalls leaned over a worktable holding an electric drill.

Mildred knocked loudly on the door. The man looked over at them and scowled. "What are you doing in here?"

"I'm Mildred Farley and this is Anne Gibson. We had an appointment with Mr. Bartholomew, but no one appears to be at the house. And you are?"

"Ferguson. Mr. Bartholomew's handyman and mechanic," he replied with a slight English accent. "The mister left with Miss Carol. Doctor's appointment."

"I hope he's okay. It wasn't an emergency, was it?"

"He took the Rolls and drove it himself, so no, I don't think so."

Mildred sighed and looked at Anne. "Marcus must've forgotten we were coming by. That's not unusual for him, but I had talked to Carol." She turned back to Mr. Ferguson. "Can I leave a message for them?"

"I'm not his secretary, but you can write it down." He hunted around the worktable and finally turned over a yellow invoice and handed Mildred a pencil stub.

Anne looked around the long narrow room full of sleek cars. Marcus had quite a variety, from sleek sports cars to elegant sedans, even a limo. And was that the Model T that her mother had mentioned there at the far end of the garage?

"Mr. Ferguson, does Mr. Bartholomew or his daughter drive a new black Porsche?"

Mr. Ferguson stared at her with an odd expression. "No, Miss. Mr. Bartholomew collects only vintage cars."

"Oh yes, I see that. Impressive collection," Anne said. "You keep them in great condition."

His stern expression didn't soften. "Fine things should be given the care they deserve."

"Here you go." Mildred gave Mr. Ferguson her note. "Thanks for passing on the message."

"That way will take you directly to the driveway." He nodded toward the far door and turned back to his workbench.

Anne fell in step with Mildred as they walked the length of the old stable. Old-fashioned wooden feeding bins still hung on the walls, and a carriage occupied a space of honor among the more modern relics of modern civilization. Anne could make out where the stalls used to be by the indentations on the stone floor. She tried to imagine the large pens on both sides of the wide aisle filled with beautiful horses.

As they reached the door, Anne noticed a small car in the corner with a white sheet partially covering it. Something about the shape of the car and the faded red color drew Anne closer.

"Where are you doing?" Mildred asked.

Anne lifted the sheet and looked under. She gasped. "It's Aunt Edie's convertible."

"Are you sure?" Mildred hurried over.

"I think so. Yes! Look here. See this tiny dent?" She pointed a spot on hood. That was caused by a baseball that Alex threw to me and I missed it. And over here by the bumper is a scratch I put on it when I was learning to drive it. I swiped that old hedge that used to be at the end of Aunt Edie's driveway."

"What are you doing over there?" Ferguson stormed toward them.

Anne dropped the sheet as if it were on fire. "I recognize this car. It used to belong to my great-aunt."

"Mr. Bartholomew gave strict orders that car is to be left alone. I give a good cleaning and wax once a year and that's it." Ferguson yanked the sheet to fully cover the car.

"But why doesn't anyone drive it?" Mildred asked. "Why is it over here in the corner?"

"None of my business. None of yours," Mr. Ferguson said with a huff.

Anne wanted to argue that it was. The car had been in her life for so long, it was almost like seeing a member of the family again.

Mildred tugged gently on Anne's arm. "We better get going. Good-bye, Mr. Ferguson."

Anne could feel the old man's gaze boring into their backs as they walked out the door and down the driveway toward the front of the mansion.

"Sorry about that, Anne," Mildred said as if she were somehow responsible. "All those years I've been coming here, I've never spoken with Mr. Ferguson. I'd see a glimpse of him but always in the background, like an extra in a movie."

"Well, he's certainly very protective of Mr. Bartholomew's cars. I'm still in shock that Aunt Edie's car is here. I was sad when she wrote me while I was in college and told me that she'd sold it. I always just assumed that she had traded it in on her new car. I never expected to see it again. Did you know Aunt Edie sold the car to him?"

"No, but I remember the day she showed up with a new car at church. I just assumed that she'd finally decided to get something more practical and reliable. I asked her about it, but she didn't want to talk about it. Poor Edie! She had an emotional attachment to the old car and seemed a little upset about selling it."

They got back in Mildred's car and Anne looked out the window as they headed back to town, but she hardly noticed the scenery this time. She couldn't get the convertible out of her mind. She had an emotional attachment to the car too and many fond memories of Aunt Edie taking her on country drives with the top down. Sometimes Aunt Edie would give her a pretty scarf to wear over her hair and sunglasses so they could pretend to be movie stars, like Grace Kelly.

When she turned sixteen, Aunt Edie taught her how to drive a stick shift in it. For the first couple of lessons, the car did more hopping than anything else, but she eventually mastered shifting gears, thanks to Aunt Edie's patience.

Then, during her senior year, Aunt Edie had been so excited that Anne was chosen Homecoming Queen that she insisted she and Alex borrow the old two-seater. Alex had been elected Homecoming King, and Aunt Edie suggested they could sit on the back of the car and wave to the crowd during halftime. Alex got one of his friends to drive the car around the stadium. It had been one of the most nerve-racking but memorable evenings of her life. She'd been so nervous when they were ready to enter the stadium. Alex had sensed her discomfort at being the center of so much attention and had given her hand a squeeze, encouraging her until she was waving at the crowd. He'd been a good friend, kind and intuitive, back then, as he was now.

Mildred's voice broke into Anne's thoughts. "I hope you don't think I'm a pest, but I can't get that fallout shelter out of my mind. When I can see it?"

Chapter Sixteen

I'm afraid that the only way down into the shelter is by a ladder," Anne said. "The entrance with the stairs is covered with dirt and construction material."

Mildred parked by the library and set the parking brake. "You're thinking I'm too old and creaky to get down the ladder?"

"No, of course not," Anne said with a laugh at the little-old-lady voice Mildred had used. Mildred was spry for her age and no doubt could do pretty much anything that Anne could do. She certainly didn't mind Mildred seeing the shelter and possibly giving more insight into what Aunt Edie might have been thinking back then.

"I was really nervous about going down the ladder myself," she explained. "The kids had no problem, but it's a good fifteen-foot drop. Alex said that he'd clear the other entrance sometime soon. But if you really want to see it now, I'll be happy to show you the entryway and then you can decide."

"*Hmm*, maybe I'll wait until the other entrance is open. Not that I couldn't get down the ladder, it's getting back out that I worry about," Mildred said with a chuckle.

"I'll let you know when Alex gets it open," Anne said, relieved that Mildred had changed her mind. Like with her Aunt Edie, this generation of strong women didn't like to be told what they couldn't do. "I'd love to show you the codebook and get your impression, but it will have to wait until tomorrow. I lent the book to Dr. Stone, a cryptologist, to see what he could figure out."

"Well, I guess I'll just have to exercise a little patience," Mildred said. "But while I'm here, there's a novel I'd like to check out of the library. Wendy put a hold on it for me and it's finally in." She got out of the car and looked toward the back of the house. "Isn't that Alex over there?"

Anne turned. Beyond the back fence, Alex and a crew of two were busy with shovels. Hershey raced around the backyard, barking his enthusiasm at all the activity.

"That's where the other entrance is. I didn't expect Alex to get started on it so soon." Anne shut her car door. She passed by Alex's pickup, which was loaded with old concrete, rebar wire, and timber.

Alex stopped shoveling and leaned on the handle as he swiped his forehead with a gloved hand. He gave her a smile. "Wendy said you'd be back soon, but I didn't think you'd mind if we got started."

"Not at all." Anne peered down into the hole where the two crew men were still digging. The top of a blue metal door peeked out from under the soil. "Oh, wow! You guys really have made progress."

"Luckily, the dirt has been softened by all the rain. We were digging through mud there for a while," Alex said. The men's jeans were caked with mud from the knees down. "There used to be retaining walls here, but they've crumbled over the last fifty years." He pointed to what must have been concrete block walls on either side of the hole. "We never would have dumped stuff on here if we'd known."

Mildred walked up, curiosity shining in her eyes. "So how much longer until we can go in?"

"Give us a few more minutes and I think we'll be able to get that door open," Alex said.

Mildred peered into the hole. "This is the most exciting thing to happen around here in years! Well, other than finally getting a library."

Anne smiled in agreement, although the possibility of Aunt Edie being a government spy ranked right up there.

They watched the men dig and then, for want of something to do to help, Anne picked up some of the branches that had been cut from the brush on the overgrown mound and stacked them in a pile.

Mildred found a round stick and tossed it for Hershey until the dog tired enough to stop barking.

Anne texted Wendy that she was back and that she was outside with Alex. Wendy texted a reply and told Anne to take her time—but she was dying to see what was going on. Anne assured her she'd let her know when she could see the room.

The sound of metal hitting metal pinged out of the hole as Alex cleared the dirt nearest the door. "Okay, I think we can try to open it. It's padlocked shut. I'll have to get my bolt cutters." He looked up at Anne. "I'm guessing you wouldn't know where the key is."

"You guessed right." Anne smiled. "I'll just get a new lock for it."

"It's rusted anyway." Alex strode over to his truck and returned with the bolt cutters. With a mighty crunch, the padlock fell to the ground. Alex pushed on the door.

"It's jammed." He put his shoulder against it. One of the workers jumped down beside him and pushed. The door creaked open. Alex pulled his flashlight out of his tool belt and shone it down into the opening. Anne moved closer so she could see over Alex's head. The steel stairs were covered with a thick layer of dust but looked solid. Alex stepped down slowly checking the walls and ceiling, both reinforced with steel beams.

He reached the bottom and opened the second door. He disappeared for a few seconds and light streamed into the stairway. He looked up at Anne. "It's safe."

Anne looked at Mildred. "Ready?"

"Always," Mildred said. Alex took her arm so the older woman didn't falter stepping onto the dirt and down the metal stairs.

Anne followed next. She looked back at Alex's crewmen who had worked so hard to clear the area. "You're welcome to come see the room too."

They grinned and followed her down.

Mildred stood in the middle of the shelter, her eyes wide with wonder as she slowly turned. "As they used to say back then, this is really *boss*." She gasped and grabbed a blanket off the overhead bunk. "This is the quilt I made for Edie when we were in home ec. I don't know if I should be perturbed she buried it underground for fifty years or touched that she wanted to save it in case of nuclear disaster." She smiled at Anne and hugged the quilt. "I think I'm really touched."

"I would be too," Anne said. "Do you want to take it? I'm sure Aunt Edie would've wanted you to have it back."

"I do, but I can get it later." She carefully folded the quilt and placed it back on the bunk. "You know, this would make a great opportunity to share that era with young people."

"You're right," Anne said. "I'm just trying to figure out the best way to do it. Originally I was thinking of just donating some of the items to the historical society, but now that Alex got the other door open, I'm thinking that maybe people might want to see this as it is right now."

"You could charge admission to see this," one of the workmen piped up. "Make some bucks, you know what I mean?"

"Like a museum," the other added.

Anne considered the idea. "I think I'd feel funny about charging admission."

"You could just ask for donations to benefit the library. Don't ask for a specific amount," Mildred suggested quietly. "Then later you could decide if you still want to donate the items to the historical society. It's something to think about anyway."

"That might work," Anne said, thinking that the extra funds could be used for a new elevator if the current one couldn't be repaired up to code.

She glanced over at Alex and the workers. The guys were examining the air purifier, discussing if it would have really worked and for how long. She shook her head. What was it about the ugly cylinder that fascinated men?

Mildred spied a stack of novels on one of the shelves. "I remember reading some of these. Edie and I would trade 'good reads,' as we called them. Some of them are classics now, but of course, they were brand new back then." She laughed merrily.

Anne enjoyed watching Mildred explore the room and was beginning to really like the idea of letting other people down here.

"We have to get on to the next job." Alex stood by the door. His workers were going up the steps.

"Thank you so much, Alex."

"Well, since I still don't have the new motor for the elevator yet, I figured I'd at least get something done for you."

Anne walked over to the doorway and looked up the stairs. "I was thinking that the wall out there needs to be rebuilt. What do you think?"

"I agree, because when it rains the mud is going to fill up the entrance again. I'll get you an estimate. Many of the blocks out there are still good, so it shouldn't cost too much. I'll call you later." He started up the stairs and then turned. "Just so you know, I told the guys to stay quiet about the shelter. Our policy is not to discuss jobs with other people anyway."

"I appreciate that." With just the excitement that was being generated with her friends, she could imagine there were going to be lots of curious people. Mildred's idea to use the shelter for fund-raising was growing on her. Part of the income could go to library maintenance and part to another worthy cause like the literacy program.

She turned to see Mildred standing over the trunk. "Is this where you found the codebook?"

"That's it." Anne walked over to her. "Aunt Edie packed mostly clothes in it."

Mildred opened the lid, and Anne showed her the little brown backpack where the codebook had been hidden.

"It was hidden in the lining," she said.

Mildred turned the bag over, looking at it carefully. "I had something similar at one time. Did you know there's a hidden pocket in the bottom?"

"Really?" Anne said. "I didn't notice."

"I think that's the point," Mildred teased. "Here, look. If you open the zipper on the pocket and put your fingers in here . . . Oh, there's something inside."

Anne's imagination went wild. What could be in there? A secret message? Another codebook? Her passport?

Mildred pulled out a piece of crackly paper with commercial writing on it. "German." Mildred sniffed the paper. "Chocolate. This is a candy bar wrapper."

Anne didn't know whether to be disappointed or laugh. "Aunt Edie loved chocolate."

"Don't we all, sweetie?" Mildred chuckled. "Well, at least you know that Edie probably carried this bag on one of her trips to Europe."

Anne held the wrapper, trying to imagine Aunt Edie buying the candy bar in Germany while being on a secret mission. She was still having difficulty thinking of Aunt Edie as a spy. Maybe she'd used the lining and hidden pocket in the backpack to smuggle other things.

Anne put the wrapper back inside the backpack. "I better go and relieve Wendy. She's been dying to get down here."

"Oh, let me," Mildred said, slapping her hands together to brush the dust off. "That way you can enjoy sharing this with your friend. These are the times you'll want to remember. Just like all the adventures I had with Aunt Edie. I just wish . . ." Mildred glanced down at Edie's bag and then gave herself a little shake. "I was going to say I wish she'd taken me with her on her trips, but if she was indeed a spy, maybe it was a blessing in disguise that she didn't."

CHAPTER SEVENTEEN

Willy Harris was still the lone man in the literacy class on Thursday night, but he didn't seem to mind. In fact, he seemed downright pleased that the women in class appeared want to take him under their wings and make sure the poor widower was taking care of himself properly. They crowded around him at the refreshment table looking at wallet photos of his grandchildren.

Willy had arrived early, waving a black book. "I brought my Bible. I want to be able to read the Scripture for church when my son and my granddaughter come to visit for Fourth of July. I already talked to my pastor and he gave me a psalm to learn."

"That's terrific, Willy," Wendy said. "We'll get started on it right away, and by the time your family arrives you'll be a pro at it."

"I'm counting on it," Willy had said and headed for the refreshment table.

Bella agreed to keep an eye on the checkout desk and take care of any library business until closing while Remi volunteered to serve as a tutor. Now that college was out for the summer, Wendy had loaded her up with literacy material to review.

Mr. Layton had arrived and was going over the student files. He seemed pleased with the progress of the class.

After Wendy taught the lesson, Anne worked with Sandy again, this time staying in the History Room at the table. Sandy seemed in a happier mood. She did well on the review material they had covered in the first class but hit a wall when it came to reading simple sentences.

Mr. Layton roamed the rooms for a while to spend some time with each student and tutor. He praised each student's achievements and made suggestions where needed. He saved Sandy for last.

He gave Sandy and Anne a big smile and sat down beside them. "Sandy, you're doing well with your phonics lessons."

"So why I can't read better?"

"Well, I was going over your history assessments from your file, and I really think you might benefit from having an expert test your reading ability again."

Sandy grimaced. "But they've done that all before."

"The tests have improved greatly. I think you may have a rare form of dyslexia, which was not picked up before. It's nothing that you did or didn't do while in school. You may just have a unique way of processing the words."

Anne gave Sandy a reassuring smile. "It can't hurt to try, right? What if they can solve the problem, and then you'll be able read anything you want to?"

"Anne's right," Mr. Layton said, "Once we figure out what you're seeing on the page, you can teach yourself to process the letters so they make sense to you. With your permission, I'm going to consult with someone who is very experienced in this type of thing."

Sandy looked uncertain. "I suppose, like Anne said, it can't hurt to do it one more time. But I can still stay in this class, right?"

"Oh, of course. I hope you do," Mr. Layton said.

"I guess that would be okay." Sandy picked up her purse and notebook.

"I'll call you tomorrow when I can set something up." Mr. Layton looked at his watch. "I've got to run." He said good-bye to Anne and walked out the door along with Sandy.

Willy shuffled into the History Room and grinned at Anne. "I read the psalm all the way through."

"And he did very well." Jen handed Willy the notebook he'd left behind.

"I'm not good enough to read in the church service yet, though. I still have problems with some words."

"But you will be ready by the time your granddaughter gets here," Jennifer said.

After the students had all departed, Anne joined Wendy, Remi, and Bella by the checkout counter.

Heather came out of the Nonfiction Room and handed Wendy a progress sheet. Anne had filled hers out for Sandy while Mr. Layton was talking to her. The form consisted of check boxes that indicated what the student covered each session and a blank space for comments. Anne had noted that Sandy was going to be referred for dyslexia testing. She was relieved Sandy had agreed to explore her options further.

"Oh, I forgot to do my report. Willy and I were having too much fun." Jennifer turned to Wendy. "Do you have another sheet? I think I left the blank one in Willy's notebook."

"Here is an extra." Remi pulled one out of a notebook she was holding. "There are pens on the counter."

"Thanks, kiddo." Jen took the check sheet over to the counter and started filling out the report.

Heather covered her mouth and yawned. "Sorry. I had to be at school at seven this morning for band practice. Anyway, I think I have another student for you. He's one of the school bus drivers and had heard about the class through a friend who uses the library. His name is Sam and he's going to come next week."

"That's great!" Wendy said. "The word about the class is spreading."

Jennifer, Remi, and Heather stayed around for a few more minutes, chatting about the students and their plans for the following week. After everyone but Wendy had gone home, Anne asked, "So how is Luke doing? I was hoping he'd come to class tonight."

"So was I, but I couldn't convince him. I think he's going to be just fine. I had him stop by my house last night for some tutoring. His daughter is precious. I'd say, according to the assessment, he's almost at a third-grade level. He just needs encouragement and some confidence. We have put him on the fast track and set up a schedule where he can get tutoring three or four times a week."

"That's wonderful, Wendy. You're an angel for taking the extra time to help him."

"Well, like Jennifer said, I think I'm getting more of a blessing than he is, if you know what I mean."

Anne thought of Sandy's shy smile and her bravery to try to overcome failure again. "I do."

* * *

Anne awoke hours before she had to get out of bed on Friday morning. She hoped this wasn't becoming a habit. But she couldn't get Aunt Edie and her old convertible out of her mind. Anne pondered again why Aunt Edie might have sold her car to Mr. Bartholomew.

Mildred had suggested that Aunt Edie may have just decided she needed a new car, but could there have been another reason? Did she suddenly need money and had gone to Mr. Bartholomew because of his known generosity and love for old cars? And in that case, was he trying to help Edie's library now? After all, this was Edie's legacy to the town.

Anne slipped out of bed and went to her closet. Outside the window, dawn was breaking. She tugged on some jeans and a blouse and headed downstairs to the kitchen. She started the coffeemaker and popped some toast in Aunt Edie's temperamental old toaster, keeping an eye on it. Anne had a newer toaster she'd brought from New York, but she liked using the old appliance that had been there when she was a girl.

She picked up Mildred's scrapbook from off the counter and set it with the file of articles and clippings she'd already collected. After their adventure in the shelter, Anne had mentioned finding some articles with Aunt Edie and Mr. Bartholomew, but the photos weren't very clear. Mildred had insisted on dropping off her scrapbook so Anne had something else to work with.

Anne spread peanut butter on her toast, grabbed a mug of coffee, and headed downstairs with Mildred's scrapbook and the file she had compiled with all the articles. She left the door open so that in case the kids woke up they would know she'd gone into the library.

The first floor was shadowy and quiet and had that special library smell that Anne loved. She went behind the counter and cleared space on the desk.

She smoothed out the copy of the note they'd found in the bush and studied it again.

Gracious Lady,

When the little girl spied the mangy dog limping over the hill toward home, she ran and threw her arms around her pet. She never knew about the fire or the act of bravery her dog did. But in her eyes, her pet was a hero for returning home. The past was forgiven and a new life begun.

A kind deed is never forgotten.

Maybe it was from having spent time with Dr. Stone, but Anne was even further impressed that the message seemed to be some sort of code. A secret message for Aunt Edie? But like with the codebook that Aunt Edie had possessed, Anne didn't have the "key" to decipher it. Or did she?

The words in the note obviously had special meaning. She typed them into the computer Internet search but nothing useful popped up.

Next, she opened Mildred's scrapbook to the page with both Mr. Bartholomew and Aunt Edie's photos and then spread out the rest of the articles she'd collected. She methodically studied the photos, sorting them into piles that contained common committees and people. She made lists of names on a pad of paper trying to see a pattern and paid particular attention to the group shots, searching the backgrounds. Of course Aunt Edie, Mildred, and Mr. Bartholomew were featured in many photos together since they worked on the same committees.

A young man whom Anne didn't recognize kept popping up in several of the photos that were dated in 1998. He usually wore overalls and was always in the background, never the focus of the photographs. Sometimes he was holding a hoe or hedge clippers. Anne noted that he only appeared in photographs that Aunt Edie was in.

Who was he? She went through the photos again and compiled six that contained the man in overalls. She focused on another group shot of a park project where he wasn't working but sitting under a tree off to the side with a book on his lap. She took it over to the scanner and brought the image up on the computer screen. After some fiddling with the photo options, she managed to zoom in on his face and make a print.

The man had dark wavy hair that needed trimming, a strong nose and, despite the deep scar that ran from the corner of his eye to his ear, he had an appealing, boyishly handsome face. Anne guessed him to be in his thirties. So what was his relationship with Aunt Edie?

In one photo he was looking down at the book in his lap and in another he was carrying it in his hand. She placed the image on the scanner and enlarged it until she could see the author's name on the book. Bonnie Tuft. The title was too blurry to interpret except for the partial word "Do."

Bonnie Tuft's Web site revealed the late author had written sixty-one children's books. Anne scanned the books for a blue cover and the letters "Do" in the title and to her delight she found one called *The Lonely Dog*.

Now that she could see the whole cover, it appeared familiar. Hadn't she read that book when she was a child? She couldn't be sure. She checked the catalog and confirmed that she didn't carry it in the library. A quick search online revealed it was out of print, but copies were for sale by various used bookstores. She noted the delivery times, and it would take three days to a week to be delivered, unless she wanted pay an exorbitant amount. But maybe there was a quicker way to get her hands on it.

She gathered everything together and went back upstairs. Liddie and Ben were still sound asleep. Anne gently woke them and told it was time to get ready for school, and then she went to the kitchen to set out cereal and milk. She went back upstairs to nudge Ben again. He yawned and sat up this time.

"Mommy, I can't find my Hello Kitty shirt," Liddie called from her room.

"That's because it's in the laundry hamper and I haven't had a chance to do the wash."

"But I want to wear it. Cindy is wearing hers today."

"Well, you can't wear it to school dirty. Remember you spilled milk down the front."

"Can't you wash it now?" Liddie's voice rose in a wail.

"No, there isn't time," Anne said firmly. "You'll have to pick something else out.

Liddie opened her mouth to complain again, and Anne shook her head. "Liddie, enough, please."

Her daughter snapped her mouth shut, but tears welled up in her eyes.

"Liddie, this is nothing to cry over. Why don't you tell Cindy you can wear your Hello Kitty shirt next Monday? Mommy will make sure that it is washed by then. Okay?"

Liddie nodded and Anne chose another shirt that used to be one of Liddie's favorites, before she'd met Cindy.

Ben was already at the table by the time Anne and Liddie got back to the kitchen. Liddie spied her favorite puffed cereal on the table and her attitude improved drastically as she asked Ben to listen to it snap and crackle when she poured the milk on it.

Anne glanced at the clock. It was about an hour until school started. She dialed Mr. Layton's cell number.

"Mr. Layton, it's Anne Gibson. I hope I'm not interrupting anything."

"I'm just at school grading papers until students arrive. Is anything wrong?"

"No, everything is fine with the class. Thank you so much for the help you're getting for Sandy."

"My pleasure. I hope she'll persevere."

"So do I," Anne said. "I'm calling because I'm doing some research and trying to locate a children's book, *The Lonely Dog* by Bonnie Tufts? It was printed in 1955. It's out of print, but I was hoping someone might have it at the school."

"I don't recall that title, but one of the other teachers, Mrs. Rich, has a collection of old storybooks in her room. I'll check with her now. Come by my room when you drop your children off."

Anne thanked him and hurried the kids along with their breakfast. Despite her early start to the day, Anne couldn't seem to get her children organized and out of the house fast enough. A shoelace tore on Liddie's shoe and Anne had to hunt for a spare. She finally took one off of her own shoes. Ben realized that he'd forgotten his math book when they were halfway down Bluebell Lane, and they had to go back for it. For some reason, the Blue Hill Elementary parking lot seemed extra jammed this morning, and it took ten minutes to find a parking spot.

Anne was breathing hard by the time she reached Ben's classroom. Ben had hung back in the hall, not sure he wanted to be seen with his mother in the class in front of the other boys.

Mr. Layton stood at the whiteboard, writing out a list of verbs. Several fourth-graders were hanging around their desks and stared at Anne.

"Sorry, I meant to get here earlier," Anne said.

Mr. Layton smiled. "You're not tardy. The bell hasn't rung yet." He set the marker down and turned to his desk. "You're in luck. Mrs. Rich had the book in her room. She said it was a popular storybook that was very useful in teaching children to read several generations ago."

Anne picked up the blue-covered book. "This is what I was looking for."

"Mrs. Rich didn't want the book to leave the school premises, but when I told her it was you, from the Blue Hill Library, she consented. She made *me* promise it would get returned in the same condition as it is now." He waved his index finger at her. "So don't get me in trouble with her."

"I will be very, very careful with it. I will get it back to you soon," Anne promised as the bell rang and fourth-graders surged in the door.

Anne had to sidestep to keep from getting bumped into as she tried to get out the door. She headed down the rapidly emptying hallway and back outside to her car. She couldn't wait until she got home. She sat in the car and skimmed through the book.

From what Anne surmised, the book was a sweet story about a girl and her dog. The dog was sometimes naughty and wanted adventure. He ran away twice, upsetting his young mistress. The little girl finally had to chain him up, but the dog didn't understand she was trying to keep him safe and he broke free. He ran away again, but this time he got picked up by a family and taken far away. During his journey to find his way home, he learned some lessons and almost died when saving a family from a fire. The family wanted to keep him forever, but love for his little girl drove the dog back home where he was loved and forgiven.

Her heart beat faster as she read the last sentences of the book.

She never knew about the fire or the act of bravery her dog did. But in her eyes, her pet was a hero for returning home. The past was forgiven and a new life begun.

They exactly matched the words in the note.

Obviously the story's theme was about loyalty and forgiveness, which must have meant something special to the writer of the note and possibly Aunt Edie, if she was the gracious lady.

Elated about her discovery, Anne started the car engine. Now that she had found the source of the note, she just needed to find out who was holding the book in the photo and maybe the mystery of the note and package of money would finally be solved.

CHAPTER EIGHTEEN

A nne, Carol just called me, and Marcus Bartholomew invited us to lunch at twelve thirty." Mildred sounded breathless over the phone. "*Today* at twelve thirty."

Startled, Anne looked at the library clock. "Today? It's almost noon already."

"I know, I know. It's short notice. I'm sorry. His daughter apologized about yesterday. The doctor's office kept them longer than planned. Her phone battery died and she didn't have my cell number. So they want to make it up to us by inviting us to lunch. I can certainly ask them to reschedule, but I thought since you were anxious to get some information, I'd ask you if it was possible. Who knows when we will be able to meet up with him again?"

"It's fine with me," Anne said. After her most recent discovery, she was even more anxious to talk to Mr. Bartholomew. "Actually, I was just thinking about taking my lunch break. I'll check with Remi and make sure she is okay with my leaving her alone." Anne set the phone down and turned to Remi, who was seated behind the checkout counter.

"I can handle things here, no problem." Remi looked over her shoulder. "Sorry. I didn't mean to eavesdrop, but it's kind of hard not to." She gave Anne a smile and went back to flipping through a photography book. Remi was seriously considering taking a college photography class next fall for one of her required electives but couldn't decide between that one and another in culinary arts. She liked to joke that both courses were creative but one satisfied the aesthetic side of her personality and the other her stomach.

Anne lifted the phone to her ear. "Okay, I can go."

"Wonderful. I'll be there in fifteen minutes."

Anne hung up and took the stairs to her living quarters at a brisk pace. She was tempted to take the steps two at time, but living in a library required a sense of decorum. When she closed the door to her private entrance behind her, she tore up the next flight of stairs into her bedroom and flung open the closet doors.

She dug through her clothes, trying to find something suitable for luncheon at the mansion.

She pulled out a summer dress that she hadn't worn since she lived in New York. Eric, who didn't usually notice women's clothing, had seen the soft pink dress on a mannequin at Macy's when they were on a shopping expedition for Ben's school clothes. Eric suggested she try it on and then insisted she buy it. Every time she wore the dress, she remembered the admiration in Eric's eyes when she'd come out of the dressing room.

She stopped in the bathroom to trade her glasses for her contacts, swiped on a little mascara, and patted powder on her shining nose. She grimaced at her reflection. If she had more time she'd run the straightener through her shoulder-length hair and wear it down. Instead she adjusted her hair clip to loosely sweep her hair up and allow for strands to fall softly by her face.

She headed down the stairs, slipping on her sandals in the kitchen before going back into the library.

Remi blinked. "That was quick, Cinderella."

Anne laughed as she picked up her purse from behind the counter. When she reached the front door, it opened, and Alex stepped inside.

He let out a low whistle. "Nice duds."

Anne's cheeks warmed. "Thank you."

"She has a lunch date," Remi told Alex.

"With Mildred, Marcus Bartholomew, and his daughter," Anne added hastily.

Alex grinned. "Good luck. Ask him if you can see his basement."

"Quit teasing," Anne said, although now that he mentioned it, she was a bit curious about that rumor of his laboratory and a time machine.

Mildred's car turned into the driveway, and Anne hurried outside to meet her.

"Pretty dress," Mildred commented as Anne got in.

"Thanks. I didn't have much time to prepare, so I grabbed the first thing that looked suitable." Anne looked over at Mildred's stylish red and black pantsuit. "I like your outfit too."

"I was at a social club meeting over at the Senior Center when Carol called. Otherwise, I would've been out weeding my garden and covered in dirt."

As they drove past the old depot, Anne recalled that Mildred had mentioned that Marcus Bartholomew's grandfather had made his fortune in the railroad. Blue Hill had a rich railroad history, and the town had flourished in the late 1800s with other local industries and factories dealing with iron, limestone, coal, logging, copper, and brass. Obviously the Bartholomews had diversified their wealth well and didn't suffer much after the abandonment of the town's railroad track in 1899.

Anne rubbed her hands on her dress, feeling a flutter of nervousness in her stomach as Mildred turned into the estate. Today the big iron gates were closed and they had to be buzzed through. Mildred parked by the fountain, and this time the ringing of the doorbell resulted in the massive front door swinging open almost immediately.

A middle-aged woman with graying blonde hair and large green eyes stood in the doorway. A silky blue dress flowed loosely over her trim figure. "Hello, Mildred. I'm so glad you could come on such short notice, and again I apologize about yesterday." She gave Anne a dazzling white smile. "You must be Anne Gibson. Please come on in. I'm Carol," she said as she stepped back. "It's such a lovely day out that we're having lunch on the patio."

Anne stepped into the foyer. The open space extended up three floors, where a huge crystal chandelier hung. A large staircase with a carved cherry wood bannister seemed to float to the second floor. In front of her was a huge bouquet of orange, white, and yellow roses in a large vase on a round marble table. The elegant buds filled the air with a rich floral scent.

"These are lovely." Mildred leaned close to the blossoms and inhaled. "Heavenly."

"Dad's pride and joy. They're from his rose garden." Carol guided them down a long hall past elegantly furnished rooms and through French doors to the stone patio by the pool. Today, one of the round tables had been set with pretty dishes, crystal goblets, and a big silver bowl filled with fruit salad.

Marcus Bartholomew sat ramrod straight in one of the padded wrought-iron chairs, a *Wall Street Journal* in his hands. He wore a dress shirt with a neat red bow tie, suspenders, black suit pants, and shiny black shoes. He looked up and slowly stood as if his joints were stiff.

"Good afternoon," his deep voice said. "How nice that you could you make it."

"Marcus! It's been way too long." Mildred stood on her tiptoes to give him a quick kiss on the cheek.

He cleared his throat gruffly. "It's a pleasure to see you too."

"Dad, this is Anne Gibson," Carol said as Marcus pulled the chairs out for each of them.

"I'm happy to make your acquaintance again." Marcus lowered himself carefully back in his chair. "You may not remember, but we met once under that big oak at the bottom of Blue Hill. On several occasions when I visited your aunt, you'd be up there reading."

Anne smiled. "I spent many summer afternoons in that tree."

"Your aunt used to brag about you quite a bit while we were working on committees together. One would've thought you were her own child. Does that surprise you?"

"When it comes to my aunt, I'm learning not to be surprised about anything she did. She was a remarkable woman."

Marcus nodded. "The world lost a gracious lady when she passed away."

Gracious lady? Anne's breath caught. Mildred looked at her and winked. Could Anne have been wrong in her assumption that the man with the book had written the note? Or maybe

Mr. Bartholomew and the man with the book were somehow connected.

Carol reached for the silver salad tongs. "Perhaps we should start on the fruit salad. Hildy will want to bring out the second course soon."

After they'd all been served, Anne said to Marcus, "I remember that when I was in elementary school you donated a whole ball field of sod."

"Did I now?" Marcus speared a piece of watermelon with his fork.

"Dad, everyone knew it was you." Carol laughed and said to Anne, "He loathes being thanked in public." She smiled at her father. "Always said it might give him a big head."

"I found it much more gratifying to give anonymous gifts. It makes it difficult for people to refuse them, and I'd rather ask for forgiveness than ask permission."

Anne took a deep breath. "Mr. Bartholomew, I need to ask about something and, judging from your past methods of generosity, I'm not sure if you would even admit to doing this kind deed."

Mr. Bartholomew set down his fork. "What is this generous deed that I supposedly did?"

"Someone left a package of money outside the library. I was wondering if it might have been you."

"Indeed, that sounds like something I might do," Marcus said with a small smile, "but I assure you I did not in this case. Is the library in need of funding?"

"Marcus, we didn't come here to ask for a donation," Mildred said. "Anne just isn't sure if it was a gift or if someone lost it."

Carol smiled at Anne. "I think it's commendable that you are even asking. Some people would've just taken the money and not said a word."

"Indeed they would," Mr. Bartholomew agreed.

"If it wasn't you who left the package, then I could still use your help. Last night I came across a photograph of a fund-raiser that you and my aunt attended, and there is someone in the group whom I can't identify. I have a hunch he may have been the one to leave the money." She explained about the note and the book the words might have come from.

"I assume you have the photograph with you?" Marcus asked.

"I do." Anne reached into her purse and brought out a copy of the news article and the scanned close-up of the man's face. "You and Aunt Edie are over by the table with the others, but I'm wondering who that man with the book is."

Mildred leaned closer to Marcus so she could study the photo too. "He looks familiar, but I don't know who he is," she said.

Marcus pulled gold-rimmed wire reading glasses from his shirt pocket and examined the two images. "I don't recall the occasion, but I recognize this man. He was a handyman of sorts and did odd jobs and gardening for me and several other people in Blue Hill. Edie seemed to have taken a special liking to the lad and helped him find employment."

"Do you know his name?" Anne said eagerly.

"My memory isn't what it used to be. I believe it was Thomas. But since I hired him, I would have made a record of his name and payments."

"Trust me, he keeps records of every penny spent," his daughter said with a roll of her eyes.

Marcus huffed. "I am a bit meticulous—"

"A bit?" Carol laughed.

Marcus turned to Anne. "My daughter would have you think I'm a penny pincher."

Mildred patted his arm. "If you are, you are the most generous penny pincher I know. You've given lots of your pennies away."

"I didn't say he was stingy," Carol said with a smile. "He spoiled me rotten. Still does. Now I want to return the favor. I've been trying to get him to turn more of the running of the company over to our business managers and get out of this stuffy old place and enjoy life more."

"And what my daughter doesn't understand," Marcus replied, "is that God has blessed me with everything I need and more. I enjoy life very much right here in my stuffy house. Always have. Always will."

Anne leaned back in her chair and exchanged a smile with Mildred. There was genuine affection behind the bantering between daughter and father. She looked out over the pool and the rolling green estate. She could understand why Marcus loved his home.

"I'll check my record books after we finish eating," Marcus said and, as they continued their meal, Mildred and Marcus regaled Anne and Carol with stories about the good old days. Anne listened with rapt attention.

After a wonderful dessert of fresh raspberries and vanilla bean ice cream, Marcus invited them to join him in his office as he looked for the name of the young man in the photograph. Carol excused herself and said she would join them shortly.

Anne got more glimpses of the house as they headed to the office. In one room a beautiful grand piano graced the center, and Anne wondered who in the family played. She passed another spacious room, which caused her to pause and gasp softly. Floor to ceiling, the walls were filled with shelves of books.

"I know. I felt the same way when I first saw his library," Mildred whispered.

Marcus's office was filled with antique furniture and had a wall of windows overlooking a beautiful rose garden. Marcus gestured to a leather couch and chair. "Please have a seat and make yourselves comfortable."

Marcus opened the door to a closet and walked inside. A minute later he came out with a ledger book and set it on his desk. He flipped through the pages filled with neat figures until he found the date he wanted. His bony finger traced down the columns until suddenly he stopped. "Here it is. Tobias McKinsey. Now I remember. The rascal ran off after finishing my rose bed and, according to this, he never picked up his last paycheck.

"That's strange," Mildred said.

"Yes, I thought so too. I never saw him again. I believe Edie mentioned he left town and that was that." He closed the book. "Does this help you?"

"Oh yes," Anne breathed. "I have a name now. That's much more than I had when I came here. Did you have a home or mailing address for him?"

"No, I always paid him cash. I don't know where he lived."
Marcus closed the ledger. "Is there anything else I can do for you?"

"Yes, Marcus, I have a question. Is that Edie's convertible in
your garage?" Mildred asked, startling both of them. Anne had
wanted to ask about Aunt Edie's car but wasn't sure how to
bring it up.

"Why yes, it is," Marcus said. "When did you see it?"

"Yesterday when we came by and you weren't home. We
heard noises in the garage and saw Mr. Ferguson was working in
there."

"I never thought I'd see it again," Anne said. "I always just
assumed that Aunt Edie traded the convertible in at the dealership
when she got her Honda. I never thought she'd sell the convertible
in the first place. She loved that car."

Marcus nodded and leaned back in his chair gazing at
a spot on the wall above Anne's head. "She did love it," he said
softly. "I was surprised too when Edie offered to sell it to me.
She just showed up one day and practically gave it to me.
I'd made several offers over the years for it, but she always
turned me down. One time she even insisted she would never
sell it."

"When did she sell it to you?" Mildred asked.

Marcus opened his account book again. "It would be in here.
Sometime in the beginning of the same summer Tobias worked in
my garden." He flipped back and forth through the pages. "Ah,
here it is. June 18, 1998. Edie wanted ten thousand for the car. I
tried to pay more for it, but she said that's all she wanted. She
seemed upset, and I told her she could buy the car back whenever

she wanted it. So I stored it in the garage thinking she'd change her mind. She never did."

Anne pulled the article copy from her purse and checked the date. June 16, 1998. Aunt Edie sold the car to Marcus right after that fund-raiser. About the same time Tobias had supposedly disappeared too. She stared at the photo where Tobias was sitting under the tree with his book.

Carol arrived in the doorway. "Dad, you have a conference call in ten minutes."

"Thank you for reminding me, dear," Marcus said.

Anne and Mildred stood and thanked Marcus and Carol for lunch and the help in identifying Tobias. Carol walked with Anne and Mildred to the front door.

Mildred gave Carol a hug. "I'm glad you're here for your dad."

"Me too," Carol said. "It's good to be home."

Anne paused on the porch remembering what Alex had said about the laboratory in the basement. He was teasing of course, but her curiosity got the best of her. She might never get another chance to ask.

"Carol, this may be an odd question and I hope not too nosy," Anne said, "but does your father have a laboratory in his basement?"

Carol blinked. "Yes, he does. Why do you ask?"

"A friend of mine whose husband is a coach at the school said that there is a rumor going around among the kids that he's building a time machine."

"I hadn't heard that rumor," Mildred said with a laugh.

Carol eyes began to twinkle. "Would you like to see for yourself?"

Mildred looked at Anne. "Of course we would."

"Come this way." Carol led them down a hall to a large kitchen. "The stairs are back here." She opened a door and they descended down into a large dungeon-like room. Part of it was used for storage, but on one side shallow boxes lined a row of tables. Tiny green plants were emerging from rich dark soil under hanging lights.

"My dad is an amateur horticulturist," Carol said, walking between the tables. "And over here must be the time machine."

A huge gray contraption with dials and gauges filled one corner. Carol opened the metal door on it and inside were shelves containing seedlings.

"What is it?" Mildred asked.

"A special plant humidifier," Carol said. "He's been tinkering with it for years trying to infuse different nutrients into the air to see if he can speed the growth up of his roses or make them more resistant to disease." She closed the door and turned a switch. The gauges and panel lit up and the machine emitted a hissing noise as steam rattled up a pipe.

"Okay, I can see how someone with a vivid imagination might think it's a time machine," Anne said with a laugh.

Carol looked up at some ground-level windows. "Kids sneak onto the estate occasionally and probably peek in there. We haven't had any property damage so we ignore it."

"I guess they weren't afraid of the tiger," Anne murmured.

"What tiger?" Mildred asked.

Carol held up her hand. "I don't even want to know."

They all laughed and headed back to the stairs. As they passed an open door, Mildred looked inside and said, "This looks a little like Anne's fallout shelter."

"That was its function originally," Carol said. "Dad had the shelter built in the fifties. Take a look if you'd like. Hildy mostly uses it to store her canned goods in now."

The fallout bunker was wider than Aunt Edie's and devoid of memorabilia. The walls were paneled. An exercise bike and a treadmill sat in one corner. Rows of canned peaches, pears, and cherries lined a set of shelves. Anne noticed some pickles too.

"Let me show you something really cool." Carol felt along the wall and pushed on a panel. A section turned inward revealing a closet-sized room. "It's a panic room that was to hide us from the Soviets in case they invaded."

"Amazing," Mildred said. "I never would've known it was there."

Carol smiled. "Old houses are just full of surprises, aren't they?"

CHAPTER NINETEEN

"So Aunt Edie never mentioned Tobias McKinsey to you?" Anne asked as Mildred parked the car by the library. They had been discussing Mr. Bartholomew and Tobias all the way back to the library.

"I've been racking my brain ever since Marcus identified him. I'm sure I must've seen him, considering he was doing odd jobs about town, but I really don't recall. Isn't that pathetic? But that summer there was a family wedding. It was just a hectic time."

"I don't think it's pathetic. If it weren't for your getting me in to see Marcus, I wouldn't even know Tobias's name. I can't even tell you how much I appreciate all your help." Anne gave Mildred's hand a squeeze.

Mildred squeezed back. "You know I'm always here for you, sweetie. Good luck on finding Tobias. Let me know what you discover."

"I will," Anne promised and got out of the car. She gave Mildred a wave as she drove away and thanked God for bringing Mildred into her life.

Hershey barked a greeting through the fence and whined. Anne walked over to give the dog a pat. She looked over at the debris pile and noticed that more dirt had been moved and blocks had been set back for the retaining wall. When had Alex done that? She felt a sudden urge to visit the shelter again. Being down in Mr. Bartholomew's basement made her wonder if Aunt Edie had a secret compartment or room in her shelter. Discovering the shelter had been surprising enough, and it never occurred to Anne that there might be more than met the eye.

She glanced at her watch and realized she was already half an hour overdue back in the library. She hurried inside.

"I'm reading the shelves," Bella said from among the stacks in the History Room. "I found a couple of other books out of place."

"I'm glad you're checking," Anne said, wondering why so many seemed out of place recently. Sometimes patrons would re-shelve books and slide them in the wrong place. Little ones in the Children's Room loved to pull books out and push them back in. That was to be expected. If it continued to be a problem elsewhere, maybe she needed to put up little signs like they did in some larger libraries making it a rule that only the staff re-shelved books.

Before she started her research on Tobias McKinsey, she took a walk through the peaceful library. The History Room was empty except for Remi, but several patrons browsed the shelves in the Nonfiction Room. She climbed the stairs to the second floor. Two mothers with several preschoolers and a baby occupied the Children's Room. One cute little girl with red pigtails was having a grand time drawing on the wall that was coated with chalkboard paint. The mothers were in deep discussion and everyone seemed content so Anne gave them a smile and backed out.

The Reference Room was unoccupied. The room seemed really bare without the usual tables that were now downstairs for the literacy class. Anne would be glad when the elevator was fixed, so they could move the meetings back up here where there was more space.

She spied Remi, who had now moved into the Fiction Room, moving slowly down the aisle examining the spines of the books on the bottom shelf. Anne felt a wave of sympathy. Reading shelves could be really tedious. She remembered how, when she first started out in college and worked at the library, she spent hours checking the shelves. That came from being the lowest on the totem pole.

Remi gave her a weary smile. "So far I've found seven books in the wrong place."

"Great job," Anne said. "But don't feel like you have to do all the shelves at one time. We can space this out over the next week and all take turns."

"Whew. I'm starting to get a backache." Remi straightened and rubbed her lower back. "I'll finish this section and quit for the day."

"Sounds good. I'm heading back downstairs if you need anything."

Anne returned to the main floor and went behind the counter, where they stored the phone book. She turned to the white pages to the *M* section. No one by the name of McKinsey was listed for Blue Hill and the surrounding area. She wasn't surprised, though, because Mr. Bartholomew had said he heard Tobias had left town. Still, she was hoping that maybe he or his family had come back.

She turned to the computer and tried running Tobias McKinsey through the phone directory for Pennsylvania but did not find a match. There was only one T. McKinsey, but the age listed next to his name was twenty-two. Much too young for the man in the photos. A dozen other McKinseys were listed, all of them women except one eighty-year-old man.

Tobias could have married, but why wouldn't his name be listed if his wife's was? Of course he could be living in another state. She set the search range to the United States. No exact match for Tobias McKinsey came up. She tried spelling the name MacKinsey in case she had misspelled it. Still no luck.

She propped her chin on her hand as she stared at the screen. Tobias had lived somewhere in Blue Hill at one time. The library had some old directories in the Reference Room but none dating back that far.

The church had membership records stored in the basement, but that would assume he'd been a member of Blue Hill Community Church. Knowing Aunt Edie, she would have invited him to church and he might have been listed as a visitor in the guest book. But Anne had no idea how long Aunt Edie had known Tobias. She supposed she could check the records for 1998, but there had to be an easier way. Maybe Michael Banks could find something about him in the police records. She started to lift the phone to call him when the door opened and in strode Dr. Emmett Stone accompanied by a lovely middle-aged woman with stylish short dark hair and vivid blue eyes.

The woman's gaze glanced about the room. "This is beautiful, Emmett."

Dr. Stone spied Anne behind the counter and guided the woman over to her. Anne rose to meet them.

"Good afternoon,. I should've called first but took a chance you'd be here," Dr. Stone said. "This is my wife, Erica."

Anne extended her hand. "It's great to meet you."

"Likewise," Erica said with a smile. "For all those years we visited Blue Hill, I always admired this beautiful old Victorian on the hill. I'm so pleased to finally be able to see inside it. When Emmett told me that it had been converted to a library, I insisted on coming along. Restoration for these beautiful landmarks is a passion of mine."

"Erica majored in architecture," Dr. Stone said with a proud smile for his wife.

"How nice. Would you like a tour?" Anne asked.

"I'd love one, but I don't want to take you away from the real reason we came. If you don't mind, I'll be quite content to roam about while you two talk."

"She'll be happy exploring on her own," Dr. Stone concurred.

"Feel free to explore then," Anne said. "The first two floors contain the library. I have living quarters on part of the second floor and the entire third, but the door will be locked."

"I see you have an impressive history section. I think I'll start there." Erica strode over to the History Room.

Anne turned back to Dr. Stone. "Would you like a glass of water or some coffee?"

"Maybe after we talk," Dr. Stone said. "I learned some interesting things about your aunt's codebook."

A shiver of anticipation ran up Anne's spine. "Remi, could you watch the counter?"

"Sure thing," she replied.

"There's a table back over here where we can sit." Anne led him to the Nonfiction Room.

After Dr. Stone settled in the chair, he opened his briefcase and lifted out the leather codebook and laid it gently on the table.

"I am quite intrigued by your aunt's book. I hope you don't mind but I made copies in case I come across something in the future that is connected to it."

"I don't mind at all. Were you able to determine what the codes meant?"

He opened the book and turned to a page. "Actually, what you see here is a cipher that disguises the code. It's not a difficult cipher to break, but more of a deterrent to a casual observer. Now, once I figured out the cipher, I realized your aunt was using a simple word substitution code. Quite effective and really secure if used just once or twice. How many trips did your aunt take overseas?"

"At least twice that I know of. Maybe up to four times . . . I still can't find her old passport."

"Depending on her mission, this code could've been used more than once. It also looks like she added more codes over time. See the slight variation in the black ink used. The beginning words are also fainter than those toward the end of the book."

The word *mission* gave Anne goose bumps. "I see what you mean. So what is the code saying?"

"Well that is difficult to interpret without a corresponding document or key. But by looking at the repetitive wording, some of these codes are directional. In other words, she used them to get from one place to the other. See here?" He pulled some sheets out of his briefcase where he had made notes. "I did some algorithms with the words. And I think the word *trail* means south. *Route* means east. I think *black tea* is supposed to be a street name. I will certainly still work on it. I hate leaving puzzles unsolved."

Anne could concur. Although she had never considered herself a sleuth or detective, she didn't like leaving mysteries unsolved, especially when it involved friends or loved ones.

"The CIA does use civilians in some cases," Dr. Stone said. "The Cold War era was before personal computers or cell phones or the Internet. Human couriers were very important for the security of passing information. They still are in some cases. Civilians were used to observe certain buildings or people, take photographs, or contact people that authorities couldn't without looking suspicious."

"Is there some way I can find out what Aunt Edie actually did?"

"You can try contacting the CIA and the State Department. Explain what you are looking for. But I warn you, it may take a long while to get results, if at all. This was serious business and great lengths were taken to protect their people. You can use my name if you'd like when you contact them. I still have a little pull. I can try too, but a family member might have more luck." He snapped his briefcase shut. "Is it possible I can take a look at where you found the book?"

"My contractor was able to clear out the main entrance of the shelter if you'd like to see it."

"I would indeed. Contrary to my wife's love of beautiful old houses, I find places like your shelter more fascinating."

Anne slid her chair back and stood as Dr. Stone looked around the library. "I wonder where Erica went."

Anne heard a whirling sound that she hadn't heard for days. The elevator! It was coming down right now and suddenly it stopped. Anne hurried over to the elevator cage and looked up.

"Hello, dear," Erica called from near the ceiling.

Dr. Stone strolled towards the elevator. "Are you stuck?"

"So it seems."

"Oh dear, the elevator has been broken. I put a sign on the door upstairs not to use it."

"Oh, I saw that," Erica said. "I figured it was just to keep kids from playing in it. Besides, I wanted to examine it more closely. This elevator is an antique. I've only seen a couple others from this era." She ran her hand over the bars. "Really well constructed and in good shape."

Except that it didn't operate right now, Anne wanted to point out. How was she going to get her out of there?

Dr. Stone turned to Anne. "My lovely wife doesn't like to follow instructions. This isn't the first time she's gotten herself in a pickle."

"I heard that, dear, and my *not* following instructions has gotten me the most important things in my life, including you."

Anne's heart was starting to pound over the situation, but both Stones appeared unfazed. Her first reaction was to call Alex, but as she reached for the phone, she remembered what she'd done when it got stuck with her laundry.

"Dr. Stone, I'm going to go upstairs and push the call button. If you would push the button down here when I say so, we may be able to get it unstuck." Anne ran up the stairs. She peered through the bars at the roof of the elevator and pushed the call button. The elevator gave a jerk and stopped.

"Okay, Dr. Stone push your button." The elevator started to descend and then came to a jerky halt again. They tried three more times and then the elevator ascended to the second floor.

Anne breathed a sigh of relief when she and Erica were face to face. She opened the gate.

"That was an adventure," Erica said, appearing calm and relaxed. "I'm sorry I caused you trouble. You okay, dear? You look flushed."

"I was just worried about getting you out of there."

Erica stepped out of the elevator. "How long has it been broken?"

"A little less than a week. My contractor has ordered a new motor. He's trying to find the original manufacturer, but they've had turnovers in ownership. The elevator and motor may have a lifetime warranty, which I'm sure hoping for. It could save the library some money."

"I might be able to help you with finding the company. When we lived in New York, I consulted with an interior design firm that specialized in renovating older buildings. I saw another old elevator like this in one of the hotels on the West Side that they wanted to keep, and we were able to renovate it with original parts. I can you get the contact information when I get home tonight."

"That would be wonderful," Anne said as she replaced the sign on the elevator door that must have gotten knocked off when Mrs. Stone opened the gate.

"It's the least I can do." Erica peeked into the Children's Room. "I love what you've done with the place. The colors are so inviting."

Dr. Stone arrived at the top of the stairs. "Ah, my songbird has been freed."

"Yes, yes, everything is fine," Erica said and turned back to Anne. "You said that part of this floor was redone to include living quarters?"

"My dear wife is hinting that she wants to see the rest of the house."

"Am I that obvious? I'm sorry. It's the architect in me." Her cheeks blushed slightly. "Oh, of course I don't want to impose."

"It's perfectly okay. I'm the same way," Anne said, thinking about her exploration of Mr. Bartholomew's basement. "Would you like to see the rest of the house?

"That would be delightful. Like I said, I was always curious about this place."

"I wasn't expecting guests, so it's not as neat as I would like it," Anne said.

"I raised children, so I know what it's like trying to keep after a family. I worked full time so the house was never the way I wanted it," Erica said. "My two sons now have families of their own and their own children to pick up after."

"Amazing how things come around," Dr. Stone said behind them.

Anne unlocked the door to the second-floor entrance to the living room and kitchen. Erica saw the old-fashioned toaster on the counter. "We had one of those when we first got married. It still works."

"If you like that era, you should see what's down in my aunt's shelter."

"I thought you'd never ask," Erica said with a laugh.

Dr. Stone smiled. "Did I mention before that my wife could be pushy?"

Erica patted her husband on the arm. "Assertive, dear, assertive. Not pushy."

Anne laughed. She found Erica Stone delightful and her avid interest and curiosity reminded her of Aunt Edie.

"I'd love showing you the shelter and see what you think," Anne said. "Since I've moved into the house, I've made some amazing discoveries about my aunt and this house, such as the fallout shelter."

"I just love these old places. They are full of history and character. Does it have a secret room too?" Erica asked. "Some of the Victorian homes from this era did."

Anne hesitated before answering. She had been maintaining the secrecy of the room, but she couldn't very well lie. "Yes, it does."

"How marvelous! Was this house on the Underground Railroad?"

"Not that I know of. This was a room where my aunt kept a desk and some photographs." Anne led them into the little sitting room to where the star quilt hung on the wall, and then she showed her the small secret room.

"How absolutely marvelous," Erica repeated as she turned slowly, taking in all the details. She looked up. "I love the little skylight."

"Your aunt may have wanted privacy for other reasons too," Dr. Stone said quietly.

Anne caught his meaning—that maybe Aunt Edie had used it while she was a covert operator. Anne had explored this room before, but maybe she hadn't discovered all its secrets.

"I would love one of these rooms," Erica said.

"Are you saying that you don't enjoy sharing a home office with me?" Dr. Stone teased.

"I was thinking more of when our sons and grandchildren visit. It would be a quiet place to escape for a few minutes." Erica patted her husband's arm and winked at Anne. "Now, I can tell my husband is anxious to see your aunt's fallout shelter."

"We can go down the back stairs." Anne led the way out of the house and to the shelter entrance. As they entered she kicked some small stones off the metal steps. "Be careful."

"You had no idea that this was down here?" Erica asked as they descended into darkness. Anne turned on the light and Erica gasped. "This is extraordinary!"

Dr. Stone studied the walls and the ceiling like Alex had. "I've been in quite a few of these, and for a home shelter this one is well constructed."

Anne walked over to the trunk. "This is where I found the codebook. I'm assuming it's been here since around 1963. Nothing in here seems to be younger than that. I'm guessing that's when she quit doing whatever she was doing."

Dr. Stone nodded. "That's a good assumption. She may have just wanted out then. It was dangerous work."

"I was hoping an old passport might also shed some clues," Anne said.

"The government might've given her another passport to travel with. It could have possibly been under another name," Dr. Stone suggested. "Like I mentioned before, I'm afraid unless the CIA or whomever she worked for decides to share this information, you may never know why she did it or why she quit."

"Your aunt didn't have any children of her own?" Erica asked as she examined the shelves of food. "Maybe family pressures caused her to quit."

"She never married and didn't have any children, but she took care of her parents when they grew frail, and then I spent a lot of time with her after school while my folks were working," Anne said. "But that was back in the eighties."

Erica looked at Anne. "This is a slice of history. Have you thought of sharing this with the public?"

Anne nodded. "I've been thinking about what would be the best way to go about it, either let people come down here or donate items to the historical society."

"Definitely keep it like this for a while and let others experience it," Erica said and then smiled. "I know I'm giving unsolicited advice, but opening it to the public is what I would do."

As Dr. Stone and his wife explored the room, Anne looked around at the walls, thinking about the hidden closet in Mr. Bartholomew's storm shelter. Was there such a place in here? The walls appeared to be solid concrete, and the steel beams didn't offer enough space between them to have a door. If there were more secrets down here she may never find them.

Chapter Twenty

After Dr. and Mrs. Stone departed, Anne returned to the checkout desk and let Remi head home. Dr. Stone had given Anne a copy of his book, *Decoding the Wars,* and she set it by the computer so she would remember to process it into the library system. Then she planned on checking it out for herself and taking it upstairs to read.

The Stones were a warm and likeable couple. Anne especially hoped to see Erica again. In addition to helping Alex track down the company that might have the original parts for her elevator, she'd offered to get Anne information on what would be the best way to preserve the items in the shelter.

Anne looked at the phone directory on the computer screen and remembered she'd been trying to track down Tobias McKinsey before the Stones walked in. She wasn't having much luck finding him. Maybe Michael would.

She called the station and the desk sergeant patched her through.

"Officer Banks, here."

"Michael, this is Anne. I think I may have found the person who left the money. Tobias McKinsey." She explained how she had spotted the man with the book in the article photo and tracked down his name.

Michael was silent for a few moments. "You know, I think you'd make a great addition on our squad, Detective Anne Gibson."

"Quit teasing." Anne laughed but felt a bit uncomfortable. She really didn't like getting involved in situations like this. She liked her world to stay peaceful and predictable. No wonder she chose to be a librarian as a profession.

"Yes, there is a record on Tobias McKinsey. Hold on, let me see. He was caught driving without a license. Got fined. And another incident of theft."

"What did he steal? Was it money?" Anne asked.

"Nope. The report says he tried to shoplift some canned goods from the grocery store. The owner didn't want to press charges after finding out he was trying to help a homeless family. The judge gave him some community work, which he didn't complete. That was a mistake."

More typing filled the background. "Nothing since 1998. Last known address is 896 County Line Road. I think that used to be a boardinghouse. I'm checking now."

Anne looked back at her screen. "There is a reverse directory on the computer that I was looking at." She typed the address into the appropriate box.

They both said "Nellie Brown" at the same time.

Michael chuckled. "Fast draw on the keys, I see."

"I know her, if it's the same Nellie Brown." Anne switched screens to the information stored on library patrons and typed in Nellie's name. Her address for her library card was listed as 896 County Line Road.

"It's her," Anne confirmed. "She and her sister, Betty Warring, come into the library every week. I didn't realize they had a boardinghouse. They've never mentioned it." Excitement shot through her. Nellie and possibly her sister may have known Tobias McKinsey, and where he was now.

"I'll give her a call," Anne said.

"All right. If you don't have any luck, let me know."

Anne said good-bye to Michael and checked the screen for Nellie's phone number. She called it, and when an elderly female voice answered, she said, "Hello. Is this Nellie?"

"Nope, this is Betty. Who is this?"

"Anne Gibson from the library. Good afternoon. I was wondering—"

"Oh dear, I told Nellie that book on Winston Churchill was overdue. She never listens to me."

"I'm not calling about library business," Anne said. "I have—"

"Nellie, that nice library lady is calling about your book being overdue," Betty called.

Anne could hear Nellie's voice in the background. "What are you talking about, Betty? We took that book back last week. Let me talk to her." There was the sound of the phone being handed off.

"Anne?" Nellie said.

"Hi, Nellie, sorry for the confusion, but I'm not calling about any overdue books."

"Well, I was trying to tell Betty we didn't have any."

The phone line crackled. "When did you say that?" Betty asked, sounding like she had picked up on another extension.

"Shush, Betty, I'm on the phone," Nellie said.

"So am I."

Anne took a deep breath and tried not to giggle. "Nellie—"

"Now, Anne, what were you trying to ask us?" Nellie asked.

"I was wondering if you remember anything about a man named Tobias McKinsey."

"Tobias McKinsey?" Betty said. "*Hmm*, I don't recall a Tobias."

"She means Toby," Nellie said, sounding excited.

"Who?" Betty said.

"That young man who stayed with us for a while? You know, the one that loved your blueberry pancakes."

"Oh, Toby, yes, yes, such a nice young man. Trying so hard to fit in," Betty said.

"He went by Toby?" Anne asked, wondering if that would make a difference in her online search. "Would you know how I could reach him?"

"No, he just up and left one day," Betty said.

Nellie sighed. "He'd paid through to the end of the month too. I packed some of his personal items away and put them in a closet somewhere. I always thought he'd be back someday. If you locate him, maybe you could return them to him."

"Do you think I could take a look? Maybe something in there would help me find him."

"I think that's a grand idea. We weren't planning on coming into the library until next week, but I suppose we can make an exception," Nellie said.

"Oh, I don't want you to make a special trip. I can meet you somewhere." Anne knew that Betty didn't get around very well, having to use a cane. The two sisters always traveled together. They had once told her they generally got out twice a week, every Sunday for church and another day for going to the grocery store, attending their senior club meeting, and stopping by the library.

"Why don't you come over here, dear?" Nellie suggested. "Tomorrow afternoon. We're having a little get-together. Just cookies, punch, and coffee. You could come a little early and I could get you his box of things."

Anne checked the schedule. On Saturdays, they only opened the library a partial day, and she hadn't scheduled anyone else to come in. "Well, I have my children with me all day—"

"Perfect," Nellie said. "Betty does her baking on Saturday morning and will have fresh cookies for them to sample if you approve. I bet they like cookies."

"And, just to let you know, the ladies coming over knew Toby too. We were all friends back then," Betty added. "They might have something helpful for you."

"Should we expect you around three, dear?" Nellie asked before Anne could get a word into the conversation.

"Three it is," Anne managed to say before they hung up.

* * *

"Is this the house with the cookies?" Liddie asked as Anne's car rolled to a stop in front of an aged, three-story brick home just outside the downtown area of Blue Hill.

Anne double-checked the address on the mailbox. "Yes, I think this is where Miss Warring and Mrs. Brown live. Let's remember to use our big-girl manners."

"Okay, Mommy."

Anne unbuckled her from the car seat, and Liddie smoothed the pretty green dress she'd chosen for the occasion. Anne grabbed her file with the photos of Tobias McKinsey and stared at the house for a moment, trying to relax. It had been a busy day. The library had closed at one, but Wendy had popped in at the last minute and they discussed plans for the next week's literacy classes. She reported that Luke had come over to her house for tutoring sessions the last two evenings, and he was flying through his lessons. Luke and Wendy's husband had struck up a friendship, and Beth loved playing with her children, so the situation was working out well.

Anne took Liddie's hand and started up the cracked sidewalk. Two spreading oak trees towered over the spacious front lawn on each side of them. A wide covered porch graced the front of the building. Wicker chairs sporting flowery cushions and a small round table were located on one side of the door. A tall potted palm graced the other.

Anne rang the bell and the door was promptly opened by Nellie. She was all smiles. "Well hello, pretty girl." She leaned over so she was face-to-face with Liddie. "I'm so glad you could come. Where is your handsome brother?"

"He's playing ball at the park," Liddie said.

"Yes, I'm afraid Ben scheduled a ball game with some friends and isn't able to make it," Anne said. "He wasn't happy that he was going to miss the cookies though."

"Well, that's fine too. It will be just us girls, right Liddie? We can send cookies home for Ben."

Liddie smiled and nodded.

Nellie stepped back. "I'm so glad you could come over. We so rarely get to visit with people outside our small circle of friends. Come and sit in the parlor. We have half an hour before Georgia and Phyllis get here."

"Thank you for inviting us," Anne said as she and Liddie followed Nellie to a sunny room that contained modern furniture pieces and a few dark antiques. A modern art painting with bursts of blues, reds, and yellows hung over the fireplace. Anne had always thought of Betty and Nellie as having old-fashioned tastes. Obviously, first impressions weren't always correct.

"I don't want to make you and Liddie wait for the rest to come to have some refreshments. Liddie, would you prefer milk, cocoa, or lemonade with your cookies?"

Liddie's expression turned serious as she considered the options. "Milk, please."

"Good choice." She turned to Anne. "I have coffee or tea also."

"Lemonade sounds wonderful," Anne said. With the sunlight streaming in the window, the room was warm.

"I'll be right back."

Anne sat on the wide beige couch and Liddie scooted up beside her. Her daughter looked around the large room, her gaze landing on a large porcelain dog in one corner. "Is that a toy?"

"No, sweetie, it's a decoration."

Nellie returned with the milk and lemonade.

"You have a lovely home. I didn't know you ran a boardinghouse," Anne said.

"Oh my, yes. We did for a while." Nellie sat on the love seat across from Anne and Liddie. "We enjoyed it too. After my husband passed away, God rest his soul, Betty decided to move in with me almost twenty-two years ago come September."

"Twenty-three years," Betty corrected as she slowly made her way into the room, her cane in one hand and a plate of cookies in the other.

"Are you certain?" Nellie frowned. "I distinctly remember Scruffy was one year old when you came to live with me, and she passed away seventeen years later. That was five years ago."

Betty set the platter of cookies on the square glass coffee table and smiled at Anne. "Notice that Nellie has to reference the cat when it comes to figuring out how long her own sister has lived here. Shows where I fall in the pecking order."

Nellie winked at Anne. "Scruffy was here first."

"Anyway, with just the two of us, this old place got kind of lonely, so we starting renting out rooms."

Betty backed up slowly and sat on the love seat next to Nellie. "We were very careful as to who we let stay here, of course. Two women living alone, you know how it is."

"We met some really nice people," Nellie added. "Mostly young people starting out in life and unable to afford an apartment or house yet. We had a schoolteacher and a nurse live with us for a while."

"There was that waitress too. Cecilia something," Betty added. "She was a sweetheart."

"Tobias was one of only two gentlemen we rented to." Nellie glanced at Betty. "The first man was Mr. Richard Daniels. Betty was a touch sweet on him."

"I was not," Betty said although her cheeks flushed pink. "Besides, he was too young for me. He was only in his sixties."

Liddie looked up at Anne with a puzzled expression, and Anne gave a reassuring smile that she'd explain later.

"His room always smelled of sardines." Nellie wrinkled her nose at Liddie. "Fishy."

Liddie giggled.

"He had a small aquarium," Betty explained. "Lots of guppies. He went to live with his sister in Pittsburgh after a bit."

"So Tobias, I mean Toby, came to live with you in 1998?" Anne asked steering the conversation back to the man she wanted to learn about.

Nellie tapped her lips with her index finger. "That sounds about right. He came around Christmas, so that would be 1997. That's why Betty and I took him in. We felt sorry for the young man being out in the snow with no place to go."

"Where was he from?" Anne asked.

"Michigan, I think," Betty said. "Ann Arbor."

Nellie shook head. "I thought he was from out West. Kansas City."

Betty shrugged. "He traveled a lot, from what I remember him saying."

"I see," Anne said, a little disappointed. She'd been hoping that maybe Tobias had headed back to his hometown, but apparently Betty and Nellie weren't sure where he was from.

"Did he ever mention his family?"

"All gone except a sister, I think. He wasn't much for talking about his personal life," Nellie said. "He was a hard worker though."

"He had a green thumb, that one," Betty added. "When spring rolled around, he worked with our roses and they bloomed so pretty. I don't think they've been as beautiful since."

"Mr. Bartholomew said he worked for him, too, in his rose garden." Anne took a sip of lemonade and reached for an oatmeal cookie.

"Yes, he was getting some work about town," Nellie said. "People liked him because he didn't complain and got the job done."

"I think he did some work for my aunt Edie too," Anne said.

"Most likely, since she was involved in the renovation of Rosehill Park's flower garden around that time," Betty said.

"Did you ever hear about him getting in any trouble?" Anne asked, thinking about the police record.

"He did, but it wasn't his fault," Nellie said firmly.

Betty sighed. "I was in favor of kicking him out, but he promised to never do it again."

"Do what?" Anne asked.

"A friend of his had stolen some food from the store, and Toby tried to put it back before anyone noticed." Betty frowned. "At least that was his story."

"That's what he told us, and I believed him," Nellie said a little hotly.

Betty glanced at her sister. "He could be a little odd. He'd be up all hours of the night. I could hear him pacing about the room talking to himself, especially toward the end of his stay with us."

"Then one morning, we got up and he was gone," Nellie said with a shake of her head. "All his things were gone too except for a drawer he must have overlooked."

"Did he leave a note?" Anne asked.

Betty shook her head. "He wasn't one for writing. I don't think he had much education."

Nellie stood. "I just hope he's happy wherever he ended up. I'll get that box I told you about on the phone."

After her sister had left the room, Betty leaned forward and lowered her voice. "Nellie treated Toby like he was her son. Her own boy died while serving in the military. I think it hurt Nellie more than it should have when Toby left without saying good-bye. After all, he was a stranger to us. But I always said that he must've had a good reason. If you do get in touch with him, please let us know how he is. For Nellie's sake."

"I will," Anne promised as Nellie came back into the room, carrying a small cardboard box.

"Here you go. It's not much, but maybe you'll find something useful in there to help you find him."

Liddie scooted closer so she could watch Anne open the box. Inside, nestled in tissue paper was a cheap watch, a pair of worn leather work gloves, a wool scarf, a sewing kit, and a Bible. Anne lifted the Bible and opened the front cover.

To Dearest Tobias,

May the words of this Book guide you through your life.

Aunt Tania

"He said his Aunt Tania passed away several years before he came to live in Blue Hill." Nellie seemed to have a slight catch in her throat. "He treasured that Bible. That's why I always believed he'd at least come back for it."

It's been a lot of years, Anne thought. *If Toby hasn't come back by now, what are the chances he ever will?* The pages of the Bible still seemed crisp and the binding tight, almost like he hadn't had a chance to read it.

"If I do find him, I'll make sure he gets this back," Anne said as the door chime echoed from the hallway.

"That would be Phyllis and Georgia," Nellie said gaily and went to answer the door.

"What's that, Mommy?" Liddie pointed to the Bible. A note was tucked in the back, but Anne didn't have a chance to read it as Nellie returned with two women, one of whom Anne recognized from the newspaper photos.

"Anne, have you met Phyllis Oster and Georgia Winters? These are two of our oldest friends," Nellie said.

"Speak for yourself." Phyllis smiled at her friend. "I'm not as old as she is."

"You know what I mean," Nellie teased back.

"Don't mind them," Georgia told Anne. "They are always picking on each other. It's nice to meet you."

Anne smiled. "Likewise."

Phyllis turned her attention to Anne. "I used to see you with your aunt around town, although you were more the size of this pretty young lady," Phyllis said with a smile for Liddie. "Edie and I were on the park committee together for a number of years."

"It's nice to meet you again," Anne said warmly. "This is my daughter, Liddie."

"Good afternoon, Liddie," Phyllis said.

Liddie put her cookie back on her plate. "Good afternoon."

"Such a nice sweet child!" Georgia exclaimed. "Are those cookies good?"

Liddie nodded. "Would you like some?"

"Oh my, yes." Georgia reached for a small plate on the coffee table and selected cookies from the platter.

"Anne has been asking about Toby McKinsey. Do you remember him?" Nellie asked, passing the article to Phyllis. "You're in this photo too."

"Oh, I really needed to rethink my hairstyle in those days." Phyllis handed the photo to Georgia. "My memory may be going, but I remember the stir he caused around here. Ungrateful young man."

"Now, now, Phyllis, we don't know what happened or why he left."

Georgia studied the photo. "I think I saw him someplace not long ago. Of course he is much older now, but it's that scar by his eye—you don't see that every day."

Anne leaned forward. "Do you remember where you saw him?"

Georgia gave her head a little shake. "I wish I did. It wasn't in person, and if I had to guess, I think it was in a newspaper or magazine. Only I don't remember his name as McKinsey. It didn't start with an M."

Nellie raised her eyebrows. "Toby was in a magazine?"

"I think it was an ad for some sort of service like cable TV or maybe landscaping." She passed the photo back to Anne.

"Poor Toby. I hope you did see him, Georgia, and he's successful wherever he is," Nellie said.

Betty patted Nellie on the arm and looked over at Anne. "So how is the literacy class going?"

Anne slid the photo of Toby back in her file. "It's going well. Of course, we're just beginning. We had six students this week and expect to grow over time." At least Anne hoped so.

The ladies exchanged glances, and then Betty said, "We were talking after church last week about doing a fund-raising event for literacy. It's been a while since we've done anything like that. It would be good publicity for the class too."

"I think that would be wonderful," Anne said, touched by their interest. She passed the cookie plate to Liddie as the ladies launched into a discussion of their ideas from selling tickets, to an afternoon tea, to an art show by local artisans, to going in with the local scout club and selling coupon books to the local businesses.

The next half hour flew by, but Liddie was starting to yawn. Anne realized Ben's game would be over soon and that she needed to get going. She thanked the women for their wonderful ideas and stood.

"We'll narrow our list down and get back with you next Monday," Betty said.

Anne picked up Toby's box, and Nellie walked Anne to the door.

"Thank you for the cookies and milk," Liddie said.

"You're most welcome." Nellie handed Liddie some cookies wrapped in a large napkin. "Those are for you and your brother later."

"Thanks again for inviting us and for the information on Toby," Anne said. "I'm overwhelmed by the enthusiasm to help the literacy cause."

Nellie smiled. "I hope we weren't too pushy. Well, I have to confess that I nudged them. You know how Betty and I love to read. We may argue which books to check out of the library, but those evenings we read to each other mean the world to me. And your trying to find Toby right now while you are holding classes is such a coincidence."

"Coincidence?"

"Yes, Toby didn't know how to read."

CHAPTER TWENTY-ONE

A nne opened the microwave door and took out the popcorn bag. Careful to avoid the steam, she pulled the ends open, dumped the contents into a bowl, and carried it to the living room, where Ryan, Ben, and Liddie were engrossed in watching a movie. Alex had stayed with the boys all afternoon for their ball game, and when he dropped Ben off, Anne had offered to make them dinner. Alex had some work-related errands to take care of, but Ryan stayed. It had been two hours since dinner and Alex still hadn't returned, so Anne fixed the kids a snack.

"Popcorn," Anne announced.

"Yummy," Liddie said, sitting up.

"Thanks, Mom," Ben said, reaching up for the bowl from his position on the floor, his gaze never straying from the TV screen.

Anne paused to watch the funny car chase for a few minutes and then returned to the kitchen. She sank into a chair. Her legs ached from running up and down the stairs carrying loads of laundry to the basement and back. Ben and Liddie had helped, but they were obviously in much better shape than Anne. At least she'd gotten most of their towels and clothes washed and dried, including Liddie's Hello Kitty shirt.

The box with Tobias's things was sitting on one of the chairs. She opened the box and picked up his small Bible.

Nellie had said that Toby couldn't read, which would explain the stiffer leather and pristine pages. How sad. Bibles were meant to be lovingly worn and soft from lots of use. Had his aunt known he couldn't read? Or was he like Luke, who tried to hide it from his loved ones and the world?

Anne pulled out the folded slip of yellow paper that Liddie had pointed out back at Betty and Nellie's home. Inside were lists of simple words with the same vowel sound. It was the same type of thing they were teaching in the literacy class—phonics! So he had been trying to learn to read. She wondered if Nellie knew that. Was she teaching him? But then, why hadn't she said so? She examined the lettering. Was that Aunt Edie's handwriting? Since the letters were printed, it was hard to say.

She opened her file on Tobias McKinsey and studied his face. So he hadn't been able to read, yet he was carrying around a children's book, which may be evidence he was learning. But where had he gotten the help? Her aunt Edie was a big advocate of literacy training. Did she have something to do with that book? Anne would probably never know unless she located Toby McKinsey.

Georgia had mentioned she'd seen him on an ad somewhere. The scar made his face unique, so it would be too coincidental that someone who looked like Toby would have a similar scar. He had been a handyman and gardener at one time, so maybe he was advertising those services. He was most likely not in Blue Hill or one of the ladies would have seen him around town. So in what kind of publication had Georgia seen the ad? Since he'd been a gardener, maybe he advertised in a gardening or landscaping or home improvement magazine. That opened all kinds of possibilities.

There had to be an easier way to narrow the field down. There were places on the Internet where people recommended services and reviewed the workers, but she didn't subscribe to them. But she still could search online. Maybe he had a Web site.

Anne got her laptop and set it on the table and did a search on handymen and gardeners throughout Pennsylvania. Either Tobias didn't work in those occupations now or he was out of state.

The doorbell buzzed and Anne crossed to the door. She pushed the button on the intercom. "Hello?"

"It's Alex."

"Come on up." She pushed the button to release the lock and went to the table.

Several seconds later Alex strode into the room. "Good evening." He glanced at the computer. "Are you working?"

"I was just doing some personal research." She blew out a deep breath and explained about Tobias McKinsey and how Georgia thought she'd seen his face somewhere. "If you were a gardener or handyman, where would you advertise?"

"The newspaper probably," Alex said. "Or maybe the *Nickel Ads*."

"I didn't think of that," Anne said. The *Nickel Ads* was a publication that cheaply produced booklets containing ads for selling things, posting jobs, and the like. It was free to the public.

"I think I have one in my truck. I'll go get it." Alex headed for the door. "Be right back."

"Thanks, Alex," Anne called after him and then checked on the children. The movie was still going, but they'd finished the popcorn. She grabbed the bowl and set it on the kitchen counter.

She had just put another popcorn bag in the microwave when the door buzzed again. She pushed the button again to let Alex in.

He entered the kitchen carrying the beige newsprint catalog. "Sorry it took me so long. It had fallen behind the seats."

"I'm just thrilled you have one," Anne said. She grabbed her file and took out the photo of Toby.

"We're looking for someone resembling him." She handed the photo to Alex after he sat at the table.

"So that's Tobias."

"Some called him Toby. Georgia said it was the scar by his eye that caught her attention."

She looked over his shoulder as he flicked the front page open. Small ads were listed down the center of the pages with more spacious ads on the side. If Georgia had seen Toby's face in the *Nickel Ads* or a similar publication, it would be in those bigger ads. Some of the ads contained photographs, such as those advertising real estate agents and lawyers. There was even a landscaping ad with a photo of the crew. She examined that one closely but didn't see anyone resembling Toby. There were still at least twenty more pages to examine.

The microwave beeped, and Anne transferred the popcorn to the bowl and took it back to the kids. She started another bag to share with Alex before returning to the table.

Alex turned the page and they studied more ads as they munched on popcorn. They reached the end without any luck, but Anne was encouraged. Maybe Tobias had placed an ad in there but on a different week. She could call the paper on Monday and see if they could help her. He might be in another kind of business by now.

"Thanks for helping, Alex," Anne said.

"Wish we could've found him. It would be nice to know why he'd be carrying around that much money."

The movie must have ended because there were squeals coming from the living room and several thuds.

"You're not roughhousing in there, are you?" Alex called. The thudding ceased. Alex grinned at Anne as he slid back his chair and stood. "We better head home or Ryan isn't going to want to get out of bed for church."

Anne helped him extract Ryan from Liddie and Ben amidst protests that it was still too early, but they were eventually appeased when they were reminded they'd see each other in the morning and Alex suggested a trip to the park in the afternoon.

By the time Anne got into bed later, she was ready for a good night's sleep. It had been such a busy week, and she was so close to finding Tobias McKinsey. She just wished she knew of his current location. If he had dropped off the money, then he couldn't be very far away, could he?

Please, Lord, help me find out the truth.

She closed her eyes, but her mind still spun. Her thoughts turned to Aunt Edie. She hoped Dr. Stone would be able to find out information on what she'd been doing with a book of codes. She still would love to find Aunt Edie's old passport or some other documents to see where her aunt had traveled. Had she ever gone behind the Iron Curtain?

Dr. Stone had mentioned that the government might have had her travel under a different name, which would make sense if she were trying to hide in plain sight. *Hmm . . .* hide in plain sight? Could Tobias McKinsey have changed his name?

Anne sat up wide awake now. She wasn't going to be able to sleep unless she could check the theory out. She padded downstairs to where she'd left her laptop and took it back to bed.

Her fingers paused over the keys. Okay, if she were Tobias and wanted to change her name, what would she pick? The possibilities were endless. She groaned. What had she been thinking?

Suppose Tobias had only changed *part* of his name? She'd already searched for businesses related to maintenance and gardening. He could be working for someone else, of course, but then why would his face be on an ad? Also, Georgia said his name hadn't started with an *M* but had sounded similar to McKinsey.

Anne played around with the letters and tried names that would rhyme with McKinsey, putting them in the search box and scrolling through the lists of links.

Maybe she was trying too hard. She tried "Mac Kinsey" and scrolled through the list, clicking on the businesses and came to a Kinsey Printing located in Brickton, Pennsylvania.

The Web site listed the owner of the printing business as T. B. Kinsey. Anne clicked the link on how to contact the business, and there on the page with photos of the owner and employees was an older version of Tobias McKinsey. Silver streaked his hair and his face had weathered and matured. And there it was. The scar on the side of his face. It slid into the laugh lines around his eye, but it was definitely there. She had found him!

Thank You, Lord.

Kinsey Printing was located about seventy miles away from Blue Hill. She made a note of the phone number and turned off the computer and the lamp. She lay back against the pillow with a deep sigh. She'd be able to sleep now.

CHAPTER TWENTY-TWO

A crash of thunder broke the stillness of the Monday morning. Rain was forecasted for the entire day. The spring storms had roared back across the regions, but Anne was in too good of a mood to let the ugly weather get her down. She softly hummed "Showers of Blessings" as she returned library books to their proper shelves.

Sunday had truly been a blessing. Pastor Tom had outdone himself with his sermon on the Beatitudes, and in the afternoon Alex and Ryan had joined Anne and her kids for a long walk in Rosehill Park. They visited the rose garden, where a plaque was dedicated to Aunt Edie for all her service.

While their children ran about and climbed on the large wooden ship playhouse in the playground, Anne and Alex wandered by the pond and fed the ducks.

She told him about finding Kinsey Printing and Tobias McKinsey's photo. He congratulated her on her ingenuity.

Anne laughed but reminded him that she was only hunting the Internet for Tobias because it was the right thing to do. She had to make sure she knew what and who the money was for. She'd be glad when this was over and she could leave the detective work to others, which reminded her that she should update Michael. She'd almost called him on his cell but then decided she should probably first confirm that it had been Toby who had written the note. She called the Kinsey business number, but the recording informed her that the printing shop was closed for the day. She'd left a message on their answering machine. Wendy and her husband and their seven children arrived so Anne had put Tobias McKinsey out of her mind and enjoyed the rest of the day with her children and good friends.

Anne shelved the last book in the Children's Room and returned to the checkout desk. Wendy had plunked down a basket full of small spongy balls. Anne raised her eyebrows. "I'm almost afraid to ask what those are for."

"Oh, I thought they'd be fun to use during the baseball story I picked for Story Time today. Don't worry, they're harmless." She tossed a ball at Anne and it bounced off her forehead. "Oops! Sorry." Wendy giggled. "But you can see the balls won't cause any damage."

Anne grinned and picked up the ball. She was so tempted to wing it playfully at Wendy, but she heard the front door open. She maturely set the ball back in the basket.

"I'll go set up." Wendy suppressed another giggle and headed for the stairs.

"Nellie, did you forget the biography on Barbara Walters?" Betty said as she moved steadily forward with a hard thump of her cane.

Nellie followed her sister with their quilted book bag. "I told you I returned that book last week. Don't you remember? It was a thick heavy book, and you didn't want to carry it around."

"Since when can't I carry a book?" Betty asked. "I'm not an invalid, you know."

"I didn't say you couldn't carry it. You didn't *want* to."

"I think you imagine these things." Betty lifted her head, and a smile broke out on her sweet wrinkled face. "Good morning, Anne. We have good news."

"That's exciting," Anne said, nearly bursting to tell Nellie that she'd found Tobias McKinsey, but something held her tongue. Maybe she should wait until she talked to Toby. No sense in getting Nellie's hopes up. Toby might not want anything to do with the people of Blue Hill. After all, he had only been seventy miles away all these years and never contacted them. There were still many unanswered questions.

Nellie set the bag on the counter and removed two books to return. "Georgia and Phyllis agreed with Betty and I that we should have a costume party right here in the library. We will sell tickets and the proceeds will go to the literacy program."

"We can have a different activity in each of the rooms, depending on the section." Betty said. "For example, in the mystery aisles they'd have to solve a mystery. We can have a history scavenger hunt in the historical and biography section. There are lots of possibilities. We'll plan it all, with your approval of course, and we'll do our best not to intrude on your busy schedule."

"I think the costume party is a great idea," Anne said sincerely, relieved that the ladies would run the event. "When were you planning on doing it?"

"We were thinking in three or four weeks. It will give us time to advertise and spread the word."

"That would work. The elevator should be fixed by then," Anne said and was struck by the thought that maybe that would be a good time to open the fallout shelter for people to see.

"We'll keep you updated." Nellie nudged her sister. "Come on Betty, let's go pick another biography. I saw one on Michael Caine I want to read."

"I'm more in the mood for something historical."

"You always want to read about dead people," Nellie said to Betty and winked at Anne. "Why do they become so much more interesting to you after they're gone?"

Betty made a sputtering sound as she followed her sister to the Nonfiction Room. "Maybe it's because their stories are complete."

Anne spent the rest of the morning catching up on paperwork and changing the book display by the counter. It wasn't quite time yet to put out the summer beach reads, so she hunted for books that had to do with the transition from schooltime to summer, such as graduation parties, proms, gardening, and travel planning.

Betty and Nellie finally compromised by selecting a new book on Margaret Thatcher. Nellie considered it a more modern biography, since the former Prime Minister had only recently passed away, and Betty liked it because her life span included many historical events.

The lunch hour approached, and Anne was about to call Kinsey Printing again when the phone rang.

"Blue Hill Library. Anne Gibson speaking."

"Hello, Anne. This is Jayne Myers at Kinsey Printing. I had a message that you called. How may I help you?"

"I'd like to speak with Mr. Kinsey, please. It's a personal matter."

There was a long pause on the phone. "I'm afraid that isn't possible. Mr. Kinsey passed away earlier this month."

"Oh, I'm sorry," Anne said, stunned.

"Thank you, we were all devastated but not surprised. He had been ill for a while. But I can leave a message for his niece, Charity Palmer. She is running the business now. But she just left for lunch. May I ask what this is concerning?"

"Yes, it concerns a package that I think belonged to her uncle."

"Okay. I'll have her ring you."

Anne thanked her and hung up the phone. Her good spirits from the morning took a nosedive. How sad. She felt like she'd lost someone she knew, which was ridiculous since she hadn't even met Toby. He was a stranger, but all that time staring at his photo and trying to find him had given her a connection with him.

And he wasn't a stranger to Nellie. Anne dreaded telling her about Toby's passing. This also meant she may never know the truth about the money unless someone else came forward.

Toby couldn't have dropped off that package himself unless it had gotten lost or hidden somewhere on the property and Hershey later found it. But did that really make sense?

She rubbed her forehead, feeling a headache coming on. She hoped Charity Palmer would call back soon.

Wendy's Story Time was a resounding success as usual. Sponge balls littered the room when Anne peeked in the door, and the little ones were having a blast.

The time came for Anne to pick up the kids from school, but she still hadn't received a call from Charity Palmer. Anne took *The Lonely Dog* to the school and returned the book to Mrs. Rich and thanked her. Mrs. Rich said the book was one she'd learned to read as a child.

Anne loaded up the kids and they were driving up Bluebell Lane when Ben leaned forward from the backseat. "Mom, who is that?" He pointed to a black Porsche parked by the library.

"I think I might know who it is." Anne parked in the doorway. It must be the Porsche that Shaun and Lilly saw driving away from the library when they'd been testing Pastor Tom's car.

A young woman got out of the Porsche and ducked under her black umbrella. She was dressed in a white stylish suit. A matching scarf partially covered her blonde hair. She wore high heels and walked with a youthful bouncy step.

"Are you Anne Gibson?" she called.

"Yes, I am," Anne answered as she helped Liddie out of her car seat.

"I'm Charity Palmer." She held out her hand, and Anne noted her pink manicured nails. "I'm sorry about all the confusion. I was doing as my uncle asked. It's quite a story."

Anne shook her hand. "I'm really interested in hearing it. Would you like to come upstairs so we can talk out of the rain?"

"I'd like that." Charity looked at Liddie and Ben and smiled. "These are your children?"

Anne introduced them as they took the back stairs. The kids scampered off to their rooms, and Anne settled Charity in the living room and offered her a drink.

"Oh, I'm fine, thank you." She sat on the sofa, and Anne took the chair.

"First of all, I didn't know that Edie Summers had passed away until my secretary told me you called. I was puzzled why you were calling about the package, so I had her do a little research. When I found out that Edie had also passed away, I decided to drive up here rather than try to explain over the phone."

"I'm glad you did. I had quite a time tracking down your uncle. I didn't even know his name."

"That note was obscure, but he said that Edie would know exactly what he was talking about. He had his reasons for being secretive." Charity's gaze searched Anne's face. "So you didn't know about him and Edie?"

"I'm afraid not."

"Well, I never met your aunt, but she saved my life." Charity smiled. "I only recently found out the story when my uncle got sick. About a month ago my uncle called me into his hospital room. He must've sensed he wasn't going to live much longer." Her voice caught and tears filled her eyes.

A lump rose in Anne's throat. She understood how hard it was to lose someone close. "Can I get you a tissue?"

"It's okay. I have some." Charity dug in her purse and pulled one out. She dabbed her eyes. "But I'll take that glass of water you offered."

Anne went into the kitchen and got two glasses of ice water. By the time she got back to the living room, Charity appeared composed. She took a sip of water and continued her story.

"My uncle told me about a wonderful lady who lived in Blue Hill and had shown great kindness to him, giving him jobs and teaching him to read. She was one of the reasons he'd later been successful with his printing business. However, he was very ashamed of something he'd done and had wanted to make it right for years." She took another sip of water and Anne waited quietly for her to continue.

"Edie Summers and several town members were putting on a fund-raiser. An auction for some project that he couldn't even remember. My uncle was working the grounds, and after it was over he went to pick up his sack lunch. Your aunt prepared one for him every day he worked for her and filled it with goodies that he would take to the boardinghouse. Anyway, he grabbed a sack in the kitchen and went back to his room where he got a message from his sister, my mother. I was about seven. My father had run out on us and my mother was in financial trouble already when they found out I needed an emergency heart valve operation. My grandmother was a widow and couldn't help much. If it hadn't been for Uncle Toby, she didn't know what she would've done."

Charity's lips lifted in a wistful smile. "They sacrificed a lot for me. I really miss them both."

"So your mother is also . . ." Anne's throat tightened and she couldn't finish the sentence.

She nodded. "A couple years ago she passed away, but she had a good life thanks to my uncle. Anyway, back to his story. He packed up his belongings and hurried to the bus station. After my uncle boarded a bus and was many miles away, he discovered the bag he thought was his lunch was actually full of money."

Anne's eyebrows rose. "It was full of money? So the money I found in the yard was stolen?"

"Oh no, it wasn't. Well, yes, I guess it was in a way it was, but the money wasn't intentionally taken. My uncle knew there had to be a mistake. They must've been putting money from the auction in a brown paper bag. He must've grabbed it by mistake, and besides, who would've believed him after being convicted of theft in Blue Hill before? And he said later that he rationalized that Edie would've given him the money if she knew about the emergency."

"So . . . he just happened to pick up a bag that was full of money?" Anne knew she sounded skeptical but couldn't help it.

Charity's lower lip trembled for a moment. "I know, I know, it sounds bizarre, but if you'd known him, you would realize that Uncle Toby was a good man. I would hate to think he was lying to me and that he intentionally robbed your aunt."

"Well, I'm having a hard time believing Aunt Edie would keep that much money around the house. But if there was a fund-raiser that day, then we might be able to find out if his story is plausible."

"Really? That would make me feel better."

Anne went to the kitchen and returned with her research file. She pulled out the article of the fund-raiser, which must have been the day that Tobias left home.

"There's your uncle." She pointed to Tobias under the tree. "Oh, he's cute," Charity said with a low laugh.

"These are newspaper articles and photos from that day your uncle left down." Anne skimmed the article. "It says that they raised ten thousand, fifteen dollars auctioning off local art. She turned her attention back to the table by the auctioneer. Was that a paper bag on the table? It appeared to be.

"So it's possible they were collecting the money and put it in a bag to take it inside the house," Anne said, willing to give Tobias the benefit of the doubt. "That supports his story on how he got it."

Charity looked relieved. "I know the ends don't justify the means, but he said he used the money to get me to the best doctors. It was touch and go for a while, but I recovered and, well, here I am. It's hard for me to condemn what he did."

"I can understand how you feel, and I'm sure Aunt Edie would've understood if he needed help and done whatever she could." Anne was pretty sure she understood what happened now. Aunt Edie had covered for Tobias, and Anne could guess where she'd gotten the money. "In fact, I think she replaced the money he stole."

"She did? What a kind thing to do." Charity sighed. "I wish he'd known that. He was afraid that if he stayed in Brickton he might be prosecuted if the Blue Hill police caught up with him. So he traveled out West and worked at a printing press with a kind, Christian couple that taught him everything about the business. He said that over the years he tried to rationalize that the money in the sack was an answer to prayer. God had helped him out in his time of trouble, but he still felt ashamed and wanted to make it right."

"He waited a long time," Anne pointed out. She was sympathetic to Tobias's plight but he should have tried to make it right sooner.

"I guess he planned to return to Blue Hill eventually, but the time passed quickly. When the statute of limitations ran out for the theft, he came back to Brickton to be with us, found some investors that believed in him, and opened a printing business of his own . . ."

"Why did he change his name to Kinsey?"

"I asked him once and he shrugged it off saying Kinsey was easier to remember than McKinsey. But later he told me that he was still ashamed of his actions even if the law couldn't touch him then. "

"But he did pay Aunt Edie back through you," Anne said, jumping ahead in the story.

Charity nodded. "He worked very hard and did very well in the business. He wanted to return the money with interest. Then his health took a hit and kept getting in the way of going back to Blue Hill and . . . then it was too late."

In more than ways than one, Anne thought. Aunt Edie would never know that he'd set things right.

"He made me promise to drop the money off. My uncle didn't want me to get involved any further. He assured me that Edie Summers would understand the note and about the money."

"Well, since Aunt Edie is no longer here, you are welcome to take back the money."

"Oh no. I couldn't. Uncle Tobias left me the printing business. I'll be fine. I'd feel much better if the money went to something that was special, like this library. It seems fitting after she taught him to read. I think my uncle Toby would've liked that."

"Aunt Edie's legacy to the town is the library." Anne explained how she'd come to live in Blue Hill again and the renovation of the old mansion. "Would you like to see it?"

Anne took her on a tour and Charity noticed the elevator was broken. "Are you having trouble getting it fixed?"

"I'm hoping to find the paperwork for it. My contractor thinks the elevator may have had a lifetime warranty. I just haven't found the paperwork. I admit I've been worried how to fund the repair." And they were running out of time with the inspection looming.

"Now you have some money to help with that," Charity said heading down the stairs. "I'm going to go down to the police station and sign it over to you."

"Ask for Officer Michael Banks," Anne said. "And the money needs to go to the library, not me."

"Okay." Charity took a quick look around the first floor and then paused by the counter and looked at Wendy's sign for the literacy classes.

"You have a literacy class going on. How cool! Uncle Toby would've liked that too. That would be a great legacy to use his money for. You will use some of the money for that, won't you?"

"I will," Anne said, knowing Aunt Edie would have wanted that too.

"I was wondering if I could get a copy of those photos you have of my uncle. I only have a couple of photos and they were taken when he was a child with my mother."

"Certainly. You can have mine if you want. You may even want to check with the newspaper and see if they kept negatives of their photos."

"I think I will. My family photo album is rather skimpy," Charity said. "I'm getting married in a couple months and hope to add more."

"Congratulations!"

"Thank you. My fiancé has a huge family, and I certainly won't be alone anymore."

"I have some of your uncle's things. They were at the boardinghouse. I'll get them." Anne left Charity with Wendy at the counter and went upstairs to retrieve the box from her kitchen. When she returned, Charity eagerly examined the contents.

"This is his Bible?" Charity opened the cover. "Oh, my great-aunt Tania gave it to him."

"Maybe you can use it in your wedding," Wendy suggested.

"That's a wonderful idea." Her eyes glistened again as she held out her hand and grasped Anne's. "It was nice meeting you, Anne, and if you're ever in Brickton, please stop by."

"Thank you and if you ever get back here, come visit," Anne said.

Charity stepped out on the porch and stood looking over the yard. "I'm trying to imagine what it looked like when Uncle Tobias was here. That big oak looks like the same tree in the photo."

"I think it is," Anne said with a smile. She handed Charity the box with Tobias's things.

"Oh, I almost forgot. I found an envelope in his desk," Charity said. "It had the name Nellie Brown on it. Do you know who that is?"

"Nellie Brown was the owner of the boardinghouse where he lived. She comes into the library quite frequently."

"Could you give this to her then?" Charity took an envelope out of her purse.

"I'd be happy to." Anne took the letter. Nellie was going to be pleased that Tobias hadn't forgotten her.

She watched Charity hurry down the sidewalk and get into her fancy car. Mixed feelings surged through her. She was so relieved that the owner of the money had been found and she could use it for the library without guilt. But she was also sad that Tobias McKinsey and her aunt Edie weren't there for the closure of that chapter in their lives.

She'd just shut the door when Charity came back in, breathing hard. "I have something else for you." Her eyes were bright with tears again as she handed Anne a book with a blue cover. "My uncle Toby said that Edie had given him this book while she was helping him learn to read. Did you know that story about the lonely dog was the first story he'd read all the way through by himself? The book was an inspiration to him to keep trying to succeed, and now I think it should be returned to where it came from." She gave Anne a little wave and headed back down the sidewalk.

Anne hugged the book to her heart and whispered, "Welcome home."

* * *

Anne stood on Nellie and Betty's porch and rang the bell again. She decided to talk to Nellie about Tobias before she picked up Liddie and Ben from school. She had dreaded coming, even though she had the letter from Tobias McKinsey. But she had sad news for Nellie and it didn't feel right telling her over the phone. She was about to head back to the car when the door opened.

"Anne," Nellie said softly. "Come on in. Betty is taking a nap."

"Oh, I should've called first. I'm sorry," Anne said, still trying to figure out how to tell Nellie about Tobias.

"Oh, it's fine. Betty likes to burn the late-night candle and hence needs the nap. I'd like some company. Let me get you some coffee. I just made myself some. Come on back with me."

Anne followed Nellie back to a large, high-ceilinged kitchen. Yellow wallpaper with bright red apples lined the walls, and the white modern appliances shone with cleanliness.

Nellie poured Anne some coffee. "Let's sit at the table." Nellie gestured to the white wooden chairs with cushions that matched the wallpaper. "So I assume you have news?"

Anne settled back on the chair. "I do, Nellie. I'm afraid it's sad news. I did find Toby's niece, but Toby passed away earlier this month."

"Oh." Nellie stared into her coffee cup.

"He lived a good life," Anne said. "He owned a printing business and helped raise his niece, who is a nice young woman. But he got sick."

Nellie looked up. "Well, I'm glad his life turned to the better after he left here."

"He wrote you a letter." Anne took the envelope from her purse.

Nellie's hand trembled a little as she took it. "This is from Toby? So he did learn to read and write. Good for him." Nellie opened the envelope and swallowed hard as she read.

Anne waited quietly.

Nellie read the letter out loud.

Dearest Nellie and Betty.

I am sorry for leaving all those years ago without saying good-bye. You both were very kind to me and got me through a rough time in my life. My time in Blue Hill is one of the most cherished memories I have. You are true Christian women, and I will never forget the lessons of love that you and others in the community taught me. I hope that you can forgive me for the wrongs I have done.

May God bless you,
Tobias McKinsey

A tear rolled down Nellie's cheek. "What wrong did he do that he needs forgiveness for? Was he just referring to the store incident?"

"Something happened that day he disappeared. Something that made him afraid to come back." Anne explained about Tobias's sister and how he'd ended up with the money from the fund-raiser.

"But nobody reported the money missing?"

"I think Aunt Edie sold her convertible to replace the money before anyone noticed," Anne said. Aunt Edie knew where to get cash quickly and that was from Marcus Bartholomew.

"Why would she do that?"

Anne gave a little shrug. "I'm sure she had her reasons. Aunt Edie did a lot of things people wouldn't expect." Like possibly traveling to Europe as a secret courier.

"She was a special lady." Nellie folded the letter and placed it in her lap. "And I'm glad Tobias's niece got his Bible. It should stay in the family. Do you think Charity would mind if I wrote her? I could share some things about her uncle, like what a great gardener he was."

"I think she would like that. She doesn't have any close family except for her fiancé's," Anne said as she stood. "I better get going. I have to pick up my children from school."

Nellie walked Anne to the door and kissed her on the cheek. "You are a lot like your aunt. A good person."

Anne drove to the school, relieved that task was over. She loaded up the kids and returned to the library. To her pleasant surprise, Luke Norris and Beth were standing by the checkout desk talking to Wendy. Anne was saying hello to Luke when a terrible hammering sound rose from the depths of the house.

"Alex is in the basement working on the elevator," Wendy explained. "He said something about the motor arriving."

"That's terrific. I'll be back." Anne hurried down the stairs.

Alex was prying off a panel on the wall. He looked up and smiled. "Hey, there. I think we can get this baby working by the end of the day."

"I'm so glad," Anne said.

"Unfortunately the cost is going to be over my estimate, but I have good news too. Your friend Erica Stone tracked the company that had provided the original elevator. Delta & Peters Elevators. It sold a couple of times and the name changed. I got ahold of the owner, and he said that most of the elevators purchased back then had a lifetime guarantee like I thought. Because the motors weren't grounded properly the way they are now, they will honor the replacement of motor and parts of the elevator."

"Do they have a copy of the warranty?" Anne asked.

"Probably. The owner said they would look in their old files, but there's a chance the paperwork could've been misplaced in the many moves. It would be much quicker if you can produce the paperwork."

"I haven't been able to find it yet," Anne said. "I thought for sure I'd seen something on the elevator when we first moved in and that I put it in a safe place."

Alex picked up an electric screwdriver. "I lose more things in 'safe places' than anywhere else."

"Well, I do have the money that Tobias McKinsey left to help pay for the repair, but I was hoping to use most of it for the literacy program," Anne said. She'd called Alex the night before and told him about Charity and where the money had come from. "I'll keep looking for that warranty."

Anne started for the stairs and then turned. "Before I forget to tell you, I decided to let Nellie and Betty and their friends put on the costume party in a couple weeks. In fact, I think I will open up Aunt Edie's bomb shelter for the evening too. Erica Stone was right. It would be a crime not to share it in its original state."

"I think it's a good idea. I'll make sure the retaining wall is finished by the stairs. In fact, I'll get right on it after I finish here."

Anne thanked him and went back up to the library to work at the desk for a while, all the time trying to think of where she could have put that elevator paperwork. But she couldn't concentrate. After having to erase mistakes on the order form for office supplies three times, she gave up.

Wendy was giving Luke a tutoring lesson at one of the tables, and Anne indicated to her she was going upstairs.

As she passed the Children's Room, she saw Liddie and Beth sitting on the floor looking at books. Above their heads on one of the shelves, Anne had displayed Tobias's book *The Lonely Dog*. She gave the girls a wave and continued to their private quarters.

She checked the box of paperwork she'd gotten from the attic again. Maybe she'd just missed the paperwork when she'd been looking through the files. She didn't have any luck. This was driving her nuts. She hated when she couldn't find something.

Oh, Lord, please help me find the warranty.

She decided to check the secret room one more time and pushed past the quilt on the wall. The faint scent of her aunt's lavender perfume lingered in the room and today it made Anne feel closer to her aunt.

Anne sat behind the desk and ran a finger over her aunt's wire-framed reading glasses that still lay on the writing desk. "Aunt Edie, you'd be amazed what your kind deed helped produce. A little girl survived and now she's getting married. And the man you helped really did learn to read and became a success. And he tried to right his wrong."

Anne listened to the sounds of the old house, comforted by the familiarity, and then realized she'd been sitting there far too long. She needed to get back downstairs.

She pulled on the desk drawer that she had previously searched, but this time it stuck tight. She yanked hard and the drawer flew completely out, the contents falling to the floor.

Anne picked up the papers, checking each one carefully. Maybe she'd been in too much of a hurry last time. She reached the bottom of the stack and discovered that a couple of pages were stuck together. She gently pried them apart. The one underneath was a document labeled Delta & Peters. It was the elevator warranty with the lifetime guarantee.

"Thank You, Lord!" Anne breathed. Excited to get back downstairs to tell Alex, she tried to shove the drawer back in. A pinging noise sounded as the drawer's bottom panel fell open on hinges. The drawer had a false bottom!

Something had hit her foot and she got down on her hands and knees to reach under the desk. Her fingers closed around a key ring and something else flat and square. She pulled out a worn looking passport. She opened to find an old passport and a head shot of Aunt Edie, but instead of Edie Summers being named on the passport it was issued to an Evelyn Strait.

A thrill tickled her spine as she turned the pages full of stamps from countries her aunt had visited. Under her assumed name, Aunt Edie had traveled in and out of France, England, and West Germany several times during the fifties and early sixties. But what Anne found most exciting were the stamps for the Eastern European countries of *Polska Rzeczpospolita Ludowa* and *Československá socialistická republika,* which Anne surmised were Poland and Czechoslovakia as known back then while part of the Soviet Union. So it was feasible that Aunt Edie could have easily slipped into Russia if she'd wanted to. Aunt Edie might've been a secret courier or spy after all.

Anne checked under the desk again to make sure she hadn't missed anything and discovered a sheet of plain stationery and another of white card stock.

Anne turned over the card stock. An American eagle emblem graced the top of the page with Edie's name below and the words:

In recognition of your service during the period of the Cold War (2 September 1945-26 December 1991) in promoting peace and stability for this Nation, the people of this Nation are forever grateful.

The certificate was signed by Donald Rumsfeld, Secretary of Defense, which meant it must have been issued sometime after the year 2001 when he was in office.

So Aunt Edie was involved in the Cold War somehow! Anne's fingers shook as she looked at the handwritten note on the sheet of plain paper.

Dear Edie,

When these certificates for personnel became available after the collapse of the Soviet Union, I thought of your contribution and contacted the office to submit the appropriate documentation. Hope you are doing well. Thanks for everything.

Your old pal,

Jim

Anne shook her head with amazement. She had no idea who Jim, the author of the note, was. But deducing from the fact that Aunt Edie traveled to Eastern bloc countries under a different name, she suspected that Jim might be associated with one of the intelligence agencies and likely Aunt Edie's coworker or boss. Maybe Anne would never know the secrets surrounding the codebook, but now she was certain that Aunt Edie had done something extraordinary.

Her heart warmed with love for the woman who continued to surprise her. Not only had she strived to help Tobias McKinsey and others in Blue Hill, she'd tried to serve her country as well.

Anne returned the letter and passport to the false bottom in the drawer. For some reason Aunt Edie had wished to keep this part of life a secret from her family, and Anne would honor that for now. She took the elevator warranty with her as she went back into the library. From the Children's Room she heard a masculine voice. She peeked inside. Liddie was still on the floor, but Beth Norris was sitting on her father's lap, her face radiant as Luke read to her from a blue-covered book. Tobias's book.

Luke turned to the last page. *"But in her eyes, her pet was a hero for returning home. The past was forgiven and a new life begun.*

A kind deed is never forgotten."

ABOUT THE AUTHOR

Emily Thomas is the pen name for a team of writers who have come together to create the series Secrets of the Blue Hill Library. *Cracking the Code* was written by Kelly Ann Riley. From her first introduction to the beginning readers with Dick and Jane, award-winning author Kelly Ann Riley wanted to be a writer. She began penning tales at an early age and received special recognition for her short stories. Later, she became a reporter and editor for her high school newspaper.

Now Kelly Ann enjoys writing romantic suspense and cozy mysteries. She lives in Alabama with her husband, two grown children, and numerous pets. She enjoys working with her church's youth group and loves to travel. You can contact her through her Web site at KellyAnnRiley.com.

A Conversation with the Author

Q. *Aunt Edie has had a lot of adventures in her life. Can you tell us about the most exciting adventure you've experienced?*

A. One of the most exciting adventures I've ever experienced was when I was a staff member on a teen mission trip in Monument Valley, Utah. It was our last day of the trip and a couple of wonderful Navajo people offered to take us on a tour of private Navajo land where visitors could not venture without a guide. The teens and staff piled into four-wheel-drive vehicles and pickups and we took off across the desert, winding between the towering beautiful rock monuments. Finally we stopped at an ancient Indian dwelling and were allowed to carefully climb up and sit in the very rooms that people had carved out of the rock hundreds of years ago. My imagination soared thinking of what it must have been like to live there in the quiet desert in all its natural rugged beauty. It was easy to feel small and insignificant beside the massive monuments under an endless sky, but there was also a peace and a feeling of being closer to nature and God. I'm so thankful that the wonderful Navajo people shared their special place with us.

Q. If you could visit Blue Hill, where would you go first? Why?

A. The place I'd most like to visit in Blue Hill would be the library. The old mansion fascinates me and I adore libraries. But, first, I think I might stop off at Coffee Joe's to fortify myself with a latte after my long drive. I'd also order a bag of delectable pastries to take up to Anne and the other library workers. Before getting back in my car, I'd spend a little bit of time walking on Main Street, drinking my latte, and absorbing the sights and sounds of the historic town. Then I'd get back in my car and head for the library, hoping Anne might have time to give me a tour. After a delightful afternoon in the library, I'd invite Anne and her children for supper at Stella's Pizza where I hear they have fantastic pizza.

Q. Anne moves back to her hometown after years in New York City. What do/would you miss about your hometown?

A. I lived in several places growing up, but I consider Centerville, Ohio, as my hometown since I graduated from high school there. It was great growing up in a small town. Our school had a wonderful little library, and I spent many hours sitting between the stacks, reading. There was a little doughnut shop downtown where they made the best glazed doughnuts and a restaurant where we would stop to get hot fudge sundaes. The area was rich with history. Lakes and parks were close by just waiting to be explored. But, most of all I miss the school, my classmates and teachers, and the great experiences I had. It was such a special time in my life, full of new beginnings, and I will always cherish the memories.

Q. *Which of your now-deceased relatives would you most like to visit now? What questions would you ask them?*

A. The now-deceased relative that I would most like to visit would be my maternal grandfather, Garfield Jorgenson. When he retired from teaching, he and my grandmother spent time as missionaries in Hawaii, Africa, and the South Pacific. I wish I'd had more time to sit down and ask more questions about what the world was like when he grew up and all the adventures he experienced later in life. My kind grandfather had a wonderful sense of humor and even when he was in the hospital for the last time he would crack jokes with the nurses. He was always trying to make people laugh, and I would ask to hear some of those jokes again. He was a wonderful husband, father, grandfather, and Christian. I'm glad I had the chance to know him.

Recipes from the Library Guild

Wendy's Blueberry Muffins

Muffins
½ cup butter, room temperature
1 cup granulated sugar
2 large eggs
1 teaspoon vanilla
2 teaspoons baking powder
¼ teaspoon salt
2 cups all-purpose flour
½ cup milk
½ cups blueberries, fresh or frozen

Crumb Topping
½ cup sugar
¾ cup flour
⅓ cup butter
1½ teaspoons cinnamon

Preheat oven to 375 degrees. Grease eighteen regular-sized muffin cups or twelve large-sized muffin cups (or use muffin liners.)

In a bowl, mix butter until creamy. Add sugar. Beat until pale and fluffy. Beat in eggs one at a time. Beat in vanilla, baking powder, and salt.

With a spoon or spatula fold into batter half of the flour, then half of the milk. Repeat. Fold in blueberries. Spoon batter into muffin cups.

Mix crumb topping ingredients together with a fork and sprinkle topping onto each muffin.

Bake fifteen to twenty minutes or until golden brown and springy to touch.

From the Guideposts Archives

This article by Fred Mayer originally
appeared in *Guideposts* magazine.

On December 8, 1941, the day after the Japanese bombed Pearl Harbor, I went down to my local army recruiting office in Brooklyn, New York, and enlisted. I was just twenty years old, a Jew from Freiburg, Germany. My family had been in America for only three years. We'd fled the Nazis and made a new home here, where we could practice our faith without fear. I felt like it was my duty to help my adopted country.

The night before I left for the army, my mother took me to our rabbi for his blessing. Afterward, we walked home together in silence. It was dinnertime, and in the brightly lit windows of the apartments above us, we saw families saying prayers around their supper tables and smelled the food from their kitchens. Most of our neighbors were like us, Jews who'd fled the violence in Europe. Now it had followed us here. Suddenly this peaceful new life with all its freedoms seemed incredibly fragile, as though it could be shattered with a single stone. My mother clasped my hands and said, "Freddy, wherever you go, whatever happens, don't forget that I will be praying for you. God always hears a mother's prayer."

I had enlisted in the infantry, but while I was in basic training I heard about the OSS, the Office of Strategic Services, forerunner of the CIA. They needed people who spoke foreign languages to go behind enemy lines and gather intelligence. I knew German and French, and volunteered.

I was paired with another young refugee, a Dutch Jew named Hans Wynberg. I was short and powerfully built, Hans was tall and slender. I was known for being loud and impulsive, Hans was quiet and scholarly. Together, we made a great team.

The OSS trained us in everything from martial arts to handling explosives. We learned how to forge documents, use code, and maintain a false identity. For practice, the OSS placed me in an Allied POW camp, disguised as a captured German soldier. It was there that I met Franz Weber, a serious young Austrian who'd deserted from the Nazi army. Franz came from a small town in the foothills of the Alps, and he made no effort to hide his hatred of the Nazis. Eventually, I recruited Franz for the OSS.

"I hope you understand the risks for you and your family," I said.

"Yes," Franz answered, "but they want Austria to be free as much as I do."

In the winter of 1945, our team parachuted into Austria. With help from Franz's family and the local resistance, I took up the identity of a German officer. Armed with false papers, I checked into the officers' barracks in Innsbruck. For three months, living day and night with the enemy, I kept my eyes and ears open. A bored officer at the bar, a chance acquaintance in the mess hall, a discarded note in the trash—all could provide me with vital information.

My primary objective was to monitor the Brenner Pass, a high mountain corridor linking Austria with the Axis armies in Italy. I made contacts in the railway freight yards and passed my information to Hans and Franz to transmit to the Allied air force from a radio hidden in a farmer's hayloft. Several important supply shipments moving through the pass were destroyed because of our messages.

In April 1945, I decided it was time to change my disguise. I took on the identity of a French laborer and went to work in an airplane factory outside of Innsbruck. I stayed in daily contact with my comrades, sending them everything I could find out about a new jet fighter the Nazis were developing. A few weeks later, on April 20, I woke up to a heavy pounding on the front door. I jumped out of bed and ran to the window just as my door burst open and eight Gestapo officers charged into the room.

"Halt or we'll shoot!" they shouted. "You're under arrest."

I was taken to a jail in Innsbruck and thrown into a windowless cell. I'd heard about the brutality of Gestapo interrogations, but I had to maintain my false identity at least long enough for Hans and Franz to escape. Word of my arrest would be passed along the underground, and even a few extra hours could help. My stomach twisted with fear, and I thought about my family back in Brooklyn—would I ever see them again?

My cell door swung open and a Gestapo officer entered, flanked by soldiers. He was a small man, wearing a meticulously pressed suit and a sneer of satisfaction I longed to wipe off his face.

"My name is Walter Guttner," he said, "I am Kriminalsekretär of the Innsbruck Gestapo."

I told him in French that I didn't speak German.

"Do yourself a favor and drop this charade, Herr Mayer," Guttner said. "We know who you are, when you entered Austria, and that you are here with two accomplices. Where are they?"

I shook my head, repeating that I couldn't understand. Guttner nodded to the guards. Suddenly my face exploded as a fist smacked into it. I fell onto the floor and a heavy metal-studded boot slammed into my stomach. Through the ringing in my head, I heard Guttner's voice close to my ear.

"Tell us where your friends are." I shook my head, stubbornly repeating my story: I was French. I had come here through Switzerland two weeks ago.

Lightning flashed in my head again. I tasted my own warm, salty blood. I was stripped and ordered to sit on the floor.

"Bend your knees! Link your arms over them!"

I heard it snap first, then saw it uncoiling out of the corner of my eye. The bullwhip cracked across my back. I barely swallowed a scream. Two soldiers grabbed my hair, yanked my head back, and poured a bucket of water onto my face. Water flooded my mouth and nostrils. Then the whip cracked again.

It seemed like it would never end — the questions, the crack of the whip, the searing pain that cut my body in half, and Walter Guttner's voice, cold and steady as a drill. Finally, I was dragged into another cell and thrown on a pile of lice-infested straw, hands cuffed behind me. Through the bars of the window, I could see the pale light of dawn. I prayed for sleep, but the pain wouldn't allow it. When I closed my eyes, all I could see were Guttner's smirk and tailored suit. I didn't know if I could face him again.

Then other images filled my mind. I saw that last night in Brooklyn—the quiet street, the families praying before dinner and my mother's face. *Mother,* I wondered, *are you praying for me now?* Instinctively, I knew that she was, and that certainty filled me with a desire to live. My parents had already sacrificed so much to make a new life for us. They wouldn't have to sacrifice their son as well, not if I could help it.

My cell door rattled and Guttner entered, a triumphant look on his face. Informers had told him where to find my friends, he said. Still handcuffed, I was taken to witness their arrest. But it was too late. I watched the Nazis break down the doors of one empty house after another, while Guttner's gloating transformed into rage. My stalling had bought Hans and Franz time to escape. *Good luck, guys,* I thought. But had their escape sealed my doom?

Over the following days, I languished in my cell, subsisting on cold soup and stale bread. Why are they keeping me alive? I asked myself.

Late one night, when I heard the guards whispering in the hall outside my cell, I carefully laid down on the floor and put my ear to the crack under the door.

"Hitler is dead," one guard was saying. "Berlin will fall any day. It won't be long before the Allies are here in Austria."

Later that night, I was shaken awake by the guards and hustled into a car. We left the city, and I watched with growing apprehension as the dark forest loomed up on either side. *Is this the end?* I wondered. We pulled into the driveway of a large country house. My handcuffs were removed, and I was ushered into a sitting room. Now I was more confused than frightened. I was introduced to Gauleiter Franz Hofer, the Nazi Party chief for Innsbruck. As I relaxed in a plush armchair, the Gauleiter told me the American Seventh Army was only eighteen miles away. He wanted me, as an American officer, to help him negotiate Innsbruck's surrender.

The next day, May 3, 1945, I drove out of the city in a German staff car, wearing a makeshift American uniform and carrying a white bed sheet as a flag of truce. I was exhausted, my face still marbled with bruises from Guttner's interrogation, but I was also ecstatic. What would Guttner say now?

Two weeks after the surrender, I received a call from counterintelligence. They'd captured Walter Guttner and were holding him in custody.

"Do you want to interrogate him?" the officer asked. I envisioned the little German standing over me and again I longed to wipe the smirk off his face.

"I'll be right there," I replied eagerly.

Guttner was being held in the old Gestapo prison in Innsbruck, the same prison where he'd interrogated me. I walked slowly past the cells, now filled with the men who'd guarded them. My hands clenched into fists as I approached Guttner. The once-arrogant Gestapo chief lay huddled in a corner of his cell. He turned his head slightly as I unlocked the cell door. Grabbing him by the shirt collar, I yanked him to his feet. He was as limp as a rag doll. The light fell across his face. I gasped. He had been terribly beaten. Dried blood covered his cheeks and mouth, and he looked at me through eyes half shut by bruises. He cringed when he recognized me and said through his swollen lips, "You can do anything you want to me, but please don't hurt my family."

Family? I paused. It had never occurred to me that behind that cold smile there could be love for another person. All at once I wasn't angry at Guttner anymore. He was no longer my torturer, but just another person caught in the vise of war, and in his eyes I saw only fear. Looking in those eyes I remembered the reason I'd come back to Europe to fight in the first place. It was so that people would never have to be afraid like this again, so that my parents, my neighbors in Brooklyn, and even Walter Guttner would be able to live and pray in peace with their families. I let go of Guttner and he slumped against the wall. I left the cell and walked out of the prison into the warm spring sun, thinking of my mother, praying that I would see her soon. And I thought of Walter Guttner. Maybe he had a mother praying for him too.

Read on for a sneak peek of another exciting book
in Secrets of the Blue Hill Library!

The Valentine Visitor

I'm going to your school today," Anne Gibson told her son as she
filled a bowl with oatmeal for his breakfast.

"Are you going to bring cookies?" Ben asked, at the same time
turning up his nose at the steaming bowl of cereal. "This goop is
too hot to eat."

"No to the cookies," Anne said. "I'll be meeting with the other
room mother and your teacher to talk about the Valentine's Day
party."

"Oh, that," he said with a total lack of interest.

"It will be fun," Anne assured him as she poured a generous
amount of milk into his bowl and let him sprinkle a little brown
sugar on the oatmeal. Ben swirled his spoon through it but didn't
begin eating.

"I like cold cereal better," he said locking his arms across his
chest.

Anne knew he got his stubborn streak from her, but there
wasn't time for coaxing on this frigid Monday morning.
Yesterday, the first day of February, had brought freezing
temperatures and a significant amount of snow in the small
Pennsylvania town of Blue Hill. She had to worry about getting

her two children to school before opening the library, and her silver Impala could be hard to start in winter weather. She made a mental note to have the battery checked, but there wouldn't be time today.

"Eat your oatmeal," she said in a no-nonsense voice. "I have to see what's keeping your sister."

"It's too hot."

What would Eric have done if his son refused to do something? Her husband had passed away three years ago, and not a day went by when she didn't wish he were still with them.

"If you're not too full when your oatmeal is gone, you can have one of the toaster pastries you like," Anne said.

She felt a twinge of guilt for using Ben's sweet tooth to hurry him along, but she had to open the library and work there alone until someone came to give her a break at noon. At least she didn't have far to go to begin her workday. Thanks to a bequest from her great-aunt Edie, the first floor, and a large portion of the second floor of the big Queen Anne Victorian house had been converted into the town's first library. The back portion of the second floor and the entire third floor had been converted into personal living quarters for Anne and her children.

"Do we have chocolate chip?" Ben asked with his spoon poised over the bowl.

"You'll find out when your oatmeal is gone," Anne said with a light laugh. Sometimes life with Ben was a series of negotiations, but she didn't think it was possible to love her usually reserved, thoughtful nine-year-old son any more than she did. "Now I have to see what's keeping your sister."

She ran up the stairs to the third floor bedrooms, calling Liddie's name as she went.

"Mommy, I can't find my red shirt," the five-year-old complained, meeting her outside her room.

"That's because it's in the laundry," Anne said. "Wear what I laid out. If you don't hurry, you'll be late for your kindergarten class."

"But I told Mandy I'd wear red today so we could dress alike."

"Sorry, sweetie, it's not going to happen." Anne smiled at the earnest expression on Liddie's face. Unlike her brother whose brown hair and hazel eyes mirrored Anne's, Liddie had curly brown hair with hints of gold and chocolate brown eyes inherited from her father.

Following her daughter into the bedroom, she watched her pull a pink tank top from her dresser drawer.

"I'm afraid it's too cold for that." Anne found a yellow sweatshirt with a bumblebee logo and started pulling it over Liddie's head.

"Mommy!" Liddie slipped into it herself sounding annoyed by her parent's help. But unlike her brother, she gave up easily, readily accepting the change of wardrobe.

"Can I take my giraffe to school?" she asked, picking up a stuffed animal nearly as tall as she was, a gift from Anne's parents.

"Not today. It's not show-and-tell," Anne said, replacing the toy on the bed.

"I told Mandy I'd take it."

Anne hadn't met her daughter's new best friend, but she couldn't help but be curious.

"Maybe she can come to play after school some day," Anne suggested, taking Liddie's hand to hurry her down to breakfast.

"No, she can't," Liddie said. "She lives on a farm."

"Well, we'll see," Anne said, knowing how complicated a play date could be with a child who rode the school bus to a home in the country. Later she might volunteer to take her home, but right now she wasn't sure her car would start to give her own children a ride to school.

"Can I have chocolate crunchies for breakfast?" Liddie asked as they hurried down to the kitchen.

"No, I have oatmeal made."

Somehow Anne managed to get both children ready to leave, hustle them down to her car, and check their seat belts for the short ride to school. Now if the Impala would start!

The starter made a grating noise, and the motor didn't turn over. Anne thought with nostalgia of her life in New York with her husband, Eric, a senior acquisitions editor at a publishing house. In the big city a car was an expensive nuisance rather than a necessity, and they'd chosen to use public transportation instead of owning one. But she'd grown up in Blue Hill, and she knew the pace of small town life. They could walk to school, but the wind had cut through her thick winter sweatpants and made her shiver in the few moments before she got into the car. It was much too cold for the kids to walk.

She tried again and wondered if a cold motor was too trivial to ask for God's help starting it.

"We're going to be late," Ben pointed out, although he didn't sound too concerned.

"I don't want to be late!" Liddie said with horror. "I'll miss play time."

"Only babies get to play in school," Ben said with a big brother's superiority.

"I'm not a baby!"

"Shush!" Anne said, sending up a desperate prayer before trying again.

Much to her relief the motor started, albeit with a harsh sound. She was even more relieved minutes later when her children disappeared inside the aging but recently remodeled three-story building that served as Blue Hill Elementary School. Ben walked three steps ahead of his sister, but he kept looking back to make sure Liddie was keeping up. As soon as they were out of sight, Anne returned home. With all the things on her to-do list today, she didn't want to take the car into the shop. Anne hoped it would be okay now that it was warmed up. What wasn't okay was the condition of the walkway and steps leading up to the library. She didn't mind a little shoveling and de-icing, but it was going to be a challenge to open the library on time.

Anne was almost through making the approach to the library safe when an ancient snowplow rumbled down the street. She watched as it threw snow across the entrance to the parking area and almost engulfed the mailbox by the curb. If the unusually harsh winter continued, she would have to hire someone to clear snow for her, but today it was her responsibility.

By the time she cleared the driveway entrance, Anne felt every one of her thirty-four years. Why had she ever thought snow was delightful? Oh yes, when she'd been Ben's age making a snowman had been great fun.

Accustomed as she was to lifting piles of books, stacks of books, boxes of books, she grunted with exertion as she shoveled snow away from the mailbox. She was just finishing when the familiar white mail truck turned onto the street and headed toward her.

Anne stood waiting for the truck to stop beside her box, then moved to the open right window where a substitute mail carrier was sorting the envelopes and periodicals that went to her or the library.

"Good morning," the carrier said, looking like Santa's helper in a bright red stocking cap and a green jacket.

"Good morning. I see the snow didn't hold you up. You're right on time."

"Truth to tell, I went in early when they called me to substitute for the regular guy. He's sick, I guess. I was up anyway because my husband had to allow extra time to warm up his school bus. He was hoping for a snow day but no such luck. I guess the country roads aren't too bad. I especially wanted a word with you before you open the library."

"Oh?" Anne reached for the bundle of mail the carrier handed to her. "Would you like to come in for coffee? You must be freezing."

"No thanks, but I have something to show you."

Anne stepped closer to the opening in the truck and saw what looked like a postcard in her hand.

"I am so sorry about this. I was fishing under the seats in the truck trying to find a quarter I dropped. This is what I found." She handed the postcard to Anne.

"It's addressed to my great aunt." Anne still got junk mail addressed to Aunt Edie, but it was a surprise to see Edie Summers's name and a personal message on the back of the postcard. "It must be from a friend who didn't know she passed away last April."

"No, look at the date in the postmark," the mail carrier said.

"February 3 — oh my, it's a year old."

"I do apologize," she said. "The post office prides itself on never losing a piece of mail. I'm really embarrassed delivering it so late."

"Don't feel bad," Anne quickly assured her. "You're only filling in for our regular carrier. And it's only a postcard."

"A pretty one, though. I'm sure Edie would've enjoyed seeing it. I knew her from way back."

"Well, I'm happy to have it now," Anne said. "It is pretty, isn't it?"

She stared for a moment at a scene of two winged cupids harvesting hearts from a tree while a third put them in a big bag. The caption was: "In all sincerity." Even without mentioning Valentine's Day, it was obviously a card designed for that day.

"Well, I'd best be on my way," the mail carrier said. "Again, I'm really sorry the postcard was lost for a whole year. Edie was a special person, and she would've enjoyed the card."

After reassuring her one more time, Anne took the bundle of mail and went to the rear entrance, leaving the shovel propped up by the door.

Going through the library mail could wait, but she was intrigued by the belated Valentine greeting. Without taking off her coat, she took it upstairs and sat down at the kitchen table to have a better look.

Even without knowing much about postcards, Anne was sure it was old. The brightly colored scene was embossed, and the card stock had an aged look. She turned it over, and the address side was even more puzzling. Besides the date that proved it had been mailed a full year ago, the postmark showed its origin: Port Moresby, PNG.

It took Anne a minute to identify PNG, then she remembered a missionary who had spoken at their church in New York. The initials had to indicate Papua New Guinea.

"Wow!" Anne said out loud. The card had come a long distance from Oceania, only to be lost for a year. She didn't fault the mail carrier, but it was disappointing Aunt Edie had never seen it.

The handwriting wasn't easy to read, but when Anne managed to read the whole message she didn't know what to make of it:

"My dear Edie, I'm so looking forward to our Valentine's Day reunion next year. I'll deliver that card in person. In the meantime, you're often in my thoughts. Sincere regards."

The signature was only a single scrawled letter impossible to make out. It could be a *D*, an *O*, or possibly a *P*. There was no return address, but the sender seemed sure Edie would know who had sent it.

Anne left the postcard on the table, but she couldn't get it out of her mind as she showered and dressed for work. Who was this mysterious friend of Edie's? The message implied that they met regularly, but where did they meet? Her great aunt had been a travel writer for many years with connections all over the world, but the sender of this card seemed to have a special relationship with her.

After hurriedly dressing in jeans with a warm white angora sweater, Anne hurried down to the library, going through the opening routine automatically.

Did the sender of the postcard know Edie had passed away? Anne could check the signatures in the visitors' book from the funeral, but it was probably a waste of time. The message made it clear her friend wouldn't see her until this Valentine's Day. Edie's faraway friend was planning to meet her in just two weeks. The question was, where? If someone were coming all the way from Papua New Guinea for a reunion with her great aunt, he would be going to great trouble and expense only to receive sad news.

Was there any way to discover who had sent the postcard? Could she contact the sender in time to save him a long trip? Who was this person who cared enough for her great aunt to go to so much trouble to see her on the most romantic day of the year? Anne suddenly had plenty of questions and no idea of where to begin searching for answers.

A NOTE FROM THE EDITORS

We hope you enjoy Secrets of the Blue Hill Library, created by the Books and Inspirational Media Division of Guideposts, a nonprofit organization that touches millions of lives every day through products and services that inspire, encourage, help you grow in your faith, and celebrate God's love in every aspect of your daily life.

Thank you for making a difference with your purchase of this book, which helps fund our many outreach programs to military personnel, prisons, hospitals, nursing homes, and educational institutions. To learn more, visit GuidepostsFoundation.org.

We also maintain many useful and uplifting online resources. Visit Guideposts.org to read true stories of hope and inspiration, access OurPrayer network, sign up for free newsletters, download free e-books, join our Facebook community, and follow our stimulating blogs.

To learn about other Guideposts publications, including the best-selling devotional *Daily Guideposts*, go to ShopGuideposts.org, call (800) 932-2145, or write to Guideposts, PO Box 5815, Harlan, Iowa 51593.